FAST TIMES
BIG CITY

A Novel

SHELLY FROME

North Carolina

This is a work of fiction. All of the characters, names, incidents, organizations, and dialogue in this novel are either the products of the author's imagination or are used fictitiously.

Published in the United States by BQB Publishing
(an imprint of Boutique of Quality Books Publishing Company)
www.bqbpublishing.com

979-8-88633-026-7 (p)
979-8-88633-027-4 (e)

Library of Congress Control Number: 2023952394

Book design by Robin Krauss, www.bookformatters.com
Cover design by Rebecca Lown, rebeccalowndesign.com

Cover artwork entitled "Times Square" by Frank Federico (1928-2018)

Editor: Caleb Guard

CHAPTER ONE

Bud Palmer slipped on his sunglasses and set off in his Ford Sunliner convertible on this balmy subtropical Saturday morning. All the while he tried to convince himself he could get this meeting over with quickly no matter what his shady uncle Rick was up to.

Then again Bud wished he'd just hung up on him. Not put up with "Can't tell you over the phone. I need you here in person, soon as possible." That way he wouldn't be driving across the MacArthur Causeway. Moreover, if his mother hadn't asked him to look out for her kid brother while she and his dad were on their Caribbean cruise, he'd never have been reminded of Rick's schemes such as hanging up a dual Realtor/ PI sign. He wouldn't be thinking of Rick Ellis at all.

As he drove on, more disconcerting images came to mind: a wiry little guy clutching a polaroid camera, hiding behind the poinsettias as some floozy snuck into a garish motel with someone's husband in tow.

Not that Bud himself was always straightforward. At twenty-nine, while his friends were married with kids he was still easing out of relationships the minute he was asked, "Tell me, Bud, how much does a sportswriter make?" Or, "I hear there's a new subdivision going up in Miramar, each house with a Lanai. Perfect for raising a family." In comparison with Rick, however, Bud was always honest about his intentions whether it be his work or love life. In contrast, when playing tennis for instance, Rick was always looking for an angle. He'd crouch behind the net ready to pounce or cut off an opponent's serve, always looking to throw the server off his game.

Bud crossed over onto Miami Beach, tooled around, passed the ballfield at Flamingo Park, eased by the pastel sidewalks taking him up to Ocean Drive and the fresh fruit juice stand at 10th Street Beach. He parked by a curb directly in line with the juice stand, got out and crossed the sun-dappled street.

Glancing around, he took in the cool tinge of fall blowing in from the ocean, fusing with the salty scent of the water. The sun's rays streamed through the fluffy clouds; the waves rippled, beckoning the smattering of sunbathers to take a dip. Everywhere Bud looked nothing had changed. Which included the sight of middle-aged women across the way in their flowery sun dresses, whiling away the hours on the patios of their pink-stucco efficiency apartments; shuffling mahjong tiles; glancing over at the white sands stretching off into the distance in hopes of spotting some lonely bachelor. It was all predictable. Even his paper, the *Miami Herald* and source of his livelihood, discarded on the empty green bench, seconded the motion. There was a photo of President Eisenhower above the fold playing golf nearby at Jackie Gleeson's country club, and a sidebar noting the U.S. was gaining in the space race with the Soviets.

Whatever Rick was champing at the bit about had to be taken with the proverbial grain of salt.

As if in agreement, a voluptuous blond in a fuchsia bikini came into view, turned on the outdoor shower a few yards away, casually washed off the salt water residue on her shoulders, and winked.

Bud smiled back, checked his watch and gazed beyond the mahjong ladies to a gap in the row of efficiency apartments at the end of the block where the weathered bungalow sat a few yards back. The one with the fading sign fronting the bamboo porch railing that read *Walk-ins Welcome: Services Unlimited.*

He crossed over, hurried past the row of squat apartments, pivoted by the sign, noted the rear end of the rusty Studebaker sitting in the carport, and nodded. It was all the same-old same-old promising more of the same. He bound up the steps, called out "Hello?" opened the screen door and walked right in.

And, sure enough, there Rick was ready and waiting, sporting that signature Charlie Chaplin mustache, flowered short-sleeved shirt and white linen slacks. The first worrisome signal, however, was his bleary, blood-shot eyes as he over-poured a carafe of steaming black coffee into a mug. He whipped out a handkerchief, plunked the carafe and mug on the edge of the desk in the center of the room, and mopped up the spill. At the same time, Bud took in the rest of the place and saw that it hadn't changed a bit, starting from the girlie calendars on the walls, milk boxes full of paperbacks on the floor; the cluttered desk topped by a scuffed black rotary phone, notary stamp, and the Smith-Corona typewriter flanked by a hat stand with a random display. To complete the picture, there was the rack of glossy magazines so that Rick could keep up with the latest, plus a wooden perch that once accommodated a talking parrot on the near side of a shaded window and a sun-bleached deck chair.

Everything was the same and not at all the same.

Slurping some coffee, Rick said, "Right . . . Bud . . . great, you made it." He moved a pile of papers aside and dug out an old photo album.

Taking a few steps further inside, Bud said, "Okay. Well, here I am. So?"

"Terrific," Rick said, clutching the album. "What a guy, after giving you only a moment's notice. And hey, look what I dug up while I was waiting here killing time. Get a load of this." Slipping out a black-and-white Polaroid, he said, "Look at you on East Flagler, walking out of the Seybold Arcade, sporting a fedora from this very rack like Sam Spade from *The Maltese Falcon*." Dropping the photo, he skirted around the desk, snatched a dusty hat off the rack and plopped it on his head. Affecting a hardboiled Humphry Bogart impression while trying to shake off an involuntary twitch, he said, "Listen, sweetheart, everybody's got a story to tell."

Countering, Bud said, "Come on, Rick, cut the tap dance. What does that have to do with anything that demands my immediate presence, making me drive all the way over here?"

When Rick didn't reply, Bud said, "What is it? God, Rick, you look terrible."

"Haven't slept. Drank too much booze for starters."

"Uh-huh, all right, go on."

"I'm getting to it, I'm getting to it." Replacing the fedora, he circled back behind the desk to the paperbacks stacked up in the milk boxes. "You looked into something for me. And not so long ago either. Went deep into the Glades, into the Fakahatchee Strand despite the swamp and alligators."

"Oh, no, not that again."

He rubbed his eyes, bent over, snatched a paperback and said, "Ta-daa! You were my Archie Goodwin. While I, with my asthma, was Nero Wolfe. You know. The armchair consultant, the mastermind while you were my leg man, my younger man of action. And you went along with it."

"I didn't go along with it. It's some old radio show, and what are you getting at?"

Not at all sure his uncle hadn't gone off the deep end, Bud began spelling it out for him. "As it happens, I didn't go to all that trouble for your sake. I did it because my mom, your sister, was worried you were getting yourself into something really dicey this time. Just to make her happy, I drove up there, slogged through the wetlands, asked around and found out the guy you were in cahoots with was a poacher."

"Not really."

"Yes really. Out to clone ghost orchids. To hook up with collectors while he propagated them in a nursery in Coconut Grove. Except for the fact the Strand is a preserve. Except they caught up with the guy red-handed and arrested him."

"Yeah, well . . . anyways, still, you did real good . . . got the knack."

"I don't have any such thing. I cover sports for the *Herald*, that's what I do. So, can we get off this and come to the point?"

Shaking his head, Rick scuffed over to the venetian blinds covering the window and started fiddling with the draw-cord.

"Come on, Rick. Will you just talk to me?"

Opening the blinds and staring out into the glare of the noonday sun, Rick began easing into it. "Okay. We got the Shriners in town. You know, those guys wearing the round, red hats with a tassel, from the burbs in Indiana, letting off steam. Get them in a card game, perfect marks—you can't miss."

"Go on."

"Naturally, when Lenny the building contractor fills me in how they're gonna develop Sanibel Island, secluded retreat and such near Fort Myers . . . if I get in now, divvy up, become a shareholder, I'm golden. No more scrounging around."

Rick yanked at the draw-cord, sending the blinds flying up. His hands shaking so bad Bud had to go over, straighten the blinds, and lower them down again. "Just break it to me, that's all I ask."

But as Rick began to hem and haw, it was near impossible to piece it all together. Something about a high stakes poker game at the nearby Tropic Isle Hotel that ran till dawn. But there weren't only "boozy Shriner bozos" playing it fast and loose. There was a sharpie from Chicago. And rounds of single malt scotch. And here is where Rick really lost it.

"Way after midnight the hicks and bozos folded . . . ante got raised, pot got bigger and bigger. But when to hold, when to fold? What's he got: a pocket queen, Ace in the hole, three of a kind? He stands pat . . . check . . . rolls his eyes . . . looks off . . . says he'll see you . . . raises, stands pat again. Could be a pair . . . can't fill an inside straight or can he? Had him . . . lost him, over and over until at first light . . . until . . . "

"Tell me," Bud said, unable to take it anymore. "Why was I summoned? Why am I here?"

"Only one way out," Rick said, turning to Bud, tears running down his cheeks. "Gotta buy a little time. It's a trifecta: a pile of money I owe, a little floozy who took off, and a briefcase. What am I gonna do?" Rick lurched at him, grabbed his shoulders and said, "You gotta do this for me, Bud. Else that's all she wrote, end of the line. They roughed me up good, got my phone number, license plate, address. But you're on your feet, bright and fit. Else they'll break my legs, wrap me in a canvas bag and feed me to the barracudas! Bury me in Biscayne Bay!"

CHAPTER TWO

Rick remained crumpled on the deck chair clutching his head, rocking back and forth muttering incoherently. Bud tried a couple of times to reason with him but got nowhere. Giving up, he stepped out onto the porch hoping that given a little time and space Rick would simmer down and come to his senses.

As far as Bud was concerned, compulsive gambling was hard to reckon with. Was it a substitute for something else? Was the pull of a change of luck so enticing, losing more and more and risking more and more to make up for your losses, all part of the syndrome? Was leaving a trail of broken promises, wrecked relationships, and lost jobs something you cast a blind eye to for the sake of the next possible sure thing: a horse race, a throw of the dice, a big jackpot that kept you going until what? Or does it never end?

It was all under the province of emotions like Bud's teary-eyed mother pleading, "You've got to at least give him a call while your dad and I are away. I can't help worrying, Bud what's to become of him?" Maybe it was all a weakness, but Bud always had a problem with getting his mind around things he could reason with.

He reached for a cigarette and remembered he hadn't bought a pack today. But what difference would it make since he didn't inhale and only occasionally smoked to be social?

He gazed out at the coconut palms and stretch of white sand to try and gain some perspective. The only upshot he'd gleaned so far was what Rick called a trifecta: three operative factors. There was a large sum of money he'd lost to a high roller from Chicago. There was some young lady who'd flown the coop. And something about a briefcase.

Settling on these tangible issues, Bud reentered as Rick's moaning and rocking seemed to have tapered off. Like a consoling coach, he got down on one knee and tried once again. "Okay, so you blew it at the gaming table and some other stuff. There's got to be a sensible way to handle this."

Rick lifted his head and said, "So you'll look into it, like I asked?"

"I didn't say that."

"I tell you I'm at the end of my rope, Bud. You gotta help me out."

The look Rick gave him was so pathetic, before Bud could stop himself he said, "All right, let's think. What about this high roller from Chicago?"

"He's waiting for you, right now."

"He's what?" Bud asked, getting back on his feet.

"Waiting for you. I told him you'd be by," Rick said, his face a bit more animated. "That's why all the rush."

"Now hold on, Rick," Bud said, waving him off.

"His name is Escobar. Al Escobar. He won't listen to me. You're my last hope."

"I said hold on. And the girl, mistress or whatever? What about her? What did you do? What did you say that made everything worse? Was it while you were high, losing your shirt? What's the logical progression?"

"Before that, maybe by the pool during the cocktail hour. Just making friends, buttering her up in case she could offer some tips. Ask Chip. He'll tell you."

"And who is Chip?"

"The cabana guy. Always around, same as last year. But

nothing's the same as last year. It's all crazy. Like some damn briefcase. I tell you, it's a nightmare. Help me out, Bud, please? You're levelheaded. Before I damn well go outta my mind!"

And here Bud was, losing ground, trying to ward off unrelenting emotionality. The imploring look on his uncle's face was so desperate, Bud was worried what he might do. Purely on impulse, Bud said, "Go to bed. Get some sleep. For God sake get ahold of yourself."

"While you check it out? You mean it? Swear to me you mean it."

Reluctant as can be, Bud said, "Maybe, for a minute, that's it."

"Okay then. Okay." Rick rose, crossed his fingers for Bud's benefit, and scuffled off, wending his way gingerly through an alcove, past the kitchenette and down to his bedroom.

Bud left the bungalow hardly noticing the mahjong ladies turning their heads and waving to him as he walked by. He considered the consequence if he bailed on his uncle—his mother confronting him the minute she and his dad returned from their cruise, her hazel eyes incredulous as she said, "But you must know. I asked you to keep tabs. What could have happened to him?"

And it was this prospect that stayed with him as he slipped back behind the wheel and drove up to Collins Avenue, hung a right just before Lincoln Road and eased into the side delivery entrance of the Tropic Isle boutique hotel. He parked and checked his watch. He'd promised his eleven-year-old niece Katie he'd take her to the Parrot Jungle this afternoon. His sister Marge insisted that Katie was really counting on it. He decided to give this situation a few minutes like he said and wangle something so everything would attain some sense of balance.

He got out and walked around to the glistening sands dotted with a handful of guests lying under their rainbow-tilted beach umbrellas reflecting the glare of the sun. Turning away from the beach scene, he took the half dozen steps up to the faux marble poolside patio looking for a cabana guy named Chip.

At first there was no sign of anyone in the vicinity of the kidney shaped pool. He fixed his gaze onto a file of blue and white cabanas that resembled a lineup of Arabian tents from some Hollywood movie. But there was still nothing.

Presently, as if on cue, a muscular little guy with a deep tan appeared through the flaps of the furthest tent, pushing a wheeled cart loaded with cleaning supplies and brandishing a handheld vacuum. Bud approached him as he ducked into the next tent, vacuumed the marbleized floor, emptied the ash trays into a wastebasket and sprayed the top of a round white table. He then reached for a spray bottle and cloth and wiped off the banquets. It seemed to Bud that this was a guy with a set routine he couldn't deviate from. Either that or he needed to look busy in order to keep his job.

Bud tried to get his attention, but he ignored him and kept going. The only acknowledgement Bud received was a nod when the guy reappeared a third time and conceded he was Chip. It was only at the front of the tent closest to the steps down to the beach that Chip finally came to a halt. "What do you need, fella?" Chip asked. "As you can see I got things to do."

"It's about my uncle Rick. He intimated you could fill me in about what happened last night. Some incident around the cocktail hour that might have led to a predicament he's in."

"Some incident, huh? Some predicament? Right. Let's say he had it coming. And while you're at it, remind him he owes me regardless."

With that, Chip walked off, half-circled the pool with his cleaning cart, and was about to tackle the color-coordinated pads on the chaise lounges when Bud caught up to him again, stepped in front of his cart and said, "What do you mean he had it coming? Look, he's in a bad way if half of what he says is true. If not, I can chalk it off as Rick just being Rick and be on my way."

"Gotcha," Chip said, trying to maneuver around Bud, but Bud held his ground.

"Hey, what is this? Am I gonna have to call the security guard?"

"Great. Call him. Maybe he'll give me a straight answer and you'll have to level about your part in all this."

"My part?"

"Attempting to fleece a bunch of Shriners in a high stakes poker game that was supposed to take place on the q.t. Look, I don't want to cause any trouble, far from it. I'd love to slough this all off and get back to Miami."

Chip eased his grip on the cart and glanced here and there. At the same time, two matronly looking women came up from the beach carrying their folded beach towels and handed them to Chip, who grinned a fake grin while saying he hoped they were enjoying their stay. He stashed the towels in a nearby bin adjacent to a portable bar as the women entered the hotel. Without missing a beat, Chip came back and grabbed a feather duster, pretended to be attending to the closest chaise pads. "All right. And what's your angle anyways? Rick once told me he had a leg man on the side but didn't say it was a nephew."

"He misspoke. Okay, let's start with the girl. What was that all about?"

"Good question. All I know is the Shriners are getting restless. Been here a couple of days, the sun's going down and they've already had way too many. In she walks, couldn't be no more than twenty-four, a chick Rick and I only ran into a little while before. She plops down on a chaise lounge all dejected while the Shriners are flittin' in and out of the cabanas getting refills from the bar and giving her the eye."

"And?"

Looking around, making sure no one was within earshot, Chip lowered his voice and said, "The deal—nothing to do with her. I schmooze around, get to know each player so Rick can size them up and be on top of his game, plus now we got the girl. He comes winging it out of one of the tents, a bit crocked by now, playing good-time-Charlie. Spots the girl who at this point is looking real sad, pouting and like that. Rick wants to be introduced and get the skinny on her. I tell him all I know is she's from Chicago, attached to that big guy we saw earlier. Rick gives her a big grin, yells out above all the racket, 'Chicago, Peoria, Des Moines, same difference.'"

"Can you get to the point?"

"I don't know what's the point except using her to wheedle the big guy's maneuvers at cards. His tells. Maybe he scratches his nose when he's bluffing. Or lowers his eyes when he's got a hot hand. Anyways, I'm serving and collecting the empties and shmoozing like I said. Next thing I know, I swing by and Rick is telling her to never mind what anybody says. She could pass for Marilyn Monroe any day of the week. A few minutes later, I swing by again and this time she's all smiles and Rick gives me the thumbs-up."

"And that's it?"

"Except when the big guy Escobar comes busting in between the two of them, yanks her off the chaise lounge and elbows her back into the lobby. Rick thinks nothing of it, says it's strictly guys all through the night in the gaming room. He got what he could from her even though I could see she didn't have a clue what a tell was. Rick rubs his hands like he can't wait to take everybody on but it may have been the booze talking."

"Okay," Bud said, "this big guy, this Escobar, what can you tell me?"

"Not much. Word has it he's in tight with the owner. Hey, it's off-season. The steady clientele don't book till a bit later, around Thanksgiving. Around about now, you take what you can get."

On that note, Chip said, "Now will that do it for ya?" didn't wait for an answer, abandoned his cart, rushed down to the beach and began dismantling a few of the rainbow-tilted umbrellas. Perhaps making up for lost time. But, then again, getting far away from any fallout.

Leaving Bud in limbo, neither here nor there. As a rule, ever since grade school it had been drummed into him that every situation was a contest. Who is calling the shots? What are the stakes? What are the odds? And how should you play it to win, play it safe or at least break even? This situation however was bordering on walking in almost completely cold, still having no clue what he might be in for. Unless he did the perfectly sensible thing, threw up his hands and left. But then he would be saddled with guilt, second thoughts and apprehension.

CHAPTER THREE

Escobar's suite on the third floor seemed to be straining to live up to the hotel's boutique billing. The living area Bud was relegated to featured a slew of abstract paintings of tropical sunsets lining the side walls, rendered in splashes of coral and powder-blue, competing with a scattering of large potted palms. Not to mention a grouping of buttery-leather lounges on either side of a black marble coffee table in the center under a raised ceiling. Continuing in this vein, a silver ice bucket containing a half dozen bottles of Heineken beer sat on the table, along with a silver bottle opener, an open box of handmade Havana Panatela cigars, and a half-smoked cigar with a sturdy light-gray ash positioned neatly on a diamond-shaped ash tray.

In addition, a white phone atop a white marble stand stood at the ready in the corner of the entrance so that occupants could shuffle over and dial an operator for anything else their heart desired.

For Bud, however, as he sat in an armless leather chair flanked by the leather lounges, all this was disorienting. He'd never waited for some obscure, stocky gambler to reappear from his noonday shower. And still had no idea how to play it to let Rick off the hook and resume his lazy Saturday.

Ensconced here, he couldn't even gain an unobstructed view as he peered straight ahead past the sliding glass doors onto the balcony. Stationed like some kind of guard was Escobar's lanky sidekick Ed, wearing a short-sleeved shirt-jacket embossed with hibiscus draped over his bathing suit. At the moment, Ed was gazing down at the beachcombers, glancing back now and then keeping track of Bud with a fixed smirk on his face, as if everything amused him and life was one loopy circus no matter where you looked. And Bud was unwittingly slipping into that circus despite himself.

Moments later, Ed stepped back inside, went over to the coffee table, snatched a Heineken from the ice bucket, snapped off the cap, took a deep pull, looked down at Bud and said, "It could be that Al is taking his sweet ol' time washing off the sand and saltwater. But my money says he's still trying to cool it down over what happened 'cause of Rick, that shifty boss of yours. You gotta admit, that Rick is one nervy piece of work."

Waiting around plus the assumption that Rick was Bud's boss was only making matters worse. When Bud didn't respond, Ed pushed it a little further. "Is he always running off at the mouth like that? If anybody should know it's got to be you. How does it feel all the time mopping up after his mess?"

At that moment, Bud wished he could just set the record straight. It was obviously established that Rick was a flaky grifter and granting him even the shadow of a doubt was out of the question. Moreover, if anything happened to him, Bud kept reminding himself that his mother would be inconsolable. Nevertheless, with no other tack firmly in mind, Bud glanced up at Ed and said, "He gets in over his head sometimes. Especially when he's had too much to drink. Add that to his asthma and his dwindling prospects, he's going to need some time to get his act together."

"Yeah, sure, right," Ed said, downing the rest of the beer. "He's heading for time six feet under like I told him." With the smirk still fixed on his face, he walked over between the potted palms to

Bud's left and tossed the empty bottle into a bin. "Tell me another one, Bud. And get out the fiddle while you're at it and play me Hearts and Flowers."

Bud let it go, not able to read Ed's sense of humor, let alone place Rick's dilemma involving not only his gambling debt but some young lady who supposedly resembled Marilyn Monroe plus a missing briefcase which, taken together, continued to remain hard to fathom.

Another few minutes went by. Ed reached into his shirt-jacket pocket, got out a stick of gum, leaned against the edge of the hallway and began chewing away.

Finally, Al Escobar reappeared from the hallway, his bulk encased in a white terrycloth robe, his blue-shadowed jaw set, along with the piercing pained look in his eyes. He passed by Ed, made a beeline to the cigar box, reached inside his robe for a cigar cutter that looked like a miniature guillotine, and thought better of it. Ignoring the half-smoked cigar on the ash tray, he snatched a fresh Havana Panatela, marched back over to Ed, pointed the cigar in Bud's direction and said, "Well, Ed? You had enough time. What do you think?"

Still chomping on his wad of gum, Ed paused for a second and then made his assessment. "The way I see it, that little weasel Rick has a good point. This leg man of his comes across sharp but neutral, like his khaki pants and button-down shirt. Not tall, not short, not heavy, not skinny. Like he don't run off at the mouth and is always sizing things up. If he was standing right next to this flaky chick of ours in some New York subway or something, she wouldn't take notice. He don't look like any of our crew back in Chicago that would spook her."

With his pained look even more pronounced, Escobar said, "So what're the odds of him tracking her down and picking up the pieces while the trail is still hot? Worming his way into this airhead's confidence right off? What the hell good is neutral with the time ticking away?"

Bud wanted to set things straight and finally begin a discussion on the matter, but didn't get the chance.

"Hey," Ed cut in. "Bud here is all right, I tell you. Knows the Cubs got nothing going for them. But gives me a tip on the Miami Hurricanes where he went to college, majored in journalism or something. This could be the Cane's year, he says. Got a great quarterback and a terrific defense. And he knows his weasel of a boss Rick slipped-up right off the bat. He knows, he knows."

Bud wondered where Ed got off making up a conversation that never took place about the Cubs and the Hurricanes. He must of gotten it from Rick shopping him off the top of his head to save his skin.

"Which still gives us what?" Escobar asked. "And why would he be up for this in the first place?"

Countering as though he was ready for this, Ed said, "You offer him enough coin up front during this slow season, a break hanging around his old stomping grounds in the Big Apple, make it interesting, what's he got to lose? Besides, maybe he don't want you to take it outta Rick's hide. He cashes in with you and still got Rick on a string as a meal ticket. What I'm saying is, chances are our boy here is as sharp as they come."

"Maybe maybe," Escobar said. "In the meantime, the clock is still ticking." Pacing around, poking the cigar in the air at some invisible oracle, Escobar said, "How do these things happen? Tell me. Something this cockamamie and all screwed up?"

It was all Bud could do to keep from jumping up. He had yet to gain enough information to have any idea what this was all about to step in and dispel all these false assumptions when Ed chimed in again.

"Come on, Al. It's not like we got some mystery here. Cause and effect. Rick, the low rent grifter, coaxes her for tips on your style at high-stakes poker all-nighters."

"We know, we know."

"So you slap her around for falling for it, ratting on you, and call her a no-talent to boot."

"And then, while my back is turned at the gaming table, she slips away and sticks it to me? Get off it, I don't buy it. I say she played me. All along figured I was a ticket to Broadway, which you should've seen right off."

Escobar grabbed Ed. Ed turned his smirk back on. "Come on, Al. You wanted pure as the driven snow. Someone who could play the part, was hungry at the last minute and available. She was available, pure wishing-upon-a-star available. What went wrong goes right back to you."

Escobar let go of Ed and began muttering to himself. "Okay, maybe when I told her the case Jack Reardon handed me back at LaGuardia was worth a thousand times more than a dime a dozen fake Marilyn Monroes . . . said after she got through playing her little part for me I was shipping her right back to the boonies . . . she snatches it and heads to the Big Apple . . ."

Clasping his hands in a fake plea, Ed said, "Exactly. Which is why that creep Rick nominated Bud here to save his neck and connect the dots."

Still totally confused, Bud hated to admit it, but a part of him was starting to become interested, actually began to wonder where this was all going, like the times he'd arrived at the movie theater late and had to somehow play catch-up.

When Escobar appeared to back off a little, Ed added, "All of which eliminates going around in circles and gets this show back on the road. Get it? Am I right or am I right?"

Ed popped a fresh stick of gum in his mouth and stretched his smirk even wider as if he'd made a terrific closing argument in front of a jury.

Escobar reached into his robe, shambled toward Bud, stopped at the marble coffee table, and snipped off the end of the cigar. He got out a lighter, took a couple of deep drags as though the smoke was flavorful. Pointing directly at Bud, Escobar said, "Your lowlife of a boss says you know your way around, especially Broadway and like that."

And here it was again. Bud got up and walked over to a splashy painting opposite where Escobar was standing, wondering where Rick got this notion. The only thing that came to mind was the time his mom took him during a Christmas vacation to Rockefeller Plaza. And all he could recall were ice skaters, long-legged Rockettes doing eye-high kicks, FAO Schwarz toy store with train sets going through endless tunnels, and constant honking cabs on the streets. And now, given the precarious fix he was in, Rick being Rick would grab at anything to save himself. Including fabricating and transforming a nephew into a seasoned tracker.

Escobar turned toward Bud. "Well? What is this? Holding out on me?" Escobar asked moving in on him.

Countering, his thoughts spinning, all Bud could say was, "But how does New York come into this?"

"Oh, that's cute!" Ed hollered over to him. "Ain't you been listening? What do you think? She took the Orange Blossom Special first thing last night!"

"I hate to tell you," Bud finally said, "but Rick was so far gone he didn't spell it out. All I got, besides the gambling debt, was some encounter with this young lady and—"

"Amy," Escobar shot right back. "The chick's name is Amy. Your boss Rick told her he read in *Life Magazine* Marilyn Monroe was sick of being an airhead. That she just now married a New York play-writer and was taking special Method lessons you only can get up there. You have to ditch the makeup and chintzy duds and get real. I mean, what kinda crap is that? We are talking jeopardizing our ace-in-the-hole here, that's what. We are talking a tight timetable we got and something that really counts in this cockamamie world. We are talking a total screwup!"

"Enough already," Ed said. "Once more and we'll dance to it. She's slipping further away, remember?"

Escobar pivoted and shot Ed a dirty look. "Right. Get the Polaroid and the snapshot. Get cracking."

The second Eddie left, still giving Bud no chance to get a word in edgewise, Escobar continued carrying on. "You are to catch the sleeper train tonight to make sure you're sharp and ready by tomorrow morning. That way you'd have the rest of Sunday to get up to speed, check out the area where wanna-be actor types hang out and she might be heading. Find some place to stay and take it from there. Ed will get on it and fill you in some more. The key, buddy boy, is a lead on an attaché case and a runaway."

Next, Escobar barked out that Bud would be paid a per diem or whatever was spelled out in an agreement Rick had handy. Ed would be waiting for Bud at the Miami railroad station at 9 p.m. with the tickets, a receipt of the initial payment for Bud to sign and the money and any further instructions. "In short," Escobar said, "you got the remaining time left today to make any last minute arrangements. In the meantime, you're to have nothing more to do with Rick or give him any chance to pull something. From now on, Rick's movements are confined. His only hope to remain in one piece was you coming through, leaving only his gambling debt plus interest. This Amy chick's fate is hanging by a goddamn thread and so is yours if you don't show up tonight. You read me, fella. Am I coming in loud and clear?"

Bud froze in disbelief.

Escobar turned on his heels and made his way down the sunlit hallway where he ran into Ed and began giving Ed the lowdown as Ed kept telling Escobar everything was going to be fine.

CHAPTER FOUR

A t first, Bud just stood there. Again, he thought of the consequences even though he wanted to tell Rick off for setting him up like this. Perhaps they could even harm Bud's sister and niece and who knew whoever else for whatever reason. At the same time, some part of him was still intrigued, as if he needed to be challenged, to solve some mystery and get to the bottom of things. Latching onto this momentary break, he rushed over to the phone stand at the corner of the suite's entrance. The least he could do was call Marge, tell her something came up—he'd explain later—but there was no way he could take his niece Katie to the Parrot Jungle. Please make his apologies and he'd make it up to her somehow. But he'd no sooner gotten hold of Marge and relayed the gist of the message when Ed returned, Polaroid camera in hand.

Bud made some quick excuse and hung up the second Ed reached his side.

"Don't tell me," Ed said. "You weren't calling that joker Rick and tipping him off."

"My sister. I was calling my sister. Had to tell her there'd been a last minute change of plans."

"Calling your sister? What is this? Like you had to get back to her? Like you're not your own man? It was some dame you got stashed on the side, right? Tell her where to get off and here you go." He handed Bud a grainy head-shot of a young woman who could easily pass for a naïve beauty contestant at a small-town fair. "Taken a week ago when she could've been taken for a poor man's Marilyn Monroe from the boonies, down on her luck."

Before Bud knew it, he was ushered out of the suite into the elevator, through the pool area as Chip gave him a half-hearted salute, around the edge of the beach and over to his car as though Ed had spotted it right off and had been expecting him. Leaning over the passenger door as Bud slid behind the wheel of his Ford convertible, Ed aimed, pressed the button on the Polaroid camera, and barely waited for the image to develop before he pocketed it.

"By the way," Ed said, "in case you're wondering, the real kicker is Al knocking her around after my handing him a telegram from my cousin Jack. But Al has a thing about sin and forgiveness which drives him up the wall so's he can't function. Which explains how he got conned into coming down early and giving an engagement party this Wednesday in Boca Raton. Which has nothing to do with you except skip his lame moves and short fuse last night, that silver case would still be under lock and key, the clock wouldn't be ticking and who needs you?"

Try as he might, Bud couldn't stop looking away, still racking his brain for some way out of this.

"Anyways," Ed went on, "I'm locked in as a point man while Al gets set for his nephew's swanky engagement party in Boca Raton to a preacher's daughter—can you beat it? For which Al is footing the bill and can not duck out. And then have a high level sit-down right here this Friday, which again is not your concern. You got all this?"

"Hardly," Bud said.

"Anyways, as far as you're concerned, call it a timetable of, say, four or five days at the most from tomorrow. So pack your bags while Al sacks out after no sleep for all these hours. The way he's going, count yourself lucky he don't order a tail on you and get a bead on who you really got on the side."

By this point, Bud could only shake his head and glare at Ed.

"Hey, don't give me that look," Ed added. "Where else you gonna make a little coin on such short notice, now that weasel Rick is out of circulation, and catch the Big Apple scene to boot? Later, pal. Show up exactly on time."

Ed left him and was out of sight before Bud could say another word.

Bud just sat there. Along with everything, he couldn't get his mind around the fact he'd not only been duped by a cagey uncle, the whole time Rick had an agreement ready for Escobar to tweak as he saw fit. As if Bud's compliance was a done deal. As if Bud had already been set up while he was driving over here.

Within seconds, the sky clouded up and it began to drizzle. He got out of the car, pulled up the convertible white top, slipped back behind the wheel and fastened it.

In the time it took for the daily sun shower to taper off, it also occurred to him that the rest of the country didn't have these little cloudbursts. They had tornadoes, hail storms, icy winter winds sweeping in from major lakes off Escobar's Chicago, droughts in the southwest and Santa Ana disturbances in L.A. All the while, visitors told him how lucky he was to always be on vacation and not have to deal with the daily grind, congestion, industrial smog and all the rest of it. In comparison, he played tennis and watched outdoor sports all year long. There were rides on the glass bottom boat, swimming in the coral caves of Venetian pool, easy bike rides flanked by the shady banyan trees in Coconut Grove or past the flaming Royal Poinciana down Ponce de Leon Boulevard. There was deep sea fishing and jaunts to the Bahamas and down to the Keys. There was always the option of excursions to Havana: the night clubs and casinos; the playground of Ava Gardner, Frank Sinatra, Ginger Rogers, and the crème of socialites. All part and parcel of an easygoing lifestyle.

On the other hand, all amounting to a way to avoid the harsh realities or postpone any rite of passage running the gauntlet. Until your number was up, that is, mired in the misfortune of having a feckless uncle named Rick.

CHAPTER FIVE

With nothing else for it, Bud began to come to terms.

Actually, taking four or five days off was no major problem. He'd accrued well over two week's paid vacation with his sports-writing stint on the paper. Nothing significant was coming up except the perennial Friday night game between Miami High and Edison in the Orange Bowl. When, in recent memory, had his alma mater even come close to losing a football game with Edison? Any stringer on the sports staff could easily fill in. All he'd have to do is intercept Russ the managing editor, make the excuse that something came up involving a runaway that called for him to take the night train to New York, and straighten things out before her situation got out of hand. So much for getting into a bind over his true intentions.

As he drove off, he kept hitting a snag. Traffic was backed up on the way to the causeway, over to Miami and down Biscayne Boulevard till he reached the *Miami Herald* staff parking lot. Frustration perfectly in keeping with the way the day was going. Next, it was a matter of getting hold of Russ, who was at a meeting.

The only good thing was the chance to confer with Oliver, the cherub-like arts and entertainment editor. Oliver seemed to be always at his desk in the city room wistfully smiling like a distracted elf.

At the moment, Bud was only interested in an advanced copy of a novel Oliver had received. In passing the other day, after Bud mentioned some new mischief his eleven-year-old niece Katie had gotten into, Oliver rubbed his chubby hands and, with a twinkle in his eye, said, "Bud, you're in luck. Have I got the book for you. Scout, the lead character, happens to be eleven, always gets into scrapes but in one scene, sticks her neck out and does some good. As if she transforms from her nickname Scout to her real name, a grownup, responsible Jean Louise Finch." At the time, Bud hadn't given the novel much thought, simply saying, "Next instance of Katie's mischievous ways, I'll take you up on it."

Now, needing a lesson Katie could buy as a possible excuse for his inadvertently letting her down, he leaned over Oliver's desk and said, "That new novel coming out with that character Scout. What unselfish thing did she do?"

"Beg your pardon?"

"The tomboy, remember? Katie's a tomboy. That character did something out of character she got lauded for. As it happens, I need something that'll tide me over and maybe do the trick."

When Oliver gave him one of those quizzical looks, Bud said, "Look, her mother, my sister Marge, teaches Sunday School and uses parables to keep Katie in line. Just humor me, okay?"

Oliver sat back in his swivel chair amid the clacking typewriters all around him, surreptitiously looking around as if about to hand over some secret document. "Well, now that you seem a tad anxious..."

"Come on, Oliver. I need a simple example of going out of your way even though you'd much rather not."

"Ah yes, Bud Palmer, always playing the angles."

"Never mind. Just humor me, will you? Crank out the basic scenario and give me a break."

Never one to pass up a little intrigue, Oliver slipped a piece of paper into his IBM Selectric and began typing away. A minute or so later, he handed him two typed sheets and said, "This is all hush hush mind. Book hasn't even come out yet. Tell Katie you obtained this preview on the Q.T."

"Whatever."

"Attaboy, Bud. Always playing it as it lays."

Bud perused Oliver's notes until he got the gist of the scene in a tiny Alabama town way back when, as Scout intercepted a gathering of townsmen hell-bent on a lynching. Bud gave Oliver a thumbs-up, folded the pages and pocketed them.

He then peered over and caught sight of the familiar lanky form behind the glass partition chain-smoking his beloved Camels. Russ, the managing editor, had returned and, doubtless, would only be available momentarily. Bud hurried over and proceeded to make the bind he was in convincing. He claimed the young lady in question had run away to New York and he had to catch up to her before she got swallowed up on the fast lane.

Giving Bud the benefit of the doubt, perhaps assuming Bud was involved with the young lady in question and, besides, had always been reliable, Russ nodded and lit up another from his pack of Camels. After taking a few drags, he noted that a substitute stringer would have to be put in place. After that, a seasoned reporter for a few upcoming major sporting events would be assigned in case Bud's mission was extended. Whisking away strands of straw-like hair from his temples, he got on the phone, glanced around the city room, and began to make the necessary arrangements.

Moving on, Bud left the city room and notified the comptroller in regard to accrued funds for a two week vacation. All told, it was late afternoon by the time Bud left the building. In fact, the fluffy clouds had turned pink on the horizon, signaling it wouldn't be long before the twilight afterglow slid into view.

The traffic had become moderate as he drove down Biscayne

Boulevard, past the movie marquees lining downtown Flagler Street to his right, reminding him of all the tales he saw as a kid. Afterwards, Bud would regale his wide-eyed little sister Marge with an upbeat retelling. But stories like Bogie as Sam Spade from *The Maltese Falcon* were old hat. They were formulaic. The jaded detective was in his element and knew the terrain inside and out. There was always the stock femme fatale to gum up the works. They were as applicable now as Rick's box of worn out capers from yesteryear he couldn't seem to part with. Like an overgrown kid and a secret stash of Marvel comics which probably was at the heart of his dilemmas.

Bud turned onto the Ta-Miami Trail heading west to the guest house behind his sister and brother-in-law's place off 22nd Avenue. Hoping he could keep a lid on things here before encountering Ed and boarding a train hurtling toward some dicey unknown.

CHAPTER SIX

Around the same time, Ed still didn't know how to break it to his cousin Jack. With his muscular build from his boxing and longshoreman days, his salt-and-pepper crew cut, square jaw, and squinty eyes, Jack had his finger into some kind of trucking and hauling and whatever else he could latch onto and was suddenly all hot to trot with this new scheme. Once Al Escobar jumped in and greenlighted it (whatever in the world *it* was) it was all systems go, assuming the capper here with Trafficante in a couple of days went without a hitch. Leaving Ed under the circumstances with Al Escobar involved with his nephew's wedding as some kind of go-between. Never taking into consideration Jack's New York was a territory neither Al or Ed hardly knew anything about, perfectly content to leave the logistics on Jack's end strictly up to Jack.

And even more iffy, some rumor floating around that Jack's pub was really a front for the IRA, that terrorist group causing all kinds of grief back in Belfast. More matters Ed didn't want to know about or waste any sleep over, let alone this screw-up over the attache`case. Talk about overloading the circuit.

Keeping things positive, if only they could put a lid on what just happened with that airhead Amy. By the same token, if this leg man Bud, who he just met, met the deadline Ed gave him of no more than a couple of days, never mind all what cousin Jack Reardon really had up his sleeve, Ed and Al would be out of the woods with no one the wiser.

He decided to come up with a progression he could handle. It had only been yesterday morning when they met Jack at the La Guardia passenger lounge before catching the connecting flight to Miami. Innocent looking Amy, who Ed had fixed Al up with, was there only because Al wanted a wholesome looking escort he could take to his nephew's engagement party in Boca Raton to make his sister happy, not look so much like a hood and fit in. Then the big meet with Traffacante, the secret partner, on Friday who would be coming down from Tampa, which was really only a hop, skip and a jump.

Ed told himself all they had was a little hitch. Keep it simple, patch it up, and they were home free.

But once again, Ed stopped himself and got the story straight. Al admitted he'd been stringing this Amy Evens on, promising her a leg up in show business, which Al knew practically nothing about. And when this creep Rick told her about Marilyn Monroe to con her so's to make nice, so's to get the goods on Al's tells at poker, that was the trigger causing this screw-up. If these wires hadn't crossed they wouldn't be in this fix.

Ed padded over to the ice bucket, pulled out another chilled bottle of Heineken, snapped off the cap and drained it. Anyways, the kicker boiled down to the silver case Jack handed over to Al like he was handing over the crown jewels. A briefcase that turned out to be not locked up in this hideaway Miami Beach hotel but smack back in Amy's little hands in New York. Where she was living, out to get even after Al roughed her up. And hopefully hadn't made out the contents and only got show biz on the brain. But Al telling Ed to keep Jack in the dark while this Bud character retrieved the case could be a tall order.

And Ed was still beside himself despite all the finagling he did in his mind.

After tossing the empty Heineken bottle in the bin next to the potted palm, all Ed could come up with to stall Jack was to spin the story a bit.

Ed went over to the phone stand and asked the operator to make the call. As he waited, he peered at the empty hallway hoping Al was still sleeping it off so he wouldn't come busting in and add his own two cents.

Seconds later, Jack picked up. But no sooner had Ed brought up the runaway chick after a row with Al's take on things and glossed it over with "but we got it covered with a leg man who's taking the Orange Blossom Special back in your direction" when Jack started flying off the handle, had no time for this BS, and slammed the receiver, cutting Ed off before he could finish the next sentence.

Shaken, Ed went over to the ice bucket, thought better of it, and told himself, if nothing else, Jack would be calling back. Ten years his senior, he'd always treated Ed as a kid from the Windy City, long on eager to please but short on the ways of big-time smarts. But this time, because of Ed's connection with Al to bankroll this mysterious caper and Jack's sudden need to pull something off right away with no one from the Big Apple any wiser must be the gimmick. Must be what this whole thing was riding on.

Ed went onto the balcony and gazed at the foaming crests of waves, fluffy clouds and seabirds making lazy circles in the sky. But unable to take the tension, he marched straight back to the phone stand and directed the operator to redial.

This time, the second Jack picked up, Ed cut right in. "Look, Jack, the thing of it is, I got a leg man all set but since she's probably just letting off steam, I mean I might need you on your end to jump in as somebody who knows the ropes so the leg man can cut this off in the nick."

There was a long delay. All the while, Ed could picture Jack squeezing one of those spring grips that make your hands powerful so's you can grab some clown and make him talk. Jack finally came back on the line, spelling it out real slow.

With his voice rasping even more than usual, Jack said, "I don't believe this. You think I got time for this? I got nothing else to do?"

"Absolutely not. I'm talking just in case it gets outta hand timewise."

"Look, Ed, with Escobar's end of it from his loan sharking, when Tarfficante arrives we got all three cornerstones locked in. No slipshod operation like Chicago with Sam Giancana hanging out with Frank Sinatra, rigging elections. You've seen the goddamn newspapers. The shooting of Anastasia in Midtown in broad daylight."

"Manhattan, right? I heard Al mentioning it."

"And did he tell you it went down at Grasso's barbershop at the Park Sheraton in the barber's chair? Five shots, he was whacked before you knew it."

"Right. There was a photo in all the papers, the body swathed in white towels."

"You got it. And who carried it out? How about Crazy Joe Gallo for Vito Genovese or linked up with Carlo Gambino? Things move around here. It ain't the Midwest or your frickin' Chicago. That's why I called and said to be on the lookout."

"I hear you, Jack."

"And you're telling me you're sending me a leg man to track down that mousy chick? If she might be in cahoots with the Genoveses or the Gambinos I might be interested."

Winging it, Ed broke in. "Whoa, no worries. She's probably just a little mixed up. You seen her. As pure as they come from the Bible Belt, all set to be an escort 'cause she was down on her luck. So all we got is a wrong move. Al lost his head, followed by her losing it to get back at him. But as soon as she gets her head screwed back on straight and the leg man catches up with her in plenty of time there are no worries. Plus we got here early on account of that engagement party is well before Trafficante shows up. I'm saying, it's what they call a grace period. She don't know what she's doing up in your territory. I sent you two polaroid shots of her plus this leg man who knows the scene. You can chip in. We got her in a squeeze play."

Jack let out a long deep sigh. "You're some talker, Ed. Always have been."

"Hey, what can I say? I'm the fixer, ain't I?"

"What is that, a joke?" Another slam of the receiver leaving Ed with only the dial tone. And right back with his suspicions about the real story, the smoke and mirrors, the IRA. Stories within stories within stories.

Ed wandered back out onto the balcony. But this time he didn't take in the sight of the waves and gliding seabirds. All he could do was realize how far removed he was from a relaxing sun-soaked stay, chock full with high stakes gaming action, keeping things laid back as Al went to this shindig of an engagement party and then met up with Trafficante.

Ed left the suite, took the elevator down, hurried out onto the empty pool area, spotted Chip the cabana guy restocking the portable bar and went right over to him. "Hey, tell me something," Ed said.

A puzzled look registered across Chip's smooth, deep-tanned face as he fumbled with a fifth of Jack Daniels bourbon almost dropping it. Flashing a fake smile, he steadied himself, wedged the bottle on the shelf behind him and said, "Yes, sir, sure, what can I do for you?"

"The girl. The one you and this Rick character were conning last night to get a line on Al Escobar."

"I'm afraid I don't—"

"Get off it. Rick told us everything. I'm letting all that go for now for a couple of quick answers. Otherwise—"

"I'll take the quick answers," Chip said, switching to double-shot glasses, wiping them with a white hand towel as nervous as can be.

"Okay then. Did she come back down here last night, around sunset when the card game was in full swing? Holding a little ice pack against her cheek, say? Asking you maybe for a little advice since you and Rick was so nice to her before?"

"I was nice because she looked so sad. But the shmoozing was Rick's play, not mine."

"Answer the question, Chip."

"Well, yeah, she did come down now that you mention it." Chip gave up on the shot glasses and began wiping the bar with the cloth to avoid looking Ed in the eyes. "But it was as if she didn't know who she was getting mixed up with. No offense. "

"Talk to me, dammit!"

"She must have overheard something. And wanted to know who Crazy Joe Gallo was. Yeah, that was it. She just overheard it."

And you said?"

"So I says 'Hey, Shriners, Crazy Joe—one big party, anybody's apt to drop in.' I mean, how do you know what was going on in that little brain of hers?"

"You tell me and we'll both know."

Ed shuffled back to the elevator. Though he could talk himself into anything, he couldn't nail Amy Evens down even though he did a helluva job billing her as a Bible Belt princess. Likewise, neither could he turn this Bud Palmer into something definite. As a matter of fact, every freaking thing was up for grabs.

Calming himself down, Ed realized he couldn't get the story straight. There were too many possibilities, too many loose ends.

All they really had going was this Bud Palmer and Ed's hunch he really was a whiz at sizing things up. Bud had his boss Rick pegged right off. He was the type of guy who looked around, watched and listened real closely and didn't run off at the mouth. The type who could round up the pieces of the puzzle, cut through the smoke and mirrors and, one by one, come up with a clear pattern of what was what, starting from here and going to there, beginning to end.

Truth to tell, given all this rigmarole, they could really use a guy like this. As long as he swept all his personal ties and crud under the rug and showed up right on time ready for work.

CHAPTER SEVEN

In the meantime, Bud was preoccupied trying to figure out how to break the news to his sister Marge, deal with tomboy Katie, and excuse himself from the usual Saturday night get-together with Marge and Dave, Bud's brother-in-law, at Cookie's restaurant in Coral Gables. How could he do this with little or no hassle so he could ease into the guest house, pack and slip off?

Speaking of which, it was ironic he had only recently agreed to rent the guest house because a tenant had broken the lease, given no notice and skipped town. Then again, everything had slipped its moorings the moment he answered Rick's call, unbeknownst to his mom and dad who were on a much-deserved Caribbean cruise doubtless assuming everything was under control, which went double for sister Marge and niece Katie before he hurriedly broke the news over Escobar's phone.

As the tinges of fuchsia afterglow held steady on the horizon, he'd no sooner pulled into the drive of the stucco guest house when Marge slipped out of the sun room behind the main house and accosted him.

"Oh, Bud, I've tried to reason with Katie. And now she's up in the mango groves and won't come down."

"Okay okay," Bud said as he got out of the car.

"What is happening? And where have you been all this time?"

"I was trying to tell you over the phone but got cut short."

"Why? I don't understand? Jill, the babysitter, will be here any minute and Dave will leave the Pontiac dealership and be waiting at the restaurant for us in less than thirty minutes."

Gazing at his sister's round sweet face, he knew he'd altered the routine which was in the realm of not-nice. Nice being the operative word. Dave, his brother-in-law, was always on an even keel and nice. All her friends were nice. The boys and girls she taught in her Sunday school class were well-behaved, which was tantamount to being nice. Katie was generally manageable, which was borderline nice until moments like this.

"I'll take care of it," Bud said, "but I won't be going to Coral Gables with you." He moved off, wondering if even dealing with a scrawny niece holing up in the mangoes was also going to be problematic.

"Not going? But why on earth why?" Marge called after him. "This started out to be such a nice day."

Even when Bud caught up to Katie, she did one of her I'm-mad-and-not-listening pouts and climbed a branch higher on the mango tree until she was almost camouflaged by the big leaves and hanging fruit.

Reaching out to her, Bud said, "Katie, I'm trying to tell you it couldn't be helped. And if you'd think about the example I just gave you, you could be grown up about it, understand and come down from there."

"Well I don't care," Katie said, poking her narrow face out through the foliage. "You promised. You always keep your promises. And when a person doesn't all of a sudden keep their promise, they shouldn't be listened to. And I especially don't care about some dumb girl named Scout in some dumb town in Alabama, wherever that is."

"Don't," Bud said, as she plucked a plump, reddish Haydon mango, tore into the thick skin, and took a big bite out of the juicy orange pulp. "Come on, Katie. You'll get it all over your blouse, it'll dribble onto your overalls and—will you stop this and listen for a second?"

"Why should I?"

"The point, Katie. You're missing the point. No matter how hard you try, sometimes something comes up and you've got to make a choice. Are you going to take the easy way out and be tomboy Scout? Or are you going to go out of your way and be sensible Jean Louise Finch?"

Wiping some of the orange glop off her face, Katie peered down and said, "She's got two names. How come? I don't have two names."

Trying harder, Bud said, "'Cause Scout was her nickname. 'Cause the writer was trying to tell us that under pressure—look, she marched straight over to the jailhouse steps and looked this mob right in the eye. Did it before they could storm the jailhouse and harm an innocent prisoner. Dropped her nickname and reminded them who she was and who they were. And said, 'Hey, Mister Cunningham. I'm Jean Louise Finch, remember? I play with your boy Walter and you brought my dad and me some hickory nuts.'"

"So?"

"So she made them ashamed. Stood up to them."

"And that's why you were late? And that's what you did?"

"Not exactly. But I wound up at a Miami Beach hotel to keep them from doing harm to your grandmother's kid brother Uncle Rick. It took some doing, called your mom and made my apologies. And, by the time I was through, it was too late to take you to the parrot jungle. And that's just for openers."

"So it's not over?"

"It could get even worse until I go to New York and—"

"Golly." Katie said, cutting in. "Then you got to tell me how you stood up to them and saved the day." She scrambled down and took off through the grove. Before he could catch up to her she raced past Jill, the freckled faced baby sitter, grabbed her mother's hand and pointed to Bud as he was catching up to her. "Hey, mom, guess what? Uncle Bud is taking on the mob!"

———

The rest was all a jumble. Jill, the babysitter showed up, got Katie to go inside, wash up and eat her dinner, then later watch the Saturday night lineup of comedy shows on the brand new Philco console's black-and-white picture tube. At the same time, as Marge got behind the wheel of the shiny Pontiac Grand Prix still shaking her head, the best Bud could do was tell her that he'd made arrangements to get Uncle Rick out of trouble. Meaning he'd have to take the next train to New York and intercede before it all spills over and "Mom gets wind of what befell her little misguided brother."

Opening her hazel eyes wide, obviously perplexed, Marge said, "I'm going to pretend this is some mix-up and you're going to smooth it all over. You are not going to have anything to do with mobsters. You're not going to let Uncle Rick drag you into any more of his foolishness, you hear?"

With that, Marge put the car in gear and made Bud promise to spell things out for her as usual. She didn't know what she was going to do with Katie now that he'd gotten her so excited about his going to where the skyscrapers and gangsters are. So Bud better simmer down and reconsider this whole thing.

As Bud watched her drive off, he couldn't help noting an abiding twinge of excitement. Not unlike the stint across the Fatahatchi Strand, poking around in order to keep Rick from going off the deep end. Getting hold of a wildlife brochure to keep from mistaking live alligators for sodden logs and other pitfalls and tracking down the elusive orchid poacher before it was too late. At the same time, his resentment turned into an adrenalin rush as one of the sodden logs actually began to slither away. And he couldn't help recalling a circus poster he once saw that proclaimed "Life is on the high wire; all the rest is waiting!"

At that moment it sure beat being seated in the south stands of the Orange Bowl, taking notes, coming up with a lead for a contest that was a foregone conclusion.

As daylight slid into night, Bud took one last glance down the street until it merged with 22nd Avenue. He knew that someday the palmettos and poinsettias growing wild amid the hibiscus bushes and mango trees would give way to other amber-tiled roofs dotting both sides of the lane. But for now, it was a haven nestled in this foliage, a refuge to come back to after a heady venture.

He parked his convertible in the carport and entered the one-bedroom, stucco guest house. He scoured around for the large overnight bag that served as the only luggage he needed for fishing jaunts down to the Keys and excursions to the Bahamas. He packed, knowing full well his V-neck cotton tennis sweaters wouldn't do the trick as fall was really coming on up north dovetailing into December. But it was all he had. He made a call and arranged for a cab to take him to the train station in plenty of time to meet Ed at eight. In the meantime, he made himself some supper out of leftovers and drank some strong coffee to keep alert as Ed gave him his marching orders.

Soon afterwards, he got out his fountain pen and dashed an explanatory note to Marge that she might possibly understand:

Marge,

We both know, if we took the time to think about it, that someday Rick's misguided P.I. pipe dream would catch up with him. That he'd really push it and get into deep trouble way over his head. When, yet again, Mom told me to keep tabs on Rick so she could enjoy hers and Dad's Caribbean cruise worry free, I promised but never dreamt it would come to this. When out of the blue, Rick called me this morning. I drove over, found him going to pieces over some high-stakes poker game. Next thing I know, he lied that I was some junior partner of his who knew New York like the back of my hand. And would catch up with some mysterious young lady and retrieve a vital briefcase forthwith. It's all as foggy as can be, I know. But to save Rick's skin, I've got this train to catch, will get back in touch soon as I get settled and will try to give you a progress report. Clarify things. In the meantime, see if you can talk Katie out of her notion about me and mobsters. Call them business associates of Rick.

Love, Bud

Bud folded the note, rushed around and made sure it protruded out of the mail box by Marge's front door. He traipsed back, paused for a moment, and cast about in his mind for a moniker. He simply settled for "reporter." After all, that was his stock in trade. He took it all in, a whole bunch of movement, deciphered it and reported back to readers in some cool, coherent form. Provided them with an access code so they could make sense of the blur of activity and what had happened be it an upset, beating, loss or a tie. Which was especially apt for something as bewildering as Jai Alai at the Biscayne Fronton. Whatever—he saw through it all. The only difference this time was a foreign playing field, a murky set of circumstances, a set of characters with hidden agendas, and an undetermined ultimate goal. And, oh yes, as a reporter covering all these shrouded goings on, he was a bona fide fish out of water.

CHAPTER EIGHT

A rriving at the train station well before he was slated to meet Ed, Bud was immediately thrown off-balance. It wasn't only that he wasn't used to finding himself in the seedier sections north of town. The darkness, smell of soot and diesel oil and the crunch of passengers, baggage and baggage handlers made it that much more disorienting.

Holding on tight to his duffel bag as people kept jostling against him knocking the bag to and fro, he started looking out for Ed, half-hoping he wouldn't show up. At the same time, he noticed most of those on the platform shoving their way for position were middle-aged men in double-breasted suits, puffing on their oversized Kaywoodie pipes, lightly sun-burned indicating they were returning from a quick business trip that afforded them some semblance of a tan. The sweet aroma of Mixture-79 smoking tobacco wafting with the diesel fuel only added to the mix.

The yank on his arm came out of nowhere as Ed pulled him away from the jostling fray. Even with the noise as a buffer, Ed insisted on talking out of the side of his mouth as if the two of them were espionage spies. Not only that, this heretofore cocky guy with a wad of gum in his mouth seemed to have morphed into someone much more uptight. After Ed handed him a manila folder, Bud had the hardest time cramming it into his bag

"It's all there," Ed said, making Bud guess he meant the train tickets and per diem for the first couple of days.

"Slight change of plans," Ed said, continuing to glance over his shoulder every time he spoke. "I mean, what do you really know about her? The girl, I mean?"

"Hardly anything. Speaking of which, what's her last name?"

"If she even told us the truth about that."

"Even so, what is it?"

"Evens."

"Okay. So we've got one Amy Evens who's got a thing for Marilyn Monroe, something called Method acting and the Actors Studio. A young lady who's skipped town with a stolen—"

"Keep it down, will you," Ed said, moving in closer. "So, like I said, there's been a little change of plan. No way are you going to cover the whole theater scene in time no matter how swift you are. So when you call back Monday around noon—which gives you a day and a half—you'll give me the skinny on the most likely territory and what that leaves us. I'm going to ask my cousin Jack to cover the rest till we have her cornered. You follow? In the meantime, Jack'll probably keep a sharp eye out for anybody who may have gotten wind of something going down and will have to be taken care of while the clock is ticking."

"Taken care of? What does that mean?"

Ed slammed Bud against a loaded baggage cart and just as quickly let go. "I told you to keep it down. What is this, some grapevine everybody can get in on?"

Brushing himself off, Bud countered with, "Maybe you picked the wrong spot to fill me in."

"Never mind what spot I picked," Ed said, as the baggage cart slid by him. "There's too much riding on this to leave any stone unturned."

Ed glanced at his watch, muttered something about having to check back with Escobar, and then said, "So, you really out to save Rick's skin or you got some ulterior motive I didn't quite catch?"

"What makes you ask that?"

"Nothing, nothing. Just taking in the fact I'm going to be the point man kinda. That's all."

No doubt Ed had changed his tune, was having second thoughts or was under some renewed pressure. At any rate, Ed was no longer a cool guy offering a fun time in the Big Apple and some extra cash. And this caper had taken on some added meaning.

Ed looked Bud over like a shopper making sure of his purchase. "It all comes down to New York, pal. How much can you handle and how quick before Jack—"

"Does what? Go on. And can I have the last name again?"

Ed waited for the longest time before he finally replied. "Jack Reardon, okay? And oh, by the way, you're checking into the New Yorker Hotel, which is a prime location so's we don't have to add where you're holing up to the mystery. Okay, right? We'll be in touch." With that announcement completed, he slipped away into the crowd.

Bud held off boarding for a moment, wondering why Ed had suddenly gotten so antsy. Then he asked a porter for directions to the sleeper cars, and made his way to his berth before the lurch of the train prompted him to get seated onto his bunk bed. And there he remained coming to terms with the cramped quarters, clickety-clack of the rails, endless rocking sensation and a new figure to keep in mind named Jack Reardon.

He flipped on the tiny fluorescent light and examined the contents of the manila folder, bunch of scribbled notes and a contract. He learned his per diem would be allotted at a Western Union subject to a progress report. Back to the scribbling, the New Yorker Hotel was noted as a good bet because it was connected to the Penn Station close enough to Midtown. Ed had also scribbled a reminder that Bud keep open to meetings with Jack or his crew at a moment's notice.

There was also some cursory advice to get ahold of the Sunday paper, maybe a show biz weekly and such—anything to get up to speed.

It was also noted that Amy Evens hailed from some backwater in Indiana and had been doing improv in Chicago as a stepping stone to "the real deal."

Lastly, Bud had to at all times steer clear of the Gambinos and the Genoveses (whatever that meant, though it may have accounted for Ed's apparent jitters).

Having accepted the cramped space, Bud got up and headed for the club car a few cars to the rear. Accepting the sway and rumble as best he could, along with keeping his balance stepping between cars buffeted by the cool night air, he was relieved to not only make it easily to the club car, but also to find a short little businessman in the far corner with the selfsame pink, sunburned, chubby cheeks and a lit Kaywoodie pipe clenched in his teeth.

There, dispensing with the standard hail-fellow-well-met chatter, Bud asked how you get from the Penn Station terminal to the New Yorker hotel.

Picking up on Bud's offhanded tone, the man informed Bud that you follow the crowds, get whatever you need up in the main concourse, follow the signs, go through the long corridor to the West Side entrance, and glance up. Puffing away, the little man added, "Piece of cake, kiddo. Can't miss it."

"Thanks."

"Good thing it'll be a leisurely Sunday when we detrain" he added. "Otherwise you could get lost in the shuffle of the thundering herd."

The little man went on about the days and hours of the week when things got a lot worse. But Bud hardly heard a word. Presently, he made his way back, returned to his cramped compartment, and soon managed to doze on and off.

In his dream, the train morphed into the crowds in the Penn

Station concourse, jockeying for position in the tunnel as he failed to find the New Yorker hotel and started over, his efforts merging with the clattering of the rails. Every now and then voices prodded him to join in and get cracking. The voices murmured they'd long since crossed the border. They do things differently here.

CHAPTER NINE

Despite assurances from the little man with the pipe, Bud found detraining on a Sunday morning like being engulfed in a moving maze that dared you to make it to the outside world. There were twenty-one tracks serving eleven platforms as everyone from everywhere was either leaving or struggling to get on board. Some twenty-five elevators took you up or down from the main concourse. And even when you reached the waiting room, you were dwarfed under a huge clock declaring "Timed by Benrus" hovering beneath a glass dome linked to a series of other glass domes held up by steel girders flanked by Doric columns. All of which hung over a set of long wooden benches in the center and a procession of smoking lounges, newspaper stands, a Chock full o'Nuts coffee counter, baggage and ticket windows, plus telephone booths on both sides of the terminal. Not to mention a myriad of signs leading down to Long Island trains or to the entrances on street level. One corridor led to a shopping arcade on 7th Avenue which must have been the one the little guy was talking about that would take him to the New Yorker hotel.

If this was what the guy called "a piece of cake on a leisurely Sunday," all Bud could assume was the people scurrying around him trying to get the jump on everyone else were conditioned as a natural way of life.

By the time he managed to work his way to one of the newspaper stands and get hold of a folded map of lower Manhattan, today's *New York Herald Tribune, Show Business,* and the *Village*

Voice, he needed a break. He added the *Village Voice* because the photo of the Circle in the Square Theater on the cover above the fold had no skyscrapers in the background. He chose it because Amy Evens hailed from a small Midwestern town and, as a newbie, would find a village more accessible.

Then again, Bud realized he knew next to nothing about the world of acting or what a thespian would need to feel right at home. At the U of M campus in Coral Gables, the Ring Theater was located west of everything. He'd only seen one play, a comedy about a football coach from a struggling college trying to lure a prize recruit away from a prestigious powerhouse program. Matter of fact, Bud never ran into a drama major except for an outgoing guy on the G.I. Bill who was thinking about going to Hollywood.

At any rate, the items he bought were a start and might give him a better idea of the territory and the current scene. He shoved it all into the outer flap of his duffel bag and purchased a container of coffee to go and a slice of date-nut bread at the Chock full o'Nuts stand to tide him over for now. He made his way back to the rows of long wooden benches, sipped the hot coffee, ate the moist date-nut bread and gathered his thoughts. At the same time, he tried to ignore the seedy-looking deadbeat with long scraggly hair in a tattered raincoat across the way who seemed to be eyeing him.

Minutes later, he'd no sooner gotten up, located a trash can and leaned over to toss away the empty cup and piece of wax paper, when the deadbeat snatched his bag and headed for the stairway leading down to the Long Island trains platform. Bud twisted around and raced after him. Always in shape thanks to the time out on the tennis courts, he caught on to the guy's maneuvers darting in and out of the throng coming up the stairway as he brushed everyone aside.

Soon Bud was weaving through his wake heading down the stairs following each slam of Bud's bag. With only a few steps remaining, Bud lurched forward and grabbed the strap so hard it tore off, sending both him and the deadbeat tumbling over. The next thing Bud knew, the deadbeat sprang up, leaped over a sprawled little old lady at the bottom of the staircase, gave Bud a gap-toothed grin yelling "A couple of days, man, is all you got!" and disappeared through the oncoming commuters.

Catching his breath, Bud propped himself up and clutched the bag while those heading up the stairs made their way around him as though they were used to the fallen who couldn't keep up. At the same time, the wizened little old lady got up, dusted herself off, and offered Bud a hand. Then she smiled, shook her gray head and said, "Out of towner, right?"

"Yes, ma'am."

"Figures. You're lucky it's Sunday and you hit an off day. But hey, cheer up. You're still young. You'll learn. See ya around maybe."

She left him there, headed back up the stairwell, as spry as the others and better than most.

Bud followed suit, still clutching the bag with the torn strap, working his way back up, then over to the 7th Avenue sign and down what seemed like an endless corridor. All the while he could sense some burly figure in an overcoat following him, pulling back every time Bud slowed down, repeating this routine at least a half dozen times until Bud hit the street.

He thought of the deadbeat's ultimatum. He thought of the burly figure seconding the motion. He put it all aside.

Feeling chilled, guessing it couldn't be more than fifty degrees, he felt engulfed by the noise of honking cabs on all sides and towering buildings blocking out the overcast sky unless you tilted your head back and stared straight up. He walked around, waited for the traffic lights to change, and asked hurrying people for directions. But most were tourists and out-of-towners themselves and couldn't offer more than a shrug as they brushed by. He headed west, tilted his head back once again when he reached 8th Avenue and spotted the humongous red-block letters at the very top that read NEW YORKER. The floors above the ground floor entrance numbered about eighteen on five sides like adjacent dominoes totaling at least ninety rooms.

Working his way to the reservations desk, glad to be out of the damp and chill, he learned he missed the tunnel that led directly from Penn Station which would have spared him this extra trouble. He was also told there were more TVs featuring more black-and-white stations in the rooms under one roof than at any other hotel. The only single occupancies available were located on the ninth floor; there was a restaurant on the main floor, a coffee shop and a smaller subsidiary restaurant. Ed had picked this hotel because he must have been advised you could easily walk up to Times Square and the theater district. Underscoring the notion was a cheerful young lady named Pam sporting a burgundy vest and matching skirt, perfect diction, and large glasses with round, matching burgundy rims to go with her uniform. She also confirmed that someone from Miami Beach had called and wanted to make sure the information he had given was correct.

Bud thanked Pam, booked a room for three nights for starters, relying on the room as a storage place for his bag. He went along with the central location idea and a place to sack out from his efforts to ferret out Miss Amy which, for the moment, was his chief goal.

Taking the elevator up, he discovered the room looked out at a sea of midtown soaring buildings blocking out everything else. But at least he was provided with a desk where he could unfold and study the map, a phone enabling him to order room service and/or request an outside line to place local or long distance calls with the operator for a fee, and a little TV set on a nightstand.

A bit worn out and sleep-deprived, he lay down for a minute realizing that, thanks to Rick, he'd been taken as a seasoned traveler who knew the ropes around the Big Apple. But, for now, that's the way things stood. He soon drifted off and didn't wake until a few minutes past noon.

But his little nap didn't alter a thing. There could be squads of deadbeats and what-not out there. There was Ed's cousin Jack Reardon and his crew lurking somewhere, Miss Amy and no clue what actually she was up to. Also been mentioned was the possibility of the Genoveses and Gambinos on the prowl, whoever they were. Add the silverline briefcase and how that figured in, plus the equally vague Method acting and Marilyn Monroe into the mix and there was no telling what was involved.

To put it mildly, Ed's smirk and gum-chewing assurances were all a passing fancy along with a swift path to rescuing Rick and a ticket back home to Miami. As a rule, Bud made sure his assignments were crystal clear and achievable in some orderly fashion. This was the proverbial different kettle of fish.

Keeping his promise, he had the operator call his sister Marge who he figured should be back from teaching Sunday school by now at the nearby Citrus Grove Church on Coral Way. She picked up right away as if she'd been dying to know if her brother had gone off the deep end due to the machinations of their deluded Uncle. So that's what Bud keyed on. Things were problematic enough without causing his sister any undue concern.

"No big deal, Marge," Bud said, affecting a casual tone. "I'm sure it's all just a glitch and a series of misunderstandings that needs to be straightened out. According to what I gleaned from Chip, that is, the cabana boy at the Tropic Isle Hotel when I went to see what it was all about and so forth."

"But you know the kind of people Rick deals with," Marge said. "Adulterers, philanderers, swindlers, and I don't know what."

"Exactly," Bud said, trying to skirt around one of her patented Sunday School lessons. "Anyways, it seems Rick had had one too many, was working his dubious charms on this man's escort and—"

"Escort? You see what I mean?"

"I know. Simply put, Rick encouraged a girl who wanted to be an actress to try her luck in New York. When her high-roller patron objected, they got into a fight and she took off with his briefcase. All I've got to do is find the girl and return the briefcase in the next couple of days. Rick is off the hook then, I hop on the next train, end of story."

"That's all? That's it? You mean it?"

"That's it. Mom is spared any concern whatsoever."

"But what about your job?"

"I've got it covered."

"Just like that?"

"Just like that. Okay?"

There was a slight pause until Marge said, "I guess. Where are you staying? In a nice section I hope where I can reach you."

"No worry on that score either. It's the New Yorker, amid the skyscrapers where everybody stays. Close to famous 42nd Street and you name it. I only have to check up on things so Rick will be out of the woods and not aggravate his asthma."

Another pause and Marge came right back with, "And the mob? I told Katie it was only a story you were talking about, set way back then."

"So she'd see why I couldn't take her to the parrot jungle and coax her down from the mango tree. It was simply a ploy under the circumstances."

"Well it's still unresolved. Are you absolutely sure you're okay?"

"Absolutely."

This was followed by some lingering chitchat and a promise to call Katie soon as he got a chance. Then he said goodbye.

But some part of him that, as a rule, was able to talk himself into things and out of them, was unequivocally unsure whether he could pull off this juggling act or any part of it.

Unable to stall a moment longer, he got down to business. Checking out *The Herald Tribune*, he noted it focused on local and state political issues, national and international current events like some fuss over revolutionaries in the mountains of Cuba, which his own paper had been covering lately given South Florida's close proximity. There was, however, a huge entertainment section and full-page ads for Broadway shows like a musical called *West Side Story*, based on Shakespeare's Romeo and Juliet, set in the Hell's Kitchen section of New York fairly close by.

Turning next to a weekly called *Show Business*, it was pre-occupied with the job market and opportunities for professional actors, singers and dancers, and notifications for voice coaches and the like, offering brush-ups for those between engagements. There were also articles about companies in nearby states in need of seasoned directors, set designers, lighting designers, etc. All of this beyond Bud's mission.

That left the *Village Voice*, which turned out to be another world. There were articles about havens like the White Horse Tavern sprinkled with lines of poetry: "The birds did warble from every tree. The song they sang was old Ireland free." There was a writer named Norman Mailer carrying on about "hip versus square . . . freethinking bohemians in the tradition of the Village villain being actively disliked." The pieces that caught Bud's eye were promoting "the liberation of the Silent Generation, fugitives from the provinces and the values of our parents and high school friends back home." One writer claimed a kinship with all free-

spirited writers, painters, and poets "out to find themselves—
romantics lowering their inhibitions, smoking and drinking
heavily, living life to the hilt while embracing free love."

But was any of this what the mysterious Amy Evens was
secretly after? And how could he navigate in a haven seemingly
in revolt against everything he'd been taught and was more or less
used to? What adjustments would he have to make?

Putting the paper down, he tried to get any of this back on
track. After she'd absconded, a small town girl who had made
her way to Chicago could have easily gotten hold of the current
edition of the *Village Voice* like Bud just did. She'd only recently
learned about a connection between Marilyn Monroe, Method
acting and someplace called the Actor's Studio through Rick who,
in turn, was high at the time, winging it and had no idea what he
was talking about. He was only using her.

Which led Bud to dig deeper until, judging from the ads in the
Voice, he saw there was a West Village, an East Village and Soho
catering to those who were out to explore whatever was trending
at the moment. Which, if nothing else, meant Miss Amy wouldn't
be put off because she too was hoping to get her foot in the door
and would probably be more comfortable operating from a less
frantic remove than the Broadway theater district.

Grabbing one of his notepads from his gym bag plus the folded
lower Manhattan map and tucking them into his back pocket, he
left his room. He took the elevator down still dressed in one of his
V-neck cotton tennis sweaters, braved the chilly air, and took on
what Pam behind the reservations desk claimed was a simple task:
locate the nearby IRT subway entrance, walk down the stairs, buy
some tokens at the booth, get on the downtown platform and
catch the subway. Then get off at the nearby Sheridan Square/
Christopher Street stop and carry on from there.

Bud nodded. Break it down to doable tasks was the ticket. Like that time out on the Fakahatchee Swamp. Taking in the territory, getting to know your way around, taking it from there.

At the outset, he got by without incident. Descending the steps down to the subway he noticed that though the crowds were still bound and determined to get somewhere, at this hour they weren't scrambling to beat each other out. He did have a momentary feeling of alienation though. Like being caught in a labyrinth with its low ceilings, barred areas, and stale air. Purchasing a handful of tokens, releasing the turnstile, and boarding the burnished steel subway cars was a cinch however, though all the seats were taken and he had to hang onto the overhead straps to keep from falling onto someone's lap. The only thing worth noting were the ads just below the ceiling of beers he'd never heard of like Ruppert and Rhinegold and the usual "I'd walk a mile for a Camel."

The one that really caught his eye though was the black and white ad for the new musical *West Side Story*. It featured a radiant young lady racing down the city sidewalks past a file of row houses, tugging on the hand of her lover, who was barely able to keep up with her. Back in Miami, a sight like that would never occur. A young man would mindfully accompany a young lady. Nothing rambunctious would take place on the part of the young lady. The mating game was subtle, no one tipping their hand or giving anything away until they were going steady, and lots of times not even then until they tied the knot.

Bud was taken mostly by the way the dark-haired girl was drawn to something irresistible in the distance.

Jarring him out of his reverie, the subway car doors slid open at the Sheridan Square stop and a slew of passengers hustled out. Bud let them go and, at the last minute, exited as well. The first thing that caught his eye this time was writing in splashy black block letters across the white-tiled wall: "God is dead, signed Nietzsche." At the same time, someone had come along with red paint and a brush and written over the inscription "Nietzsche is dead, signed God."

Perhaps this was part and parcel of what the *Village Voice* alluded to as the newly minted free-spirit way of life.

CHAPTER TEN

Bud climbed up the stairs in the wake of all the passersby, shivering once again in the brisk cold air but happy he could see the sky had turned a softer tint of gray over the smaller buildings and narrow cobblestone streets. The streets themselves seemed to meander here and there, totally unlike the wide streets by the New Yorker hotel that crisscrossed sharply as if designed by someone playing a massive game of tick-tack-toe. Needless to say, the cobblestones and the quaint brick buildings were a welcome revelation unto themselves.

The first thing he came across was a marble statue of General Sheridan with the dates 1853-1888 duly noted as a marker in his attempt to get the lay of the land.

At the same time, it quickly came to him that not only was he a shivering stranger but hungry to boot. He spotted a diner across from a low-lying book store at the corner featuring oversized Evergreen paperback books on Existentialism (whatever in the world that meant). One more unique item to add to the list.

The traffic was comparatively light as he crossed over and found the diner empty save for a slight, baldheaded man behind the counter wearing a white apron with a distinct glint in his eyes.

"Ah," the man said, "the last customer of the day and decidedly out of place judging by the looks of the flimsy tennis outfit, suntan and shivering to beat the band. Missed your connection, I'll wager.

But how you wound up so far from the trains, buses, and boats I couldn't venture to say."

Having no idea how to answer this garrulous man with an Irish brogue, Bud sat down at the nearest stool, took him for a manager, short-order cook or what-have-you, and ordered bacon, scrambled eggs, hash browns, toast, and a hot cup of coffee. As Bud got out his pocket-sized map to study the Sheridan Square vicinity, the man kept smiling and proceeded over to the flat-top grill. In turn, Bud studied the map for a moment and put it away, realizing he had no idea how to proceed. It wouldn't be at all difficult to strike up a conversation and get a few pointers. His first task, as he saw it, was to take in his surroundings and get acclimated vis-à-vis Amy's possible world and location in order to call Ed back by tomorrow morning to offer a progress report. It was already well after two and he was clearly disoriented.

With the bacon sizzling and the man only a few yards away, Bud said, "Is there any chance you could fill me in a bit? About the ins and outs of Greenwich Village I mean?"

"To while away a few minutes before you rejoin your tour and wend your way back to wherever it is you received your tan? Is that it? "

As the cook scattered the dehydrated potato shards with a spatula, Bud thought it over. In his profession, like everything else, he'd always been adept at reading people and establishing a rapport. And he certainly didn't want to turn this fellow off. "Actually," Bud said, "I can't go back to Miami till I find a certain young lady. Which clearly is a tall order for someone who's never been in this position, in a strange place, with time as a governing factor."

The glint in the man's eyes returned as he covered the strips of bacon, maneuvered the oil, and pressed down on the potato shards with his spatula. "Well now, if I take your meaning, you've a mind to gadabout after a young lady, shivering in that flimsy getup and catching your death of cold whilst desperate for a guide."

"In fact, it happened at a moment's notice, I had to catch the train, and a cotton tennis sweater or two is all I had."

"I see," the man said, the glint now joined by a broad smile. "Larkin is the name, by the way. Conor Larkin. And you'd be . . . ?"

"Bud. Just make it Bud."

"Fine," Larkin said, deftly working with the spatula, flipping and pressing down again on the hash browns. "Not to play the nanny, mind, but you're going nowhere till you get yourself a decent sweater and jacket. Maybe even a jaunty cap. Otherwise you'll be taken for a square, which won't get you the time of day."

"Oh, I see. I get it."

That said, Larkin got the toaster going, cracked some eggs in a bowl, scrambled them, poured it onto the grill and flicked it around. He retrieved the toast, plated the order and served it; plucked up a steaming carafe of coffee and filled Bud's mug as well. Then added pads of butter and strawberry jelly and stood in front of him waiting for a reply.

By now Bud was so hungry it wasn't until he wolfed most of it down and asked for a refill of coffee that he said, "Okay, what do you suggest?"

"You mean what would do for a suntanned, shivering bright-eyed lad who's obviously out of his element."

"Right."

"For starters, I'd say something a bit warmer and, as I said, keep those hereabout from giving you dubious glances."

"But in the meantime, I was wondering—"

"First things first. What I've got in mind is a bit of quid pro quo, one hand washes the other. You see, I too am under pressure so to speak. For openers you're to go to Peter's Glad Rags just around the corner. I'll be closing up but will wait for you and hand over a jiffy lay of the land in tandem with what you will do for me. As it happens, Peter will be closing as well, but if you hurry you'll catch him. And oh, by the way, he's gay. Will that be a problem for you?"

"Not really," Bud said as he paid the tab and left a generous tip.

"Well then, a hop, skip, and a jump down Fourth Street at the corner of Barrow. You can't miss it."

Realizing Larkin had an ulterior motive, but with nothing else going for him, Bud left the diner and turned down Fourth. He immediately got chilled again as the sky had turned completely overcast and a breeze kicked up.

Actually, as he picked up the pace he only had a vague idea what a gay person was. There was talk that chubby Oliver back at the entertainment desk of *The Herald* was effeminate. Bud overheard him once say 'I'll have you know I am not gay, just festive.' But Bud had had no experiences along those lines. And certainly didn't know how to get by this Peter character where being gay apparently was just run of the mill and part of fitting in.

Nearing a lavender sign, he climbed the worn wooden steps, opened the lavender door which set off a tinkling bell, stepped inside and peered around. At first there was no one in sight. Just racks of gaudy jackets, blouses, pants, and skirts.

Seconds later a slim figure appeared from the back of the store dressed in a white blouse, lavender vest and baggy linen pants. A shock of dyed blond hair and a haughty look completed the picture. He sashayed toward Bud saying, "Sorry, my dear, about to close up."

"I know," Bud said, casting his gaze here and there. "But Conor Larkin said if I caught you in time . . . Just need something that's more appropriate and will keep me from shivering. I was thinking of an army field jacket but anything you've got on hand will do."

"Hmm? I am Peter by the way, love."

"Hi. I'm Bud."

"Well, Bud my dear, as for what you're wearing, unless they do a revival of that campy musical at the Cherry Lane—the one about ditsy flappers and their idle boy friends—Conor is absolutely right."

"Look, I know, I know, but as I explained, I had to leave Miami in a rush."

Another "Hmm?" followed by "I see."

"Look, I'll settle for any kind of jacket and warm sweater." Recalling the article in the *Village Voice,* he added, "as long as it helps me blend in and not be taken as a complete square."

"Something butch?"

All Bud could do was shrug.

"As in macho?"

"Just a regular seeker around here from the hinterlands and outer banks."

"All right, hon, I'll see what I can dig up that might do."

Peter sashayed into the racks, separating hanging items here and there, down one aisle and up another. At once point he called out, "What would you say to a worn but still serviceable corduroy jacket with leather patches on the elbows ?"

"Anything you can come up with."

Moments later he returned with a forest green jacket and a thick charcoal grey sweater and asked Bud to take off the tennis sweater and try them both on. As Bud complied and then looked in the full length mirror, Peter said, "It once belonged to an artist who bequeathed it to a southern writer. In turn, the writer lost his way imbibing, engaging in sexual adventures, and burning the candle at both ends and, disheveled as can be, retreated to Mississippi. And here, bless your heart, we have a sturdy outdoor type with a glowing tan in his place. Goodness gracious, who will it be bestowed upon next?"

Self-consciously gazing at this image in the full-length mirror, Bud said, "At any rate, I suppose it'll do the trick for the next couple of days."

Instead of another 'hmm?' Peter made do with an arched eyebrow and took Bud's sweater in trade as an additional campy item. Bud paid him the balance, thanked him for his trouble and made for the door.

Peter immediately stopped him and said, "Do let me know, sweetie, how you're faring. I take a motherly interest in all my garments as they make their way out into the world." Slipping a lavender business card into Bud's jacket pocket he added. "But more importantly, if you've a mind to swing both ways or at the very least give Bi a try."

Bud shrugged, having no idea how to respond to that remark.

"Bisexual. My my, my dear, where have you been?"

Bud let it go and proceeded down the steps back to Larkin's diner, hoping for the promised crash course in navigating the Village in his pursuit of star-struck, possibly thieving Miss Amy. Unable to shake the notion that, dressed as he was, he wasn't going to be able to operate strictly as an observer as planned. Somehow he'd been slated to leave the viewing stands, come down, and fill in as some kind of player.

CHAPTER ELEVEN

Except for a quick approval of Bud's outfit, Conor Larkin and Bud were getting nowhere as far as coming to some kind of quid pro quo was concerned. Then Larkin finished sweeping up, came back, and leaned over the counter.

"Listen, boyo, to come right down to it, the long and the short of it is I'm a writer in a sea of writers here and about, except being a transplant from across the sea gives me an advantage. Others notice things but I'm the only one with a gift of the gab to boot who really sees it all. The upshot is my *Tales of the Village* could use an additional slant before submitting the manuscript to the publisher. I've been dealing with those who are here to find or lose themselves but you, on the face of it, seem to be another kettle of fish. Do you follow?"

Nodding, Bud said, "After something entirely different."

"Right you are. In pursuit of some long lost love, a last chance or something in that realm."

As Larkin carried on with his sales pitch, Bud started thinking of some way to retain him as a guide to make up for lost time. To offer something while, at the same time, obtaining a possible link to this world of Method acting in time to give Ed a crackerjack progress report regarding Amy's whereabouts.

Off the top of his head, Bud cut Larkin off and said, "Okay, what do you think of this?" On my end we'll put it under the umbrella of 'Chasing Amy.'"

Larkin leaned forward and said, "Go on, go on. I'm open to any blessed grist for the mill."

"As you've already established, a shivering tourist will get nowhere in these parts. I need a crash course, get to know my way around here, picking up clues as I go. By latching onto a seasoned person who could usher me into the world of the Method which has drawn Miss Amy to this town."

Larkin looked up at the low-hanging ceiling as if waiting for divine guidance and nodded to himself. "Chasing Amy, is it?"

"A working title, provided we don't get in each other's way."

"Hold on now," Larkin said, the glint in his eyes returning. "Let's have a go at it this way. A scavenger hunt, is it? But there's got to be something worth the bother. Something in need of my services as an unemployed angel, if you will, that will give it shape and thrust and purpose. Not totally unlike my aid to the winsome, forlorn spinster at her wit's end over a grifter who'd relieved her of all her savings and ran off with the comely Dutch maid. That was my last effort, mind, leaving me in need of only a signature piece as the capper for my colorful expose's to submit to the publisher. So, what is it really? Darlin' Amy slipping from your grasp? You, so smitten, you've dropped everything, even the warmth of the tropics for this bailiwick as it slips from the nip of fall heading into the chill of winter? Let's have it, lad."

Larkin was so taken with this overblown scenario, Bud was not about to let on what was really going on. "Fine," Bud countered. "For openers, in order to track her down I'll need that crash course and a contact who will give me a line on a winsome young miss from the Heartland following in the footsteps of Marilyn Monroe. As she and her whereabouts become less mysterious to me, I will fill you in."

Bud reached into the inside pocket of the jacket and handed him the small Polaroid.

"Ah," Larkin said, "a bit innocent I'd say. Possibly a bit fragile."

"But hell bent to follow Marilyn into the Actors Studio."

"A bit fragile and an untrammeled dreamer. And you, seemingly on a practical errand as a ruse, but filling me in as our tit for tat proceeds."

Handing back the Polaroid, reaching behind the counter, Larkin came up with a handful of index cards, got out a ballpoint pen and began numbering them and making a few jottings. Dispensing with any more hype, Larkin said, "It's vital that you be strictly observant in keeping with your new garb in order to pull this off. Plus, as an acquaintance of mine, following in my footsteps, you're making my very same rounds in order to take some soundings. In other words, it's imperative you not give yourself away. Do you have the gumption to take in the free spirit and new wave, in a manner of speaking?"

"Absolutely."

"And you'll be sure to be filling me in as we go so I'll have something pertinent to hang a topper of a tale on?"

"You bet."

"Well all right then. That's grand." Larkin grabbed the broom and dustpan, walked away, and tossed them in the corner closet. It struck Bud, no matter how it was construed, they were using each other. Both in need of a way to get from here to there. Both in a rush. And it certainly wouldn't hurt to have an older sidekick who knew his way around.

"Just one little question," Bud said, perusing the numbered index card. "The last card you marked. I assume I'll be ending up at a Sunday open house where dyed-in-the-wool theatrical types congregate. If nothing else on this trek clicks, I'll at least wind up with a vital lead."

"That's the plan. By the by, that outfit Peter foisted on you would surely be fit for a disciple of Tennessee Williams. The playwright. Author of classics like *The Glass Menagerie* and currently residing in Key West. Thus we link the previous owner of the jacket, your Florida tan, and to whom you owe your presence here."

"I don't do impressions."

"None needed. Keep a low profile, be offhand about it. Then come by after the lunch hour tomorrow, fill me in on your prospects and provide a leg up on mine. Fancy, if you will, we are collaborating on a tale well told."

Bud pulled back for a second. So far, Rick pawned him off as a leg man who knew his way around Manhattan. Ed and Escobar had him under a racketeer's payroll. And Larkin booked him as an inspiration for a Village short story while posing as a laconic dramatist in league with Tennessee Williams. Shaking his head, Bud said, "Fine. Whatever."

Breaking into an easy smile again, Larkin said, "That's the spirit," shuffled the index cards, and pointed out the exact progression of his personal jaunt, starting with the Beat-poet rehearsal at the nearby Circle in the Square Theater, proceeding to the goings-on at Washington Square, then to Cafe Rienzi on MacDougal Street and circling back to the White Horse Tavern, "and checking in with Reilly, the red-bearded bartender and raconteur." By that juncture, a bit more with-it, primed for the open house, he was to seek out the seasoned Method actress Stella Parsons. Upon leaving the open house, all he had to do was catch the uptown subway and be back snug at the New Yorker hotel in time to go over his findings.

Before Bud left, Larkin had one more bit of advice pertaining to Carmen, the hostess of the Sunday do. "Are you acquainted with free love, lad?"

Bud had no reply.

"Ah, and it's another of your missed opportunities is it?

Leading to your wayward dilemma I'll wager. As Peter surely must have indicated, you needn't stand on ceremonies, which I take it is a custom of yours amongst the swaying palms. A wild rover should always have a few dalliances under his belt before he settles on his one true love."

"Uh-huh" was all Bud could come up with.

"You see," Larkin went on, "the subject is bound to come up the second you run into Carmen, lady of the house, she of the ample figure, wearing a tent of a caftan, reeking of perfume reminiscent of an Arabian brothel. You'd be best off with an inoffensive reply at the ready."

"I'll keep that in mind."

"And remember, go with the wave, in the direction things are rolling."

"I'll keep it all in mind."

Larkin handed over Bud's itinerary, shooed him off and began to lock up.

Minutes later, standing on the cobblestones facing the Circle in the Square Theater, Bud set his sights on Larkin's beaten path—a quick way to supposedly get acclimated and, while he was at it, keeping his eyes peeled for suitable accommodations for skittish Amy away from hectic Midtown. That is, if his hunch was right and she needed some sense of small town America in order to pull back and get her bearings.

Soon enough, he found himself standing in the back of the dark little theater save for a spotlight focused on a swarthy looking guy in a red-and-black checkered flannel shirt playing bongos off-beat. Judging from the photo outside, the guy must be Kerouac, the featured performer. At the same time he was backed up by a skinny fellow with long curly hair and sideburns, wearing a baggy brown suit, blowing on a saxophone, touted as *Angelo and his Progressive Riffs*. Presently, Kerouac began calling out things in a deep husky voice about taking in the entire state of Nebraska like guzzling a deep swig of whiskey. In turn, Angelo responded on the sax in his own inimitable way.

Kerouac may have been attempting to catch the pulsing rhythms of Manhattan during his rendition, both of them coming up with some kind of jazz-poetry. Except for the fact the words didn't rhyme and Angelo's riffs never came close to a tune or melody. Perhaps they were fooling around, tossing out whatever came to them to see what would happen. Perhaps that was the whole point.

It didn't take long for Bud to decide he'd be at a loss for words if the subject came up at this evening's open house. He knew nothing about poetry except what he'd been forced to read in grade school and this was far and away nothing like that. As for jazz, the closest he'd come was hearing some friends of his saying "that's cool" while listening to, say, Frank Sinatra belting out "I've got the world on a string, sitting on a rainbow" on their record player. And the tunes always had an easy beginning and end and lasted no more than three or four minutes. Here there was no telling what Kerouac and Angelo were up to as Kerouac kept fooling around with the beat on the bongos, Angelo going his own way, Kerouac reminiscing off the top of his head about some trip he took. All of it the complete opposite of anything safe and predictable.

Bud left the theater, went back out into the cool overcast afternoon, glanced at Larkin's cards and then his map, and kept walking east along West Fourth Street. Momentarily, he came upon a series of large, unframed stretches of canvas propped up on easels, leaning against the sides of a brick stoop. What caught his eye were the vibrant spatters and drips of bright colors. He had no idea what medium was being used except it came from a can and definitely not squeezed out of a tube. In no time, someone wearing a raincoat splattered with the same colors came traipsing down the steps saying, "Well? Hey, what do you think?"

All Bud could say to the guy was, "What's it going to be?"

"Come again?"

He could have guessed it was the initial sprays of a meteor shower but didn't want to seem presumptuous. "When it's all finished I mean."

"What are you, pulling my leg? And what's with the tan? Wait, don't tell me. You're slumming, right? Checking us all out, nothing better to do."

"Not at all. Matter of fact, I was just taking in Kerouac's road trip with a sax player chiming in."

"The sax player wasn't chiming in, man. Besides, why the lame question? We got jazz/painting too. Jackson Pollack's wild brush strokes with Miles Davis or Charlie Parker on the turntable as he takes a whack at a humongous canvas. Is that what you're getting at? My smaller pieces winging it with Dizzy Gillespie on an LP can't compare? Size is everything? You some out of town critic gonna write-up us small fries? Well, I got news. Art is instant, man, no matter how you slice it. Just 'cause I don't have no loft and yards and yards of canvas to tack up on the wall don't mean nothing. And who are you anyways?"

"Easy," Bud said, stepping away from him. "Just passing by and was only wondering."

"Well don't."

"Fine."

Spotting a red haired woman wearing a Poncho marked with blue and orange horizontal stripes, the painter waved to her, turned back to Bud and said, "Okay, we're cool. Just watch it next time."

Bud nodded. Unlike sports or any activity he was used to, he was beginning to see the rules weren't openly defined. For all he knew, there were no rules. For all he knew, that also pertained to chasing after Amy.

Moving right along, he noted that Washington Square was only a block away and kept heading in that direction. He took in the display in a jewelry shop window featuring silver rings, necklaces, and bracelets of various thicknesses and twisted shapes, as though the jeweler too had allowed his designs to go wherever they will.

Shortly, he found himself gazing at a giant archway and the words from George Washington: "Let us raise a standard to which the wise and the honest can repair." At the same time, he ran into a gaggle of young people streaming through the archway. Following the sound of strumming acoustic guitars, he made his way down to a large gathering around a circular spewing fountain, all dressed casually: the girls in crew-neck sweaters and corduroy slacks, plaid jumpers, and flowing blouses; the guys mostly in red windbreakers, suede jackets, denim shirts over undershirts, fringed leather vests, jeans, and desert boots. No short hair Miami style in sight. Everyone wearing their hair long: the males with sideburns and mustaches, some with stubble or scraggly beards; a few girls in ponytails or headbands, most of them letting their hair hang loose around their shoulders.

Seemingly all at once the strumming began to consolidate as everyone joined in singing "This land is your land, this land is my land . . . " Followed by "Michael row the boat ashore, hallelujah . . ." and so on.

A sense of community perhaps but far different from what Amy probably experienced in the boonies. Far different than she found in Chicago also and worlds removed from touristy Miami Beach or, as it happened in Bud's Miami.

His gaze drifted over to a long row of benches at the edge of the

Square on either side of concrete tables. As he walked over, he saw there were chess boards on the tables, old men in drab baggy suits and floppy wool hats, pipes clenched in their teeth sitting across from each other, contemplating their next move, completely oblivious of the fact that the strumming had picked up tempo. Glancing back, Bud saw that a group of young girls had sprung up, held hands, and had broken into some folk dance, stepping out and crossing over, moving away and returning. Others swayed, spun around and clapped with their arms over their heads. Still others were making undulating motions. All the rest were clapping their hands in front of them as the beat picked up, singing what sounded like "Tzena tzena tzena . . . listen to the drum beat . . . they're calling us to dance and play . . . "

Bud was so taken with this outburst, in contrast he couldn't help recalling that single time as a kid watching the Rockettes at Radio City Music Hall. Thinking they must have been trained by a drill sergeant: every hair in place, every smile identical, every eye-high leg kicking in precision. He'd wondered what would happen if one of them had to scratch her nose or sneeze. But if you're trying to be like a drill team in the service, that strictly wasn't permitted.

As the "Tzena" song ended, someone started singing "Good night, Irene . . . Irene good night . . . " Soon the entire gathering joined in and began to sway to the dreamy tempo. Bud remained motionless for a while, losing track of time. Perhaps "the wave" was a leap forward and backwards and every which way, continually open, nothing set in its ways. Perhaps that's what Larkin meant, as if everything was an act of becoming and you simply had to keep on your toes.

He kept going, wending his way down MacDougal Street. The scene he'd just witnessed stayed with him as he entered Café Rienzi, the third stop on Larkin's itinerary, and readied himself for the next experience. Every one of the twenty-five or so little tables were taken in this smoke filled room, a large expresso machine hissing away, the crowd somewhat older and better dressed than the singer/dancers at the circular fountain, most of the women in dark cowl-neck sweaters. Everyone was animated, chatting away, using their lit cigarettes for emphasis while the waitresses in white blouses and long black skirts scurried here and there. One caught his eye and shouted over the din there might be a vacant table any minute now as the couple in the far corner were going over their bill.

In the meantime, Bud glanced at a bulletin board by the foyer laden with all kinds of notices hanging from thumbtacks. The most prominent one advertised a sublet on Perry Street, available immediately for two months. The price, two bedrooms, and the only rental listing was the clincher. Even if Amy had heard something promising about the Village and took the I.R.T. down here, there was little chance of her quickly landing quiet, single quarters to hole up with a strange roommate while she got her act together. Doubtless if she had gotten hold of a *Village Voice* she would have noted there were no rooming houses or rentals of the sort listed.

As he crossed Amy and the Village off his list and continued to keep his distance from the chattering, smoking, gesturing crowd, a girl dressed all in black came over to him—long black hair, dark eyes, blouse, skirt and stockings, her white makeup creating an eerie contrast. She offered him a Gauloises cigarette as she plucked one out of a bright blue package, lit it with a Zippo lighter, took a deep drag and, raising her voice over the noise, said, "French. Strong Turkish tobacco. Much deeper aroma than the run-of-the-mill brand everyone's smoking now. Picasso smoked them, did you know that? Lots of other arty types too like Maurice Ravel."

He couldn't tell how old she was, probably somewhere in her

mid-twenties like Amy but absolutely nothing like Amy, and he hadn't a clue what she was up to. She could be killing time waiting for a table. To humor her, he raised his voice as well and said, "I only smoke to be sociable. Matter of fact, I've been so distracted, I left a brand new pack of Luckies back in my hotel room."

"Ah." Eyeing the bulletin board, picking up on the sublet notice, she said, "Just a room is all you got, huh? How about it? What do you say we take it?"

"What do you mean?"

"Two bedrooms only blocks away. You're staring straight at it and are stuck in a hotel room uptown I'll bet. So I'd say it's a natural."

"And, just off the bat, you're making a—?"

"Proposal. Proposition, take your choice."

Looking around for the waitress, trying to get her attention, Bud said, "Interesting idea. Thanks anyway. I'm only taking soundings and, besides, will only be around for a couple of days."

"That's what we call a brush-off, buster. Your loss. You don't know what you're missing." Giving him a suggestive smile, she lingered a few seconds more and made straight for the front door. At that point, she turned back, took a deep drag from her French cigarette, blew the smoke in Bud's direction, pivoted, and was gone.

Bud sloughed this off as an example of what Larkin called free love. He was beginning to see how taking in the lay of the land included dealing with constant distractions. You had to keep your mind on what you were doing at all times and take the rest with the proverbial grain of salt.

He waited a few minutes more until he was notified by the waitress that the far corner table was available. It was a challenge to get by all the table hopping as people seemed to know each other, shouting, "Hi. Did you catch so and so? Did you hear about

. . . me too . . . What did you think of . . . really? Are you kidding?"

He ordered a cappuccino, having no idea what it was, having no reason to hang around, wanting to get on with his quick tour. Moreover, after barely catching any sleep on the train, he was beginning to feel groggy and overtired again.

He yawned, barely closed his eyes when the couple in the table next to him began carrying on about Marlon Brando's "great moment in the film *On the Waterfront*." And this was where the woman with the gaunt face and bifocals really began carrying on with her companion in the horn-rimmed glasses looking off, barely paying attention.

"But don't you see, Elliot?" she asked, almost shouting over the noise. "It was an accident, a mere happenstance that she dropped her white glove. It was so cold in that New Jersey park you could see their breath. Brando, through pure instinct, picked up the glove and instead of giving it back to her, held onto it. Slipped part of it on his hand. To hold her there despite the damp and cold. She was pure, trained by nuns. He was a dock worker, crude, uneducated. Obviously not good enough for her."

"You mean it wasn't rehearsed that way?" Elliot said, perking up a bit.

"Of course not. You know how Kazan works. Whatever happens, you use it, keep it alive."

"Ah, yes."

Bud seemed to recall Brando playing a rebellious motorcyclist in a movie that had a limited run in Miami; a movie, needless to say, he had no interest in. Unable to hold himself back, he leaned over and said, "Excuse me. Couldn't help overhearing. Is that the Method? Being impetuous? And does Brando happen to be a member of the Actors Studio?"

The gaunt-faced women glared at him and said, "Ah, the Studio, where shall we start? Beginning with Stanislavsky's Moscow Art

Theater before the turn of the century? Then segue to the Group Theater here during the Depression? Then, years later, Brando's study with—?"

"Sorry," Bud said. "Just curious. Didn't mean to butt in."

Elliot patted the woman's hand but to no avail. She grabbed the check, Elliot left a tip and they abruptly left almost banging into the waitress carrying Bud's cappuccino on a tray.

The waitress, who Bud noticed wore no makeup which enhanced her plain, nondescript features said, "Pay Doris no mind. She's a critic for the *Village Voice*. Loves nothing better than to put out-of-towners down."

"No problem," Bud said, eyeing the steamed milk floating on top of the small cup. "This is coffee, isn't it?"

"The steamed milk tones down the shot of espresso, which is highly concentrated coffee."

"Great, just what I need." As she turned away, Bud said, "Wait a second," deciding to take one last stab at any possibility Amy might have been in the vicinity. He got out her snapshot and said, "Did you happen to see her hereabouts yesterday or today?"

"You a detective or something?"

"Not exactly." Bud took a couple sips of the cappuccino, trying to decide how to put it in some offhanded way like Larkin advised. "She took off the other day from Miami Beach and I need to reach her."

The waitress studied the snapshot and said, "Naïve, right? You know. A believer, trusting, depends on the kindness of strangers. Like Laura in *The Glass Menagerie.*"

"Tennessee Williams' play?"

"You got it."

"Well?"

"Nope. Haven't seen her. That type is hard to come by nowadays."

As the waitress walked off, Bud couldn't help nodding to himself. It was a lot better to be looking for a poor man's Laura than some hazy, wanna-be actress and briefcase thief lost in the big city fog and clatter.

But he was still light years behind. And what did Brando's impulse to pick up a glove and hang onto it have to do with anything? Why did that sort of thing appeal to Marilyn Monroe and cause Amy to drop everything, steal an attache' case and try to latch on as well?

If nothing else, he was alert, getting specific and not taken in by every distraction he came across. If nothing else, he was back in gear, zeroing in.

CHAPTER TWELVE

Bud circled back over eight blocks to the White Horse Tavern on the corner of Hudson Street with its distinctive paintings of white horses heads set in a file of windows high above the sidewalk. At first nothing of note happened. Inside the woodsy bar, surrounded by all manner of white horse replicas and sketches and photos of a poet named Dylan Thomas, he sat down at the nearest bar stool. He declined a pint of brown ale on tap and ordered an Irish coffee laced with John Jameson Irish whiskey. He did so to stay alert now that the slight effects of the cup of cappuccino hadn't done the trick.

Half-expecting to run into Larkin, he was soon informed by Reilly, the ruddy-faced red-bearded bartender, that Larkin had dropped in earlier for a pint of Guinness and would be making a second pass around supper time for another pint and to join in the singing. To illustrate, Reilly broke into a chorus of "Roddy McCorley" bellowing with his deep baritone "Never a tear in his blue eyes, both sad and bright are they. True to the last, true to the last—"

This rendition was broken off by the commotion caused by a number of men in white cable-knit crewneck sweaters giving someone at the curving end of the bar a hard time.

"There she goes again," shouted one of them as Bud took a sip of his mug of steaming Irish coffee topped with whipped cream. "All right, lass, put your money where your mouth is."

"Right you are," shouted another one. "So what's the alternative, Kathleen, if this country is too peaceful for you?"

"Come on, come on, let's have it," yelled a third.

Straining to get a look at Kathleen, Bud leaned over and finally spotted a pixie-faced female with black cropped hair who had elbowed a few men aside as if groping for air. "I'll tell you what, if you'll back off and cut me a little slack. I have it on the best authority Fidel Castro has been gathering women as well as men up in the mountains of the Sierra Maestro. That's Cuba if you didn't know. And that's common folks wanting freedom as much as the Sinn Fein in Northern Ireland. But Castro's revolution is amounting to something. "

"And how are you going to contact them and when?" the first burly fellow guy chimed in again. "I suppose you'll need a course in Spanish, plane ticket, and combat fatigues. And what are you going to tell the dictator Batista? 'Oh, hello there. I was only passing through and thought I'd better dress appropriately in case I run into any insurgents'?"

"No just-in-case," Kathleen countered. "They're welcoming new recruits, I'll have you know. I ran into some gals in the Bowery who are thinking of going over so I'm thinking of joining them as well. Sure beats killing time with you all running-at-the-mouth fellas."

"Right you are, Kathleen," someone piped in. "Wake me before you embark. I'll drink a ruddy toast to you."

The ensuing laughter and shouting drowned out any more rebuttal on her part.

As the bickering tapered off, Bud had to admit he'd never encountered any female taking on a bunch of guys, shades of Scout in *To Kill a Mockingbird*. Never encountered anyone breaking into a heated argument over foreign uprisings for that matter, let alone being a little drunk and enjoying the encounter to boot. As far as he knew, in this Eisenhower era, it was unheard of.

Reilly returned and said, "In case, from the looks of you, you're wondering, perhaps this is the place you vent your ever-lovin' ache for the old sod, glory days and such whilst keeping an eye out for the changing times. Sentimentalists and realists, the lot of us. And what's more natural than to down a few pints, holler at each other, and sing some darlin' old songs?"

"Conor Larkin, too?" Bud asked.

"Maybe yes and maybe no. On one hand, he's one of us, a dyed-in-the-wool romantic. Only wanting all of Ireland together and free of the Brits—one grand Emerald Isle, Protestants and Catholics together. But look you now," the bartender said, affecting a conspiratorial tone. "We're not in league with the IRA terrorists who think nothing of blowing things up in Belfast to drive the Brits out—never mind the casualties, innocent bystanders, women and children included."

"Pro-Irish but no terrorism and collateral damage," Bud said, trying to catch on to the gist of Reilly's spiel.

"That's the spirit," Reilly said, patting Bud on the shoulder. "But don't you go mentioning what's going on close by in Larkin's ear, or in Reardon's pub either."

"Jack Reardon?"

"One and the same. Especially don't waken Larkin from his cozy dream. Don't dare mention Reardon's banner with the golden ploughshare and sword. Or the sewn words 'Pride of the Irish' and the rendering of a green raised fist. Plus the green, white, and orange flag with the lettering 'Freedom First, Brits Out!' You see Conor knows but he doesn't let on. Left the troubles behind him, as it were. Knows this great port of New York is a crossroads and we're right at the cusp. With a surge spilling over across the great waters but him hiding behind this cozy, village nook and his stories at the same time. But not his own stories, mind. Oh no, let's have none of that."

As the man spoke Bud realized Reilly and Larkin were at odds and Reilly had it in for him.

"And don't dare mention Castro," Reilly went on, "and his ragtag army either. Don't spoil things by bringing things up that might be a bit troublesome, reminiscent or as dear old Dylan Thomas would put it, 'things that go bump in the night.'"

As Reilly emitted a deep sigh, threw up his hands and resumed his position at the center of the bar, Bud got out his notepad and ballpoint pen from his inside pocket and jotted some of this down. Why, exactly, he had no idea. Even though nothing Reilly was carrying on about would take him one step closer to a Laura lookalike on the loose. Nothing that would pertain to inklings he hoped to pick up from theater folks at the open house in a few minutes. Back at the hotel, he'd peruse any notations that did pertain for his report back to Ed tomorrow about the issue at hand and buy some time.

But still and all, Reilly had impressed upon him that there was much more to this venture than met the eye. As he jotted down the little altercation here at the White Horse he noted it was only a matter of fleeting signals and signs even though he didn't believe in signals and signs. Some part of him that wouldn't let go sensed a deeper and wider scope than a trek after a misguided Laura-like missy who had inadvertently pilfered a silver attaché case on her way to learn "the Method" which, in turn, would enable her to set her sights on the bright lights of Broadway.

Like it or not, whatever Ed and Escobar were up to leading to some big meeting this Friday at the Tropic Isle Hotel had major ramifications. He couldn't dwell on it or other ramifications either. That would completely overload the circuit. But he couldn't dismiss it all out of hand either.

Putting his notepad back in the inside pocket of his writerly corduroy jacket, he buttoned up his jacket, waved to Reilly and left. Aware of the overcast sky, nip in the air, and diminishing daylight, he picked up the pace and navigated the winding warren of cobblestone streets. Along the way, returning to the immediate matter at hand, he tried to picture those congregating at the open house right now. Do Village bohemians gear up for the Monday morning work-a-day rush like the rest of the city dwellers? Or does everything they say and do bear watching closely, and can he actually hang back, get a lead, and not give himself away as Larkin suggested?

It was the old Catch-22. The harder you try they say to keep things simple, the greater the chances things could fly off on a tangent. But the more you lay back, the further behind you get to the point where you're no longer in the game. The old Catch-22 never pertained to Bud Palmer. He was too sharp and focused operating in laid-back Miami. Nothing of the sort ever pertained till now.

Continuing on, Bud saw that Larkin had devised the five-point itinerary so that he would wind up at Patchin Place only a few blocks north of the IRT Christopher Street express subway stop from where he started. Which left his primary task, namely getting some inkling what drew Amy to Manhattan as an escape valve while following in the footsteps of Marilyn Monroe. Getting a lead but more specifically thanks to Larkin, making a contact and calling it a day.

Soon enough, he found himself at a courtyard made up of a

few gray-brick two-story dwellings with Carmen the hostess'
place located right in the center. As advertised, while gaggles of
people dropped in and out, Carmen accosted him the second he
entered, her ample body sheathed in an oversized flowered caftan,
reeking of a perfume reminiscent of crushed gardenias. "Ah, a
newbie I see," she said, affecting a sultry tone as she kept brushing
up against him. "As it happens, it's going to be a cold winter and
there's no cozier haven than my place. If you get my meaning,
darlin."

"Thanks," Bud said, trying to look past her. "But the fact is I'm
only on a fact-finding mission for a few days and then heading
straight back to sunny Miami." Normally he never would have
been so abrupt but at this point needed to ward off the plethora
of deflections. He made his apologies and retreated through the
foyer to a table laden with hors d'oeuvres positioned under a high
ceiling.

He now had to find someone to point out the actress Stella
Parsons as Larkin had suggested and introduce himself. In the
meantime, he satisfied his hunger and washed the hors d'oeuvres
down pouring some white wine in a Dixie cup. With nothing else
for it, he began to mingle, noting some of the males around his age
or a bit older were also wearing corduroy jackets in fall colors of
green and beige or thick woolen sweaters with leather patches
on the elbows. And so were the females in the same age range,
comparably dressed in woolens and corduroy. Whiffs of Carmen's
overpowering perfume filtered in and out as she pursued other
males in her never-ending quest.

It wasn't long before Bud realized he was the only one not
smoking and pouring hard liquor in the Dixie cups. And as others
formed a group discussing theories of acting, Bud slipped into the
rear remaining as inconspicuous as possible. Then another small
group formed a band of males and females exchanging dreams,

revelations, and insights they'd received from their respective analysts as freely as comparing trips to the dentist. Bud had never known anyone who went to a "shrink" as some of them put it. The closest thing he could relate to stemmed from an old movie where Gregory Peck had to check into a clinic in Switzerland to unblock some recurring nightmare about ski tracks and a murder. That was just another Hollywood potboiler but here some woman was talking about dredging up a hidden resentment. She was informed according to her analyst that she secretly hated her sister, which came in handy during rehearsals for a new play she was in which required her to distrust the leading lady.

Soon a very pushy guy chimed in. "Right, right. Don't you see, don't you get it? The salesman in Arthur Miller's play bought that bill of goods from society—'keep smiling, if you're well-liked you can't go wrong.' But how long can you keep that mask on and that messy stuff inside you at bay? That's what you have to grab onto, that underneath stuff, to play any decent part. No more cardboard characters nowadays. That's why we go to an analyst to mine all that stuff underneath. Otherwise you're wheeling and dealing and doing your sellout tap dance for commercials and stuff that's not worth the candle."

Bud took all this as some vague clue to Method acting and the reason you had to come to New York to study. And wasn't Arthur Miller the name of Marilyn Monroe's new husband who was going to get her into the Actors Studio? The place Amy Evens apparently had her heart set on? Which made it even more imperative to get a line on Miss Amy in terms of her possible movements.

Shortly after, as a few people prepared to leave, opening up space in the middle of the hors d'oeuvres' table, he spotted his quarry in the far corner. Or what he took to be the very lady with her open face framed by short, honey-brown hair, keeping her distance and the look of a person who had seen it all—the one

Larkin said could fill him in if he played it right. She was clad in a leather vest and peasant blouse, nonchalantly holding a wine glass displaying a wan smile and easy wisdom, a lady who had to be none other than Stella Parsons.

As he approached and saw that her greyish eyes kept focused on the small group ventures in psychoanalysis, he asked if she'd mind if he took the seat next to her. When she languidly shook her head, what followed was an awkward exchange.

"Hi. I'm new in town. Conor Larkin thought you possibly wouldn't mind giving me a few pointers."

"Oh?" She reached over for a Chianti decanter set in a wicker casing, poured a bit into a wine glass, placed the decanter back on the side table, and switched her gaze directly to him. "As to what specifically may I ask?"

"Well, it's a little hard to explain." He stifled a yawn and noted the contrast between the animated conversation a few feet away, other people mingling who were just as animated, along with still others smoking, drinking, and streaming in and out, and Stella Parsons as blasé as can be as though she'd long since outgrown it all.

Pressing on, Bud said, "The long and short of it is, I've only been in town a relatively few hours all the way up from Miami. Admittedly, I was a bit frazzled when I caught up with Conor Larkin at his diner. One thing led to another and we came to an agreement. I promised to help him with the gist of a short story and he, in turn, offered to act as a guide in terms of the new wave of acting and he put me on to you."

Reaching inside his jacket for his notepad, he said, "I mean, I do have notes so far but now what?"

She gave him a longsuffering look and said, "Why? Why are you here? Why now and so what? What's the big rush?"

"I know, I know," Bud said. "The funny thing is, taking things in stride is my stock in trade. But for reasons I'm not at liberty to disclose, my project involves catching up with a young woman who suddenly took off with her heart set on learning the Method like Marilyn Monroe, and winding up at the Actors Studio. The big question is, where do you start?" Bud again reached inside his jacket, pulled out the snapshot, and handed it to her.

Taking her time, she studied it for a few seconds and said, "At first glance she seems extremely naïve and vulnerable."

"Exactly. That's what the waitress at Café Rienzi said. Like Laura in the Tennessee Williams play *The Glass Menagerie*."

Stella pulled back for a moment and then said, "Tell me something. Where is she from?"

"Some small town in the Midwest, I was told. Recently went to Chicago, was acting in Chicago and then—"

"Was told it was all happening here, especially on television. The ultimate proving ground. And you're looking out for her, I take it. Or do you have some ulterior motive and are not at all helping Conor Larkin with his plot or whatever out of the goodness of your heart? Moreover how, exactly, did Miss Naive from the Heartland get hold of Marilyn's new plans?"

Amy found out about Marilyn Monroe, Bud reminded himself, only because of Rick's bungalow newsstand full of the latest trends he might parlay into an angle. The way he latched onto the rare orchid craze and on and on. But Bud couldn't possibly tell her any of that. Instead he said, "Let's settle for the looking out for her option."

Stella sipped some more wine and, competing with the group in analysis shouting at one another, raised her voice a bit, saying, "While we're on the subject, what TV shows do you watch in Miami?"

Raising his voice as well, Bud said, "I hardly ever watch it. But my sister's got a brand new Philco. She tunes into shows like

Father Knows Best, I Love Lucy, Ozzie and Harriet and the *Colgate Comedy Hour*."

"Of course. All harmless, avoiding any hint of reality. During the commercial break, housewives are offered frost-free refrigerators, freezers, laundromats, and clock radios to keep them sedated. However, when word slipped out about programs like Playhouse 90, Studio One, the U.S. Steel Hour and so forth—live, shot on location in New York..."

She paused for a moment and nodded. "Ah yes, New York. Like a lady carnival barker, enticing, promising endless opportunities for the starry-eyed."

Smiling, pausing once again and then adding, "Seekers get on the buses and trains before they too turn into Ozzie and Harriet. Willing to learn and catch the brass ring."

Her words were lively but her tone remained as casual as referring to new ice cream flavors at Howard Johnsons. Then her slender body rose. She peered down on him and said, "Tell you what. I've got to go feed Zelda my Persian cat and brush up on a reading for a new play. Where are you staying?"

"Got a room at the New Yorker."

"Perfect, the hotel that features the most TV sets. As it happens, my friend Constance has the lead on *Naked City* at nine tonight. Think you can stay awake that long and tune into Channel Four? As I was saying, these shows are live, one shot and they're gone, vanished into thin air."

"But why?"

"Then forget it. How can anyone from Miami who knows nothing of live, deep-delving TV, rushing up here for some hidden motive, possibly be worth my time?"

She walked away. Bud held still as long as he could, rose up and quickly caught up to her, willing to latch onto any lead. "Okay okay, what's the deal? Anything within reason."

Pausing at the front door, taking her sweet time, she turned back to him. "Like everything else . . . ?"

"Bud. Just make it Bud."

"Like everything else, Bud, it depends upon the spirit of the moment. The quest for truth apart from all the masks and reaching for the brass ring."

"I hear you," Bud said, although this could be all a snag leading him nowhere.

Nodding, she broke into an all-knowing smile.

The upshot was, Bud was to key on the realities, meet her at ten the next morning at the Automat at Times Square which was within easy walking distance from his hotel. She happened to be making the rounds of casting agents in the vicinity after eleven. They'd have coffee. Provided he'd had a glimmering of what she was talking about, she'd provide him with a possible way of getting in touch with the starry-eyed young lady in question as part of her never-ending crusade.

However, if it was all beyond him, if he didn't appreciate what Constance had to offer, it simply wasn't worth her time.

He nodded again, still having no idea what the kicker was, followed her out, thanked Carmen who was greeting new revelers, and wished her all the best. Carmen, in turn, gave him a dirty look.

Outside, before parting ways, Stella smiled and said, "Are you sure you want to go ahead with this?"

"If it gets me on the right wavelength, you bet."

As she drifted off, he felt emboldened, as if he might be getting somewhere. But as the streetlamps flicked on and he neared the IRT Christopher Street stop in the late autumnal chill, he began to have second thoughts. Stella Parsons might just be playing him for her own amusement. Larkin ran a diner and dabbled in human interest stories for his own amusement in his quest to be regarded as a bone-fide Village character as his whimsical way of coping.

Bud was totally out of his element and despite his track record as a sharp sports reporter was truly unfit for this venture all along no matter how hard he tried to make the best of it.

Stifling another yawn, Bud braced himself and descended the concrete steps into the dank subway hoping he wouldn't run into another deadbeat. Hoping he could work his way through to what Stella called the realities. Hoping he could get to the crux of it all.

CHAPTER THIRTEEN

Early that Monday morning, there was a sidebar on the copy of the *Herald Tribune* delivered to Bud's hotel room noting the progress of the Cuban Revolution. The complimentary paper was accompanied by incessant honking outside his window along with a cacophony of other strident noises. In addition, there was a feint acrid odor meshing with the engine fumes seeping under the gap in his window emitting from whatever was being manufactured across the Hudson in New Jersey. But none of this surpassed the lingering impression that live TV crime show still made on him.

He assumed it was called *Naked City* because whatever was happening was raw and unfiltered. Shown in black and white like a documentary, it was totally unlike the play he once saw at the U of Miami's Ring Theater, which was obviously rehearsed. For that matter it was totally unlike a play at all. The camera seemed to be in suspense as it followed a determined woman in a rumpled raincoat, about Stella Parson's age, hurrying down a local street. Soon, she turned and entered a police precinct like she knew her way around. Hesitated and waited while a desk sergeant was on the phone. Then, to avoid him, she drifted over to a flight of stairs, worked her way up to the second floor, burst through the door and confronted a trio of detectives in baggy suits seated at their desks pecking away at their typewriters. Without warning, she pulled a gun out of her raincoat pocket with her left hand and dared anyone to move.

Thrown off guard, the detectives stopped typing, glanced at one another and back at the woman in the doorway in total disbelief. The camera zoomed in on her face, the close-up revealing a set of glaring eyes, her face framed by short, thick greying hair.

Mesmerized, all Bud could do was wonder where she was coming from and what she had in mind. What was she feeling and what might she do? Moment to moment, the tension never let up with no clue how this all would play out as she announced she was after the chief detective who, supposedly, was due to arrive any moment.

When she spoke, sometimes her lips broke into a sneer, her street-wise accent emitting things like, "Wise-guy, huh?" In fits and starts she revealed that she held the chief detective responsible for the fate of her husband, a convict who had just died of bullet wounds. Again without warning, she began to reminisce, her eyes softening, her voice becoming wistful, daydreaming about being in love, confiding she was pretty once. At other times, she would abruptly spin around and shout things like, "You shut your mouth, mister!"

All of this like a ticking time bomb as the minutes slowly went by, the tension built, the chief detective's deaf wife unexpectedly entered looking for her husband and found herself caught in this twisty situation as the stress rose another notch.

Bud kept pondering over the scenario this morning, not only because Stella Parsons would be quizzing him. What had taken place also served as a slice of life. A cautionary documentary hereabouts revealing where, without warning, a stalker could be coming at you, a concealed weapon under their trench coat, looking for trouble. A warning underscoring what he was letting himself in for if he didn't keep a sharp eye out for Crazy Joe or one of his ilk. His reverie was cut short by the ringing phone. As he picked up the receiver, the noises and odors continued to egg him on as if prompting him to get into gear.

Though he was calling long distance from sunny Miami Beach, Ed's tone amplified the morning tempo outside Bud's window. "Come on, come on, let's have it. What you been doing? What did you find out? You were supposed to pare it down so my main man up there, so cousin Jack can aid in getting a bead on the chick. So talk, what have you got for me?"

"But the deal was I had till noon today to report in."

"Tough. Al is climbing the walls. I gotta give him something to tide him over for the time being, understand?"

"But—"

"But me no buts. Al got up at the crack of dawn, pressed me again and I had to fill him in some more. Tell him she had drilled the cabana guy about Crazy Joe Gallo. Took off soon after Al whacked her around. Which fit right into Al yelling that Crazy Joe gets the briefcase over Al's dead body. So now he's figured she's on the run and maybe trying to parlay this Actors Studio thing with a handoff of the briefcase to who the hell knows what. So, you read me now? I'm saying the bill of goods I've been selling myself and my cousin Jack may not be holding water."

Though there was no way he could get the gist of what Ed was going on about, Bud said, "I hear you."

"So where we at? Tell me you got the agreement straight in your head. And that means, even though I keep telling Al it's early days, we got to have that slim silver briefcase right back in our hands at least by Wednesday before Jack even knows it's missing. You getting this or what?"

"Jack doesn't know?"

"Right. What he don't know can't hurt him. All he does know is she's Al's problem on account of some engagement shindig."

"Oh," Bud said, trying to take in this change of circumstances.

There was a pause as Ed seemed to be simmering down a bit and collecting his thoughts. Then he picked it up again right where he let off. "Okay. At the moment, Cousin Jack probably only has a bead on you for openers. But, given his short fuse, that could change any minute he gets as antsy as Al, which is for sure if you don't deliver. The last thing we need is him barging in where you're at, raising all kinds of hell and throwing everything out of kilter. So, cooling Al down a smidge is the ticket for right now. So, like I said, fill me in."

Bud told Ed to hang on, located his map of lower Manhattan, studied it for a moment and said, "I covered the Village yesterday, chalked it off the list. No suitable places for rent. Part of the new wave, however, so it does have that going for it."

"What the hell is that supposed to mean?"

"Jazz, painting, gatherings on Washington Square . . . discussions about Marlon Brando at Café Rienzi . . . a feisty gal at an Irish pub threatening to join the Cuban revolution and—"

"Hey, hold it. I don't need no guided tour of no village. Process of elimination strictly."

Bud studied the map more closely. "At present, the way I see it—"

"Hey, quit jerking me around, will you?"

"Fine. Given her main objective in following in the footsteps of Marilyn Monroe, at this point, you can cross off Little Italy."

"Go on. I'm writing stuff down being that I ain't ever been there."

"Understood. Plus Soho, the Bowery, Chinatown, and back up to Gramercy Park." Bud hesitated, making sure in his mind some possibly innocent girl wouldn't be corralled and harassed at those locations. At any rate he said, "I'm looking into the rest."

"What rest? You're supposed to be closing in."

"Look, Ed, I've got a potential contact, meeting with her at ten and I don't want to miss out on my only tangible lead. By the way, how is Rick holding up?"

"I told you to forget about Rick. That's our lookout."

Bud didn't like the sound of that but let it go. "Fine. Give me a call first thing tomorrow. I should have something definite by then."

"Just get on the stick, pal, you read me?" The warning was followed by a click and a dial tone.

Bud searched his wallet for Rick's number and had the operator make a long distance call even though he had mixed feelings bordering on deep resentment. Keeping his uncle in one piece for his mother's sake was the only justification for the bind he was in. Except for the pressing mystery regarding the elusive Amy he was eager to solve.

Rick picked up on the third ring. "Bud? Is that you? You got a bead on her and the silver case?"

"Not yet."

"Well hurry it up, will you?"

Barely able to put up with him, Bud said, "Are you okay? That's all I want to know."

"Okay? Do you call being holed up with no car okay? Having to walk to Tabachnik's for groceries? Being waylaid by the mahjong ladies, then hanging out on the beach, listening to my radio the only source of entertainment at night unless I want to dance a little on 14th Street Beach, which puts me smack back with the mahjong ladies. Now add this Ed character checking up on me like I was some potential fugitive. Try it some time and tell me how you like it? At least tell me you've got a hot lead so I can sleep better. At least tell me that."

It was all Bud could do to keep from slamming down the receiver. "Knock it off, Rick. Okay?"

"What are you, sore at me?" Rick asked, cutting into the dead silence. "Think of it like some big adventure. Your mom was all the time saying what a great time you had up there in New York and was dying some day to get back." After the next delay, Rick jumped in with, "Look, the girl turned out to be a two-bit thief. Think of it that way. It's like making a citizen's arrest, righting a big wrong, words like that."

Instead of putting up with him a second longer, Bud muttered "I'll get back to you" and hung up the receiver.

He thought about mobsters Ed mentioned, including some hood called Crazy Joe Gallo, the Genoveses, Gambinos, and being in tandem with Cousin Jack who was in close proximity. All of which certainly muddied the waters.

He got out the so-called employment agreement, sat down in a plush armchair, and stared at it. All his life play-it-safe truism's had been drummed into him like *When in doubt don't do it*. He had given them all short shrift because they never applied. He was too savvy to ever find himself in those kinds of circumstances in sleepy Miami. Never even dreamt of being in an overpowering urban environment where everything's chancy with no hard and fast rules anyone would need to keep in mind.

He wished the girl would materialize. And be worth the effort and a leading role in Larkin's final tale. Then at least he could devote himself to her plight and keep Ed's pestering at bay.

Back in Miami Beach only a short time later, Ed was trying hard to fend off a call from his cousin Jack who was having none of it and starting to catch on.

"Get off it, Ed. We spotted the leg man, but so what? What does Al's problems with some engagement shindig have to do with me? Like she'd be wandering around in my territory. Or Chinatown, Soho, or the Bowery. What for? You say this leg man knows his way around. So if he knows his way around why should I keep an eye out on my turf? No way she'd be hanging around this neck of the woods if she's out to be a wannabe actress like you say. No way I should get sidetracked while I'm up to my eyeballs in logistics and got no time for this bull."

"Just in case, Jack."

"Like hell. What you really mean is maybe your boy Al is some kind of loose cannon. And what do you know about this guy Bud? What do you know about anything except fronting for Escobar's rackets in Chicago as his chief flunky? How many unknowns we got here? I've been getting this feeling in my gut so come on, out with it."

Ed felt himself breaking into a cold sweat. He realized he couldn't keep it from Jack any longer but had no idea how to let the cat out of the bag. As a fast talker who oftentimes had to wing it, he let it just come to him on the fly.

"I tell you, Jack, when it comes to fallout, when it rains, it pours. For openers, Al's been stiffed by this weasel Rick who set this Amy chick off in the first place, bugging Al so much he hauled off and whacked her one and the next thing you know—"

"Uh-huh uh-huh. What's the clincher, Ed?"

"Well, it goes something like this. All I can figure is, when Al checked the wall safe for some reason, it was gone. She must've snuck into Al's room whilst he was at the all-nighter poker game the other night, used the key he stashed in the nightstand drawer, grabbed her travelers checks, spotted the silver attache` case, had heard it was real important and was so hot to trot to get back at Al—"

"Don't tell me. Just don't tell me."

"But it's not as bad as it looks. The leg man already has the jump on it. All he has to do is add the silver case—two birds with one stone if you get my drift. I mean, chances are there's no way she's coming back here for the shindig, but as soon as he catches up with her, the silver case will be back on its way in plenty of time."

For the next few seconds all Ed could hear was traffic noises and Jack cursing like mad. Then Jack came back on the line barely able to speak.

"Here's what I want before I take it out on somebody's skull. Because I'm up to here tending to business and gotta strike while the goddamn iron is hot. I want that silver case in my man Liam's hands in no time so he can fly back and guard it with his life. So he'll still be guarding it for Trafficante to sign the second he shows up on your end—that's first thing Friday, Ed, as you well know. Plus you on tenterhooks every second till then. And also, given the word on the street, Crazy Joe Gallo is maybe not satisfied with icing Anastasia, and Genovese, or Gambino or who knows wanting to cut in on the action or anybody else around here. I'm talking desperate about picking up the pieces. I'm talking this leg man on a short leash. I'm talking about you worrying your head over somebody I send down there to wring your goddamn neck!"

"The leg man is on it, Jack, I just now called. It'll be like nothing happened, your way, absolutely, you got my word."

The slam of the receiver was no surprise. What was a surprise was how Jack bought Ed's story about just now discovering the case was gone instead of since Friday night. Because Jack wanted to believe it. Because Jack needed to believe it.

To ease his panic over shopping his story, he opened the glass door to the suite, snatched the morning edition of the *Miami Herald*, checked down the hallway to make sure Al was sleeping it off, and scuffed over to one of the lounge chairs on the sunbaked balcony. He needed to get his mind off Jack's threats and Al who was still climbing the walls over runaway Amy. How much can a person take?

Skimming through the news, he half-noticed there was

mention of some guy named Castro's guerrilla campaign in the mountains of Cuba. Plus his trusty lieutenant by the name of Che Guevara. Like some storybook. Which could make things a million times worse if Castro cut loose. After all Ed had put up with back in Chicago, by now hadn't he earned some peace of mind? Well, hadn't he?"

Then something else crossed his mind. This Castro guy and Che Guevara in the mountains. What were they actually up to? It couldn't have anything to do with Havana itself, could it? Perish the thought. He pictured Bud Palmer—cool, calm, and collected. College grad no doubt. Just what the doctor ordered. Sorting through it all. Coming up with the kicker. Playing it as it lays. Because he was under the gun, under contract and had no choice. Which in this business was as good as an ironclad insurance policy.

Except, that is, for damn Fidel Castro. As if they didn't have enough loose ends and guys like Crazy Joe lurking around. How much can a person take for crissake?

"Hey, no worries," he muttered to himself. "Our boy Bud said he was closing in. He'd goddamn better be."

CHAPTER FOURTEEN

Threading his way up the jam-packed sidewalk with the huge Hotel Astor coming into view on his left, Bud soon came to realize everything was vying for attention, bending over backwards in an attempt to get the teaming throng to look up. In fact the looming billboards were so massive, in contrast the Times Square sign jutting out of the lamppost at the crossroads was totally eclipsed. As if it might have been a relic from a long-ago era before everything had given way to a contest for the most outlandish outdoor ads. Here, high above the rooftops to Bud's right, was a massive Pepsi bottle doing its best to block out the sky, not to be outdone by an equally outsized bottle top on its side. Further ahead as the Square verged into a tip of a triangle, other billboards joined the fray, starting with a domineering Admiral Television and Appliances sign, topped by a Canadian Club whiskey sign, topped by a Chevrolet sign, awaiting some future contestant to join in. All but eclipsed, a lesser billboard around the corner advertised the musical West Side Story—the very same black-and-white logo with the girl ecstatically racing by the tenements pulling her boyfriend along. Other logos and marquees took part by marking the street entrances to buildings so that the Statler Hotel sign beyond the peak of the triangle didn't stand a chance.

At the same time, fighting off the prospect of becoming overwhelmed, Bud couldn't help wondering if Amy had been among the rushing pedestrians who had gotten off the buses and trains. Had they too gotten wind of small town dreams—Stella Parsons' call of the enticing lady carnival barker promising never ending opportunities?

As he turned east on 42nd street, he told himself to keep ignoring all the outlandish distractions a thousand times more insistent than anything he'd encountered in Greenwich Village. He did still notice the overcast sky hovering high up above the midtown buildings, the acrid aroma wafting in from workday New Jersey, and new concerns (thanks to Ed) about the presence of plotting mobsters and shady characters lurking somewhere. Speaking of which, there was no way he was going to be employed by Al Escobar. He certainly didn't need the money. And the loss of incremental deposits at the Western Union, unless he made progress reports, would only convolute the situation that much more. He didn't know how he was going to break it to Ed but that was another matter.

As he approached the Automat, he focused solely on the live TV episode he'd watched the night before. He selected scenes and moments that made the greatest impression and hoped that would impress Stella Parsons enough. Hoped it would prompt her to help him in his pursuit of the ever elusive Amy Evens and somehow keep her from inquiring about his own supposed writerly plans. He also hoped nothing happened that would keep her from showing up.

When he entered this sea of spindle-back chairs and round and rectangular tables like an oversized cafeteria, he paused. Surely at a quarter to ten, the place would be almost empty and he and Stella could have a quiet chat. But over half the tables were full and there were lines of people by a wall of chrome and glass, under a series of signs that read *Coffee, Pies, Pastry, Sandwiches* and so on. He stood aside and watched for a minute until he began to get the hang of it. There was a cashier booth where you exchanged dollar bills for a handful of coins. Depending on what you wanted, you dropped a coin into a slot, turned a knob, the glass door clicked open and there it was.

Under the circumstances, the best bet would be to fling his jacket over a chair in the far corner by the front window at a two-seater table, get change from the cashier, grab a tray and limit his purchase to a Danish pastry and a cup of coffee, hurry back and hope he timed it so he could catch sight of her the moment she came through the glass doors.

And he did just that, pleased the line was moving along as most others too seemed to only want something to tide them over before lunchtime. He did dawdle a bit at the coffee stand, taken by the aroma of the fresh drip-brewed coffee and the brace of brass spigots in the shape of dolphin heads.

Then, seated at the little table, all he could do was wait. She wasn't on time. She didn't come bursting through the door at ten or even a few minutes after. He began to realize how little he knew about theater people. Perhaps it was fashionable to arrive late. Then again, there was little he knew about the habits and maneuvers of any big city dwellers, let alone the machinations of Ed's cousin Jack and that ilk. But there he went again, letting his mind drift off to some hazy big picture when all he could do was play it one step at a time and simply stay the course.

Then, well after he'd finished his Danish and coffee and was about to give up, she finally appeared. True to form, she didn't rush in or nervously offer her apologies. As self-possessed as ever, she took her sweet time entering, looking about and merely smiled when she spotted him. Impeccably dressed in a fashionable belted beige wool coat, her face framed by the same slightly-lacquered short honey-blond hair, she sauntered over, seated herself, emitted a sigh and said, "How nice. It's truly a miracle when an out-of-towner actually finds his way here and about."

Unable to respond at first, not only because she made no excuses but her unflinching gray eyes were fixed on him as if he was auditioning for her approval.

Reflexively, Bud rose up, gathered his empty cup, plate, and tray and said, "What can I get for you?"

"A cup of coffee would do fine with a dash of cream." She glanced at her watch indicating he'd better hop to it because she had much more important things to do.

He deposited his cup and saucer, inched along the line, fixed her coffee the way she liked it, and held her cup and saucer as still as possible on the tray. He returned, served her, sat down, and waited.

"Well?" she asked after she'd taken a few sips without so much as a thank you.

Determined not to fall into her judgmental ploy, taking the upper hand he said, "You know what amazes me? After only a little over twenty-four hours, I now find myself questioning my answers. That is, anything and everything here is subject to change. Nothing is dyed in the wool, cast in stone or whatever the cliché is."

A flicker of amusement flashed across that haughty look of hers as she said, "I'd say you may have potential to pick up on things that quickly, Bud."

"It's funny," he said, attempting to get right down to the business at hand. "In comparison, I was thinking about a play I saw back in Coral Gables. This actor was waiting in the wings, not getting ready or anything like it. Just flirting with the usherette as the lights were dimming. Then, when he heard his cue, he burst onto the stage, the audience applauded. He said his lines loud and clear, walked where he'd been told to walk and, during intermission, there he was, back at it with the usherette."

Glancing at her watch, she said, "And so? Did you see

Constance at work? Can you note any of the things she did? If so, I may be able to narrow your pursuit. If not, you and this young woman you're after obviously don't speak the same language and it would be best to spare either of you the strain of a sudden encounter."

"But that's what I'm trying to tell you. Unlike the actor who basically had a thing for the usherette, Constance was involved in the given circumstances. She wasn't acting. There was no audience. She was really there on the city streets, really after something. You had no idea where she was coming from or what had just happened. Everything was a surprise, including bounding up into the precinct entrance, easing past the desk sergeant climbing up the stairs. Then whipping out a gun, startling the detectives. Something was eating at her. And when you thought she was some kind of lowlife, her voice softened and she got dreamy, talking about being pretty once and in love. Next thing you know, she caught one of the detectives trying to drop a note out the window, broke into this nasty smile and said—"

"'Wise guy, huh?'" Stella cut in. "And she stalked him and smacked him across the cheek with her gun."

"Right. Really on edge."

"Volatile."

"Tough and vulnerable. In the moment. Words like that."

Stella took out a cigarette, tapped the end against a cigarette case, flipped her lighter, took a slow, deep drag and smiled. "Don't look now, Bud, but you may have some potential. If you can crank out teleplays like that and provide actors with material they can sink their teeth in with little or no rehearsal. So tell me, what's the story here? What's going on between the two of you?"

Bud didn't know what to say. He couldn't bring up his uncle Rick, Ed, and Al Escobar. It was all so amazing. First Rick tried to pawn him off as a sidekick, then Ed picked up on it, then

Larkin wanted to use him as some kind of idea man or writing partner, and now Stella was prompting him as an up and coming script-writer.

Picking up on it anyway, "You see," Bud started in again, "her plight really got to me. You saw her photo, how sweet and gullible she looks. I couldn't turn my back on her without making sure she wasn't getting in way over her head. I just couldn't turn a blind eye."

Stella's penetrating gaze softened. "All right. If I were you, I'd take your photo of a would-be Laura, go over to the Actors Studio on West 44th past 8th Avenue and speak to Chester the custodian. A Studio member but between gigs when you take into account his lanky form and slow, western drawl. Not much work around here for those of his breed. At any rate, tell him I sent you."

"Right," Bud said, starting to rise up. "The Method and getting to the truth dovetailing into the girl's plight."

"Now now, Bud, let's not confuse the Method with everyday life. A good script is a heightened compression leaving out all the glitches, false starts, and unfocused stretch of dull, trivial moments."

Sitting back down, Bud said, "Of course. Good tip. Got to keep that in mind."

But before he had a chance to thank her for the lead, she snuffed out her cigarette, rose up languidly, and slipped out as casually as she'd slipped in without so much as a nod or a wave goodbye. Leaving him wondering about his next move before hurrying back out into this world of constant motion. And overall moveable playing fields springing from here and Chicago to Miami Beach and who knew where else.

Which made Stella's basic comment all the more apt. What were the heightened realities? It was convenient for Ed to envision this escapade as a simple chase with Amy making a beeline for the Great White Way, getting a jump on everyone following in Marilyn Monroe's footsteps. But what did Ed really know about her except at first glance she seemed gullible and naïve? And, of course, he knew zilch about Monroe's plans and circumstances. For all anyone actually knew Amy might very well have been overwhelmed by her first encounter with Manhattan. She might have retreated, completely at a loss, holed up in some less threatening borough going over the error of her ways. She might even be there now contemplating a retreat back to the Heartland. Or, taking a page from Ed's putdowns, contemplating selling the silver briefcase to the highest bidder to underwrite her new lease on life. Making Stella's tip meaningless.

But what were the options? What else did he have going for him? The Studio was relatively close by and the only tangible lead.

"Good point," Bud said to himself. Then muttered, "Keep your eye on the ball, kid and watch your step."

He realized a few of the nearby diners had lowered their coffee cups and didn't know what to make of some tourist talking to himself. But he paid them no mind, got up and proceeded straight out the door.

CHAPTER FIFTEEN

I n the meantime, it was all Ed could do to hold down the fort until things got back on track, which had better be real soon.

Hearing the shower going full blast down the hallway was the signal Ed had been waiting for that Al was functioning almost on an even keel. After all, this three-prong caper was all that mattered no matter how much Jack kept blowing things up concerning the New York crime scene. The three-prong timetable could be met as long as Bud the leg man came through. He'd never thought of Al as a big baby before, probably because everything had gone Al's way or else. And even then, Ed had always stepped in to smooth things over so they could move on. So all Ed had to do right now was put Jack's threats on the backburner, give Bud the benefit of the doubt, and think of himself as a right hand man for the short run. If only for once he knew exactly what was going on caper-wise and Al would simmer down and take off for a few days as planned.

As Al finally appeared with his wet black hair slicked back, dressed in a white terrycloth jacket, matching shorts and sandals, Ed stepped down off the balcony and decided to nonchalantly broach the subject. "Heard from Jack. Not to worry. I mean not to get bent out of shape as long as the leg man handles it on the other end."

Al didn't respond, stopped by the marble coffee table, reached for a fresh Havana Panatela cigar, snipped off the end with the cutter, engaged the lighter, and puffed away till the pungent aroma wafted across the air-cooled room. And then all he said was "So?" faking a cool, with-it pose he couldn't quite bring off and proceeding out the double glass doors to the elevator.

Though he'd promised himself to not let Al get to him like Jack did, Ed reached inside his flowered jacket for a stick of juicy fruit gum, unwrapped it, stuck it in his mouth, and rushed after him. He slipped inside the elevator a second before the door closed. Al told him to press the B button, Ed complied and asked "What for?"

"The gym."

"I mean, how come?"

"To keep in shape, that's how come." Al took a few more drags from his cigar. "To look good in case I come up with an okay substitute while I knock this engagement party off my goddamn list."

"Oh, come on, Al. What, are you gonna pick up some available broad on the prowl, get her to act nice for the shindig, and not give the charade away? Who are you kidding?"

"I got to do something," Al said, puffing away, walking off as the elevator door opened, Ed close on his heels.

"Hey, just face it," Ed said. "That Amy was one of a kind and can't be replaced."

Shaking his head, in seconds Al was on the treadmill, Ed standing on the terrazzo floor close by, thankful there was no one else there. "Listen," Ed said, "like I was trying to tell you, I've been on the phone with Jack, who gave me my marching orders pretty clear about this predicament. So I've been thinking."

Despite the fact that Al had increased the speed of the treadmill along with his smoking and breathing, Ed raised his voice, determined to get through. "You got too much on your plate, Al, with you tearing your hair out over what happened, seeing to the shindig for Wednesday. Plus, keeping tabs on Trafficante, making sure he'll be back from wherever, and getting here on schedule. Plus keeping track of the back and forth to me from Jack and from me to this Bud character to get the damn briefcase here on time. Plus reports from me about keeping this Rick bozo on ice. That ain't no way to operate no how."

"Says who and so what?"

"Will you cut it out and start listening to me?"

Al cut the speed down a tad and said, "All right, so spill it already."

"First off, you say to everybody this Amy is sick. She's got the flu real bad. You break it easy to your sister and nephew. Which leaves you free so's in the meantime you concentrate only on Boca Raton. Rent a car, see to all the arrangements. I mean, what good is it if you're still busting your chops over this screw-up plus chasing after some bimbo who don't fit the bill even if you landed one, on top of everything else? What are the odds you yourself come down with something and wind up flat on your back to boot?"

Al didn't reply for the longest time. Then, when he was really having trouble catching his breath, he slowed the treadmill way down, shut it off and, still holding on to the handles, turned to Ed. "Since when? Where do you get off telling me what to do?"

"Suggesting. I'm the go-between, right? Ain't I the one who Jack got in touch with first, checking into how good your rackets were doing, feeling you out so's he could lay his proposition on you the second all systems were go? The way I see it, from Jack to me first makes me up in the pecking order. However, all you and Jack do is toss me bits and pieces. Wouldn't I be a better cog in the wheel while you're away if I at least knew exactly what the score was while keeping the ball rolling?"

Al got off the treadmill and headed back to the elevator.

Right on his heels, Ed said, "What's your answer, Al? What's the holdup? I say it's perfect. Ease up between the both of us on our end down here and keep all the grief up there."

"Back off will ya? I'm thinking, Ed. I'm thinking."

It didn't take long for Al to give in a bit. Back in their suite, he got out a map of the streets of Havana from his leather suitcase and placed it atop the gleaming white writing desk under the crystal chandelier. Ed was almost as taken with the setup in this master bedroom as he was with the prospect of getting let in on things. After all, who ever heard of a white-marble Jacuzzi in addition to a spacious walk-in shower, to say nothing of the plush humongous bed? With the chandelier and fluorescent lights going full tilt illuminating the parchment-like map, with a little stretch of the imagination, Ed might be second in command glancing at a key to a lost treasure.

Not about to come across like some kid from the south side of Chicago with his jaw dropped open, Ed said, "Okay, Al, lay it on me. What's this pot of gold at the end of the rainbow you've been keeping under wraps?"

With the dregs of his cigar clenched in his back teeth, Al began pointing at spots on the map. "Okay, I'm not gonna spell it all out. Only give you a taste of what's coming if Trafficante gets here, the briefcase gets back in time, Trifficante comes through with his tie-in with Batista, and a whole bunch of what-ifs I don't want to go into."

"Tie-in with who?"

"Batista, Batista. The general who took over in a military coup. All right?"

"Yeah, sure, go on."

Moving his finger across the map faster than Ed could keep

up, Al began rattling things off as if he himself didn't know much more about it and would have to wait till Trafficante showed up to spell out the details. "So it's like this," he said, biting down even harder on the cigar stub. "What we got here is the Hotel Lido in Avenida Consurado in Centro Havana. Only a few blocks from the Gran Teatro and Trafficante's Deauville. We're talking close to the seawall where everybody hangs out and promenades, remember? We're talking the high life, jet setters, rhumba dancers, roulette wheels, thirty slot machines, fifty tables. We're talking the gambling concession, raking in millions a month, paying off the government officials. Battista's take and all has to be worked out when Trafficante shows up with the final figures. Which depends on the goddamn missing briefcase. So, you gonna stop bugging me and back off?"

Al brushed the map onto the shag rug and shoved the desk against the wall. He rose up, tossed the desk chair as well, and shambled out of the room.

Ed was left shaking his head. He had some notion what was at stake on their end, but had no idea how it fit in with Jack's scheme back in the Big Apple. And even on their end, couldn't tell what Ed's job would be, how Al's rackets back home would stay operational. It was way too much to take in, let alone being in cahoots with some money grubbing Cuban dictator.

Anyways, he imagined some breathing room if Al would buy taking off to Boca Raton minus a wide-eyed go-between. At the same time, Ed himself would pick up on the friendly-broad-on-the-loose ploy, sun and surf, and drop in on weasely Rick to keep him under wraps.

Ed tossed the wad of gum in the golden wastebasket, popped a fresh stick in his mouth and debated whether to straighten up the furniture or start things off taking a dip in the ocean and looking for some chippie with a nice figure who wouldn't mind a little company. "Nice and easy," like the Sinatra song, is the gig down here.

For a second Ed felt guilty that the leg man was up there risking his neck not knowing Jack was now close by fit to be tied. Then he shrugged it off. That was the business Bud was in. Hitting the mean streets and blind alleys came with the territory. All Ed had to do is hit him harder, making sure he was on the stick, and put the details of whatever Jack was really up to out of his mind.

Ed repeated this to himself several times until he bought it and came to terms. Everybody in place doing their thing.

CHAPTER SIXTEEN

Crossing over 8th Avenue heading west toward the river, Bud noticed that not only was the area much less congested, the acrid aroma coming from the Jersey docks was more pronounced, the overcast sky that much hazier, and the breeze that kicked up much chillier. Not only that, the buildings were rundown with rows of dingy-brown tenements with rusted fire escapes. From some piece he'd read in the *Herald Tribune* there were gangs this side of town like those dubbed the Sharks and Jets featured in the current running musical *West Side Story*.

As if to illustrate, Bud caught sight of a shaggy-haired teen dressed in a sloppy gray sweater and torn blue jeans running across the street, stopping and starting, all the while looking back over his shoulder. Then, with a quick burst all the way to the end of the block, he reached up and yanked until the bottom of a rusty-iron ladder slid halfway down above the sidewalk. The teen leaped, scurried up the ladder to a landing framed by iron bars, reached back, drew the ladder up to its original position, and lay on his stomach masked only by the railing.

Soon after, other teens, looking somewhat the same except for their hooded sweatshirts, came tearing down the street two abreast—ignoring the cabs who also seemed to be in hot pursuit after someone or something—zipped past the fire escape, heading for the river.

Bud shrugged off the incident, however much it fit in with the street life depicted on *Naked City*. Yet he felt it meant something.

And so did the *West Side Story* poster, which seemed to keep cropping up.

Walking further down, keeping his mind solely on the business at hand, he took in the immediate terrain. The only break in this rundown section was a small former church to his left, constructed in Greek Revival style with a white circle above a white wooden door. The black lettering in the circle read *the Actors Studio*. Bud took the front steps in stride, opened the door, and began looking around for Chester, the caretaker/actor/member Stella told him about.

Finding no one in the musty foyer, Bud entered the doorway to his right, peered down the limited rows of theater seats, and spotted the lanky form he assumed belonged to Chester. He was leaning up against the apron of a stage no more than thirty-six feet deep, the handle of a push broom by his side. Just as Bud had pictured him, he wore denim overalls, a faded denim shirt, and cowboy boots. His face was angular, his eyes a bit wary, his loose hair the color of faded straw. All of it highlighted by the single spotlight trained on him as if he was about to confide something personal to a handful of spectators.

But he didn't speak, even after he looked up and noticed Bud signaling to him. He continued rolling cigarette paper up and down with his thumbs, licked the glue strip, struck a match against a little box, and stuck the handmade cigarette in his mouth. Still taking his sweet time, he lit it and took a slow deep drag while sizing Bud up. Then he said, "What can I do you for, friend?"

"Stella Parsons said you might be able to help me locate a certain young actress from out of town."

"Oh, yeah? You know Stella, do you?" he asked, flicking the ashes into his palm.

"Not really. Just met her at an open house in the Village last night and had coffee with her a short while ago this morning and got to talking."

"So, why she put you on to me?" Chester asked while going over to a slatted bin in the corner and stubbing out the cigarette as if he never wanted it in the first place.

"Well, for one thing, because I appreciated Constance's acting on *Naked City* last night, the way she switched moods like it all suddenly came to her. And maybe because Stella feels I'm sincere in my pursuit of a stage struck young lady and appreciative of Method acting to boot."

"Sincere, huh," Chester said, chuckling. "Same thing she said after she saw me play Jimmy, the slow-witted kid in *The Rainmaker*." Widening his eyes as if he suddenly came upon something startling, he muttered, "Golly, mister, can you really bring rain?" Then, switching it off, he gave Bud a hard look and said, "So, what's the story with this missing gal that got Miss Stella to send you over to me? Make it snappy 'cause I got stuff to do here."

Doing better this time, Bud said, "Some people are concerned the person in question might go off the deep end. I'm concerned because in thinking she's following in the footsteps of Marilyn Monroe she could wind up on the wrong end of things having never come up against this city. All told, somebody's got to look out for her before she gets in real trouble and that chosen somebody turns out to be me."

"I know you're busy," Bud added, taking out Amy's picture and going down to him as he began working the push broom across the floor. Then, using the dust pan, emptied bits of sawdust in the slatted bin. "But if you'd give it a few seconds of your time. Stella thought, under the circumstances, you'd be the perfect one to go to in case she actually contacted the Studio recently."

Stopping, giving the photo a cursory glance, Chester nodded and said, "That's the one all right."

"So you saw her?"

"How could you miss? Saturday morning, Geraldine on stage, on her knees, having a private moment, chocked up over her mother's passing in the play she was doing. Then I spot this one. Everybody's seated of course, but she's standing up there right where I just spotted you. Short blond wavy hair . . . "

"Spitting image of Marilyn Monroe's kid sister, not to mention a stand-in for Laura in *The Glass Menagerie*."

"Maybe. Which is why I hesitated. Her looking like she was entranced or something and never seen nobody go to pieces on stage. As quiet as can be, I slipped behind the seats atop the center row and ushered her back out to the foyer. Yes sir. Saved the day as Geraldine went on sobbing and didn't notice a thing."

Finished with his little report, Chester got out a rag and began dusting off backs of the seats, starting at the bottom row of the far aisle and working his way over and up.

Holding still, careful not to press him, Bud said, "And then what?"

"What do you mean?"

"Is that all there was to it?"

Bud had to wait until Chester reached a couple of rows higher. There he stopped his dusting, gazed up at the ceiling like a kid reaching for an answer at a spelling bee, and finally said, "No, come to think of it there was more. I was itchin' to get back to Geraldine's emotional memory exercise, but that little gal wouldn't let go. 'How did Marilyn get in . . . did she get to do one of these private moments too to prove there was more to her?' She kept pestering till I told her Marilyn has a special deal on account of her being married to that *Death of a Salesman* playwright. Marilyn is getting private lessons from Lee Strasberg, head of the Studio, and gets to show the results here doing a scene some Saturday morning. But this little gal is gonna have to follow the route of every other nobody like me—sign up, preliminary call back if she's lucky. Then, if she fits the bill, called back once more to do her thing in front of the whole company. In the meantime, she'd best take some Method lessons so's she don't try her luck cold and come up empty flat on her face."

Chester went back to his dusting. Bud went up the far aisle and hung back until Chester had had it. He let out a big sigh and spelled it out for him.

"This is the deal, fella. Your little gal needs to hook up with Greta Hagen, who is the only Method coach worth her salt still taking anybody on. But is real fussy and looking for raw talent who ain't been ruined by some college voice teacher and all. Your gal can sign up on the preliminary audition sheet here, but at this late day all that's left is as an alternate. Will that do it for you?"

"That's great. I'll just need an address or phone number to get in touch with this Greta Hagen so I'll have some way to contact Miss Amy or leave a note."

"Bank Street. Below Chelsea. You want me to draw you a map, drop everything and take you there to boot?"

"No no, of course not."

"Say, why are you really so all-fired after her? And why was she so antsy? What kind of trouble she in exactly?"

"Could possibly be in. It's a long story. Thanks for your help. I appreciate it."

Bud left him alone, scoured around the foyer until he found a signup sheet tucked away on a cork bulletin board. There, sure enough under a heading marked *Alternates*, was Amy Even's careful signature plus a little note:

Will leave a telephone number soon as I check into the place where I hope to stay.

Which gave Bud the best lead yet and enough to do to keep his mind off larger concerns, including the current activities of denizens of these mean streets, listed under the heading: Persons of interest.

CHAPTER SEVENTEEN

Before setting out again, Bud stood on the front steps of the Actors Studio and glanced in all directions. Not because he expected more scruffy teens running for their lives or in hot pursuit. Only because he wished the sky would let a few sunrays stream through to soften things a bit or loosen things up. Though he'd never considered signs and signals before, he was used to clouds and sun doing a playful dance in his subtropical home town. But the sky up here, along with the abiding chill, seemed reflective of a situation hovering in suspension.

At any rate, he got out his mini-map of lower Manhattan and perused the area below Chelsea searching for Bank Street. Soon enough, he found it on a direct line from where he was standing, still in the western edge of the Village, close to the river and the piers. In fact, it wasn't more than five blocks north of Larkin's diner and Sheridan Square. All he'd have to do is double-back to the IRT subway line near Times Square and catch the express south, gird himself for the work-a-day jostling down the steps, through the turnstile dropping in a token, hanging onto the overhanging straps, and dashing back up to the world of smaller buildings, slower pace and a less obstructed skyline.

But even if he did locate Greta Hagen's place, what could he hope to find at this time of day and then what? And what if he came up empty? Would he really have to ask Larkin for more tips to jumpstart him again?

At the same time, he was reminded of something his dad used

to say when he began to falter. Like pacing himself in competition at Venetian Pool. Each time his dad would shout out, "Come on, Bud. No points for slackers. You are what you do!"

In due course, scouring around Bank Street looking for Greta Hagen's workshop, he noticed that this edge of the Village wasn't at all like the area around Sheridan Square and Christopher Street, let alone Carmen's quaint, snuggled courtyard where she held her open house. Here all the three-story brick buildings were attached like a continuous wall, set off only by an occasional one-story former livery stable or narrow living quarters highlighted by pastel window frames and forest green fire escapes. He did make note of a recessed Viennese tea and pastry shop fronted by a stone walkway and wooden railing. None of this meant anything except as another signpost in case he had to backtrack.

Then, finally, he spotted it. Shaded by overarching elms whose leaves had long since fallen. It was the only façade made up of flat, pseudo ancient-Greek columns below the ubiquitous faded brick walls. There was also a small white sign above a charcoal grey door that read Studio H and clinched the deal.

From the no-nonsense, spectacled secretary in the outer office, Bud learned that call-backs would be summoned tomorrow morning at 11 a.m. At that time the makeup of Ms. Hagen's professional class would be determined. Yes, Ms. Hagen is open to promising newcomers but at this late date admission was highly unlikely. No, she wasn't permitted to give out the name of the finalists and No, she wasn't allowed to say how many young lady aspirants fit the bill regarding his photo. Now, if he would kindly excuse her, she had best-of- luck notices to send to those who didn't make the grade before the mail carrier arrived. Which, to Bud's mind, meant the odds of his quarry showing up tomorrow—whether or not she reminded anyone of Laura in *The Glass Menagerie* or Marilyn Monroe's fictitious kid sister—

was anyone's guess. However, despite knowing less than nothing about the odds of an unknown wanna-be impressing a renowned actress and Method acting teacher, Bud told himself that after all this, something had to pan out.

Which left a few items on today's to-do list. The first was walking over to Sheridan Square and consulting with Larkin over what Bud had gleaned so far and his next move. Because even if by some miracle Amy was there as a call-back, what possible excuse did he have for barging in on Greta Hagen's final tryouts? In any event, he also needed to call long distance from the privacy of his hotel room to appease Katie, his disgruntled niece. Afterwards, he could get a bite to eat in the hotel's dining room or bar area, retreat back to his room, and assess the situation so far.

Once more, he blocked out his link with Ed, Al Escobar, and Ed's nefarious cousin Jack who was stationed somewhere in the vicinity. Not to mention interested mob characters. Not to mention having to deal with Ed over the phone and report in. In the back of his mind he'd been telling himself that just locating Amy's whereabouts would be a major coup.

He no sooner set foot inside the diner when the lone occupant apart from Larkin confronted him. This grungy little man with bloodshot eyes looked up from the counter stool and said, "Wait, don't tell me, this is the guy, right? The one coming by for another confab I'll bet you anything. So's I'd have to beat it, you said. The guy chasing some little chick who's on the lam. The guy come all the way up from the Everglades or whatever, maybe up to something juicy. How am I doing so far?"

"Oh great," Bud said, glaring at Larkin. "But hey, let's not keep this to ourselves. Let's let everybody know. There's an artist I ran into yesterday who spatters paint; and Peter at Glad Rags, of course, close by and all his friends. In no time flat the word will get out everywhere. How homey can you get?"

In turn, Larkin was so flustered, he scraped the hot plate splattering grease on his apron. He cursed, whipped off the apron and stormed back into the kitchen yelling, "Lovely. Thank you so much, Walt. It's what I get for putting up with the likes of you!"

Holding up his hands in mock surrender, Walt got up, grabbed his tattered overcoat off the hook and hollered back into the kitchen. "Come on, Conor, no need to get all hot under the collar." Then back to Bud as he sidled up to the front door. "No offense, mac. Conor was mopping the floor, giving me the bum's rush, see? I says, is it a dame or some dude coming by to fill you in on some juicy shenanigans? Strictly hush-hush on the Q.T.? But Conor don't answer so I figure I touched a nerve and says it's a guy, right? But that still don't tell me what's he doing here. Larkin snaps back 'He's lovesick, come all this way from the swamps, will that do it for you? And you'd best be going while the going's good.' So naturally that's how I come up with the Everglades. I've been around, see? I know when something's up."

"So do it, be on your way, why don't you for pity sake?" Larkin hollered back. "And the devil take your blathering!"

Shaking his wooly head, Walt exited as Bud headed straight for the kitchen to confront Larkin. By this time, Larkin was leaning over the sink muttering to himself, turning on the hot and cold water knobs, sprinkling the apron with Rinso White soap flakes and Old Dutch Cleanser, replacing them both on a shelf and attacking it all with a scrub brush.

"Okay," Bud said, standing over him, "let's have it. How many others have you tossed out tidbits to see if my flimsy tale has the makings so far?"

"It's not like that, boyo," Larkin said, wringing the soapy water out of the apron. Straitening the apron out and hanging it up to dry on a makeshift clothes line, he added, "That Walt is a bleedin' freeloader. Comes in here from time to time. Offers me one of his lame poems that don't rhyme like Kerouac, as though we're on equal footing, mind. Can you believe it? Some say he lives in the homeless shelter near Cooper Union or the Henry Street Settlement or the saints know where. Everyone says he's touched in the head and that's an end to it."

"Let's hope."

"Not if any of it gets around. Then I'm really in for it I'm telling you."

Larkin grabbed a clean apron out of a drawer, fastened it and stalked out again, Bud close on his heels. "Leave off, will you?" Larkin said, covering up. "Let's just say it's of no consequence whatever Walt can conjure up with his sorry brain and leave it be. And so," Larkin added, ushering Bud to a center stool and returning to his usual place behind the counter, "it would be grand if you could say what has turned you from a cool observer to one who flies off the handle. What has led to this wary side of you, if I may be so bold?"

"And what is it that has gotten you so shook up in point of fact? Reilly says—"

"Oh, pay no mind to what Reilly says. It's the gift of the gab. Isn't it enough to keep to our own kind and give the devil his due on his own patch, for feck's sake?"

Bud could see that Larkin was really still shaken. Though Bud was ready to let his little outburst go, Larkin was doubtless fearful things might get really out of hand. Bud waited a few beats and then tried to ease his way back to their hitherto seemingly whimsical bargain.

"Well, Mister Larkin, it might interest you to know that Stella thinks there's something to my quest, theatrically speaking.

Which makes me more than some lovesick suitor in your tale, if that's what you've really been thinking."

"Readily understood. Relatable is what I'm looking for. Not going off here and there with one eye on the pot and the other up the chimney. Anyways, so it's Stella now, is it? Fill me in as I make you a simple omelet with bits of bacon and green pepper, toast, and a mug or two of my freshly roasted coffee. Tell me, if you please, without going off on some tangent and starting things up again."

If nothing else, Bud realized he'd have to skirt around the fact that Walt had hit on something with his guess about "some chick on the lam." And how convoluted things might get if word actually got out that Larkin was in on it. If the Genoveses and Gambinos and Ed's cousin Jack Reardon might somehow be in the mix or whatever Larkin might be wanting to keep under wraps. Meaning that Bud had to ward off anything problematic while looking for advice how to track Amy down vis-à-vis Greta Hagen's studio H if, by some chance, she wound up there tomorrow morning.

While Larkin was working his magic on the flat-top grill and serving up his omelet, Bud told him how he conducted his rounds as Larkin prescribed and over to Carmen's place. All the while he had brandished the photo and found the girl was reminiscent of Laura in Williams' *The Glass Menagerie*. And, because he appreciated Stella's friend Constance's live TV performance on *Naked City* last night, this morning Stella put him on to the caretaker at the Actors Studio who put him on to Greta Hagen's nearby studio workshop. Tomorrow morning, the final auditions were slated to take place and that's where Bud was stuck.

It took a little while longer until Larkin seemed to have calmed down a bit. Larkin cleared the dishes but left the counter and began pacing as if Bud had inadvertently struck a nerve at some point, tapped something deeply hidden and brought it to the surface by Reilly at the White Horse. Then finally Larkin stood still and came right out with it.

"You see, it's always been bits and bobs with me. Back in Dublin and all around the counties. I was a short order cook, took photos and added captions for a number of tourist guides. I've run the gauntlet, boyo. Even took a turn playing Joxer Daly, the ne'er do well, in O'Casey's *Juno and the Paycock*. But it's still bits and bobs because Joxer would slip in and out the window, stay for a moment downing a few pints, talk a load of rubbish with the captain and then, in a twinkle of the eye, he was gone again. I also read bits of my poetry here and there but, in a sense, did so well playing Joxer, I never stopped."

"What are you trying to tell me?"

"I'm getting to it, I'm getting to it. Before you know it, I took to drink, fell in with a surly lot who, by and by, turned into ruddy arsonists flirting with the hangman's noose. Before long no one wants to know the likes of me, not in Dublin, County Clare, nor dear old Donegal—nowhere. So, before long while I still had my wits about me, I stow away on a cargo ship bound across the waters and arrive in this land of the second chance."

"But what does that have to do with me? What does that have to do with anything?"

Larkin began pacing again because either he had lost the thread or he didn't know how to break the news. Then he stood stock still again. "Look at it this way, will you? This diner is a quick stop not a way station. I am an onlooker not a nursemaid. Like my photos and captions, like my poetry, I capture things on the fly. The sketches in the book I'm writing are just that, sketches, vignettes, not some soap opera on the radio with an announcer saying 'Tune in again tomorrow for the next continuing chapter of Guiding Light.' The upshot is, you came barging in here, I gave you a few pointers but I don't know you, never saw you again if anyone asks."

"Great. So where does that leave me?"

Larkin threw up his hands. "If you want my advice for the very last time, you'd best continue mining the Tennessee Williams thread. You've got the corduroy jacket which helps you fit in and Key West an excuse for your tan. You've also the fact that Tennessee drove up recently from the Keys to try out a new work he'd recently developed in a playhouse in Coral Gables. Plus I got word from Stella he'll be doing a tryout here in New York. You see how one strand leads to another if you keep to your own little bailiwick? So give out, will you and give me a ruddy break!"

"Except that even if by some miracle she shows up tomorrow, I have no business there. They'll throw me out or at the very least bar the door before I even get the chance to find out if she's there."

"Not, damn your eyes, if you're armed with a copy of *The Glass Menagerie* you're now about to cross the street and purchase. Not if you're daft enough or canny enough to pursue a little would-be actress all the way here and pass Stella's test to boot. To cozy up to a star-struck lass who herself is daft enough or canny enough to get her foot in the ruddy door."

"But—"

"Off you go now," Larkin said, easing Bud off the stool and starting to edge him toward the door. "But wait a second."

Larkin began rummaging around behind the counter, came up with a pad, rubber stamp, and a stamped envelope. He pressed the rubber stamp against the pad and then against the envelope and handed the self-addressed envelope to Bud. "Here."

"I don't get it?"

"You're to send me a thank-you note on a piece of your hotel's stationary. The note will include a short caption indicating the outcome. The girl is going to stick it out or return home to lick her wounds or whatever. For my part, you blew in here, I provided a bit of tourist advice, you thanked me, posted this, and wended your way back to the swaying palms."

In response to Bud's quizzical look, Larkin said, "The letter is a bit of insurance I'll expect to receive in a day or two. For my services rendered as a guide, that's all. In case some surly character should come barging in disturbing the peace."

Shaking his head, Bud pocketed the envelope and left the diner. Moments later he found himself standing by the statue of General Sheridan as gray and darkened as the sky. He could swear there was a figure in the shadows close by Larkin's diner. But he shook it off and put it down to the lingering effect of Larkin's stowaway tale after his stint with his countrymen hell-bent on mayhem.

But still and all, he couldn't discount the fact that he had flown off the handle at Walt and Larkin, something he never did. And what's worse, Larkin had introduced that diccy element that Reilly had underscored, that there was so much more to this than meets the eye. That he could tell himself to take it one step at a time but in truth he had no idea how far this whole venture goes.

But he shook it all off as best he could.

He crossed the street, entered the sprawling Evergreen Book Store, looked for the drama section and came across *The Glass Menagerie* in paperback. Close by, he also noted editions of Arthur Miller's early plays, the same playwright who recently married Marilyn Monroe and whisked her back to New York so she could learn how to act. Thus accounting for the glossy expose` on Rick's magazine rack he drew from while tipsy, attempting to be one-up on Escobar at the gaming table thanks to Amy's tips. But unwittingly set her off and running, igniting this quandary that kept spinning off in all directions and just wouldn't hold still.

CHAPTER EIGHTEEN

Back in his hotel room, right before he placed his call to Katie, Bud glanced at his notepad with his jottings of barkeep Reilly's view of things. Was everything really at some turning point up here or, as Larkin put it, just an Irishman's gift of the gab? Underneath it all, were people like Ed's cousin Jack on some kind of brink and, judging from Larkin's sudden skittishness, how soon before things reached a breaking point? How much time did Bud have to come to terms with this assignment before things began to unravel?

At any rate, he turned his thoughts to the next item on today's to-do list, something normal and simply doable. He placed a long distance call to Miami keeping in mind Marge said Katie was still miffed over Bud's behavior and sudden departure.

"Well, it's about time," Katie said, immediately picking up the receiver. "This isn't at all okay, you know."

"Whoa, kiddo, simmer down. Tell me calmly what isn't okay."

"It isn't okay for a young person to have to wait for over two days to talk to an uncle who let her down because of some Rick business. Not good for a young person to sorta get it and not get it at all."

"All right, go on, I'm listening."

"It's just that Mom says one thing, you said something else and things are all messed up around here without you. I mean, isn't this Rick, who is supposed to be some kind of relative, way too old to be misbehaving? When I misbehave, I have to learn my lesson and change my ways or else get punished. Like no comedy shows on the new TV till I clean up my room and apologize for not telling mom whose house I was at the whole time I snuck out. Being late for supper and all I mean. I'm saying, have you even heard of a person almost as old as grandma who still hasn't learned his lesson?"

"No. But I did meet a man up here who had gotten into trouble a while back in Ireland who changed his ways."

"You see, you see? Then how come this Uncle Rick is still doing it? And instead of making up for it, you have to—have to make up for his goofs, go all this way, take on the mob after not taking me to the parrot jungle and everything? Is that fair? And how come grandma can't hear about it and set him down soon as she comes home and straighten him out once and for all? How come there's all this pussyfooting around? How come you didn't say in the first place he'd made his bed and has to lie in it like mom always says? Have to take your punishment and grow up?"

All Bud could come up with was, "Rick *is* being punished. He's grounded and they've taken away the keys to his car."

"Who is doing it? The mob right?"

"The one who, because of Rick's careless big mouth, took off with some boss's briefcase. When I find it—only because I don't want to worry grandma and ruin her vacation—when I return real soon after straightening everything out, I'm going to straighten Rick out too once and for all. If he doesn't straighten up and fly right, I am going to tell grandma, his big sister, and he'll really be in for it. Okay?"

"But why should you have to go to all this trouble? And who cares about a silly old briefcase anyways? Just go out and buy another."

Feeling more and more flustered as he tried to placate Katie, Bud himself took a moment to wonder what was so urgent and special about it. Then, shifting back to his cool, knowing tone, he said, "As it happens, I'm up here because Rick can't be trusted and would probably try to skip town and get into even more trouble. I don't know what's so special about the briefcase but the sooner I retrieve it, the sooner things get back to normal and you can stop thinking about broken promises and older relatives that can't grow up."

"Boy, I at least know why Mom stays clear of Miami Beach. You never can tell who's gonna show up and ruin your life."

"You said it. So I'll see you real soon, we'll talk some more. Maybe have you yourself set Uncle Rick straight till grandma comes home."

"Boy, that'll be something."

"You bet. And tell your mom I'll get back to her as soon as the smoke clears or words like that."

Katie said, "All right, gotcha" and hung up as if she couldn't take any more of the nutty world of adults.

Bud changed his shirt, grabbed the Tennessee Williams paperback and spent the next couple of hours down in the hotel's featured restaurant amid the art-deco marble-and-polished brass and oversized murals on the walls of boats steaming into the New York harbor during more placid times.

Then he moved away from the murals that reminded him of Reilly carrying on about things spilling over the ocean to Belfast and the troubles. Put it clear out of his mind and chose a far corner table so he could concentrate on the world of *The Glass Menagerie* replete with an intro, and set his mind to going ahead with this charade. Posing as a theater person in keeping with Larkin's off-the-top-of-his-head ploy enabling him to wheedle his way into Greta Hagan's final tryouts should Amy in fact appear.

While eating his pot roast special, doing his best to avoid the occasional glances of family members and couples chatting away at the nearby tables and occasional interruptions of his waiter angling for a tip, he started to get the hang of it. According to Williams, the playwright, he learned that audiences and actors had to identify with the life depicted on the stage; that the family strife, the misunderstandings between the son and the mother over fragile, dreamy sister Laura, had to seem to be happening moment to moment and not acted out. Similar to what Constance was going through on *Naked City* the night before. Similar to that splattering painter's "art is instant" declaration. It was all taking place in front of your eyes.

Though he'd never seen a playscript before, he began to get involved. Through the first six scenes he cared about the sad situation playing out in this lower middle-class apartment, in the rear of a building in downtown St. Louis, overlooking a fire escape onto an alleyway.

He got the gist of the situation, especially in the search for a solution to fragile Laura's plight. A childhood illness left her a cripple, one leg shorter than the other held in a brace. Everything contributing to her inability to face the harsh, workaday world out there, leaving her to escape into a dream world if she doesn't have some last chance for real companionship.

It gradually all came to him by Scene Seven. There he came upon Laura's encounter with a "gentleman caller" named Jim (who was not unlike Bud) and Laura's delicate figurines, her glass menagerie. In this scene, Jim kept referring back to the high school he and Laura had attended. In fact, the caller sounded like he too had graduated from Miami High and lived up to all the precepts of Bud's compliant generation. He too sometimes cited the school yearbook that listed him as most likely to succeed and subscribed to the need to build your self-confidence in order to compete and climb up the ladder of success, here offered as an antidote to Laura's inferiority complex.

At this point, Bud put the play aside. If he ever had to go on stage and get away with it, this was the perfect part. More importantly, he really was concerned about this fictional Laura more than the young women he'd dated who were preoccupied with finding a suitable mate, settling down and raising a family in some nice, sun-washed Miami subdivision. If Amy Evens was half as Laura-like as she appeared in that snapshot, he could dismiss the counter view—the conniving thief Ed and Al Escobar made her out to be. He could hear her side of the story, retrieve the briefcase, and keep her well out of it. It would all amount to a hunt for a wayward girl unwittingly up against the harsh realities with Rick etc. way in the background. This whole situation could transform into one of those "nice" stories his sister Marge preferred, like one of her Sunday school tales. Something he could readily relate to.

But, of course, he was just daydreaming. He hardly ever lost focus like this, never mind pictured himself taking part in some nostalgic scenario of a bygone time.

He put away the play, left a tip and took the elevator back up to his room. To clear his mind, he fiddled with the clock radio until he came upon a station dedicated to upbeat Broadway show tunes and melodies. Programmed, no doubt, to help New Yorkers forget their cares of the day. Picking up with at this moment the opening bars of Gershwin's *Rhapsody in Blue,* with a jazzy clarinet solo wailing a welcome to the dawn over the big city skyscrapers, as if promising untold happenings. Along these same lines, the lyrics of the following segments ranged from "wouldn't it be loverly?" to "everything's coming up roses." Presently, an announcer informed listeners the next selection was from the current hit musical *West Side Story*. As if reverting to the Gershwin clarinet solo, a male vocalist declared something was coming. He couldn't tell what it was but it was going to take them far away to a place where star-crossed lovers could be left in peace.

Bud couldn't help picturing that ubiquitous black-and-white poster, the one with the girl leading the way as she pulled her boyfriend past the tenements with a look of wonder, about to catch up to whatever was beckoning.

This time, Bud held on to that image long after he turned off the clock radio, got into bed, and shut off the nightlight. Soon however, in the darkness, with the beeping car horns outside his window, as Stella Parsons would put it, reality was not about to offer any such thing. The beat goes on. Factions clash. The odds were in nobody's favor. All you could say was it is what it is. And he was slated to receive another call from Ed first thing demanding a progress report. Ed would brook no talk about some Laura-like creature. He was part and parcel of a seedy world added to Reilly's take on strife and rebellion across the waters. In comparison, the *West Side Story* poster didn't have a chance.

Bud got out of bed, turned the nightlight back on, got out his notepad, and continued keeping score: *Possible Amy-Laura ploy; no more Stella Parsons, Larkin link and reliable contact. Which leaves us where in addition to the toss of a coin?*

CHAPTER NINETEEN

Sure enough, early the following morning the phone rang. Sleepy and groggy, Bud picked up the receiver and Ed started right in as if Bud was the flunky and Ed was in command. And no matter how Bud tried to fend him off, Ed kept it up.

"What do you mean you're getting closer?" Ed asked. "And what's with tossing out sections like Little Italy, Chinatown and the Bowery which, according to Jack, are his own territory. Plus there's no way she'd be holing up anywheres near there I'm told. Has nothing so-ever to do with our little runaway with the hots to be an actress."

"Uh-huh," Bud said, still only half-awake.

"Listen, I hate to spring it on you, hate to rouse you out of bed, pal, but Jack knows. He coaxed it out of me that something was wrong and I made out that we just now found out she made off with the silver case on top of everything. And he wants it back in his hands yesterday, if not sooner, so's he can make sure it's ready, locked and loaded in plenty of time for the big meet."

"Big meet . . . just found out?" Bud said, starting to come out of it.

"Meaning you gotta step on it. Meaning Jack ain't just minding his end of it while you futz around treading water. Meaning the schedule is tighter than a goddamn drum and Jack ain't exactly buying your act."

"Look, I was only referring to those sections as a frame of reference while I took on the Village." When Ed didn't seem to be buying this ploy, Bud threw in, "As nearby locales she may have found affordable housing away from all the hustle and bustle."

Bud recalled that actually he'd been reaching for a way to keep this Jack person from breathing down his neck. Plus he couldn't admit he'd only been making a stab at it based on what he'd gleaned just then from the Sunday paper. More and more he was beginning to sense the pros and cons of this balancing act of appearing to be something or someone he wasn't.

"Are you listening to me?" Ed hollered over the phone. "Do I got to remind you you get no per diem unless you fork over a progress report that better be damn good?"

"Of course not."

"You think what's going down is gonna shift to neutral till you get on the stick? Or she sends out an SOS what she might be doing with herself or maybe shopping the briefcase for a lot of coin? Get off it, get with it, and wake the hell up."

"Understood. The pressure has been heightened. The briefcase is the main object more than ever. And just as soon as I get a bead on it—look, I've got to go. It's all a matter of timing as you've indicated. If I miss out right now, it's back to square one and surely nobody wants that."

"Are you messing with me? Giving me some lip?"

"Except to point out you promised me a lark while I was at it. But it turns out to be anything but, far from it. You talk about a contract, which I never signed or agreed to. You keep talking about a cousin named Jack who I've never met and seems to be cut from the same cloth as Escobar. So give me a break and tell this Jack person to sit tight and cut me some slack, will you?"

"Look, pal, it's going down first thing this Friday or else there's no Trafficante, no Havana, no nothing, and we are screwed!"

"Trafficante? Havana? What are you saying?"

"Never mind. None of your goddamn business!"

"Okay, fine," Bud said and hung up. But he didn't understand, not at all. Thinking over Ed's slip of the tongue, he'd only gotten inklings of Cuba from Kathleen, the girl at the White Horse, who wanted to join other women recruits. But what did that have to do with Ed, this Jack person, and Al Escobar? And then toss in a character named Trafficante? You take one step forward here and you find yourself more steps behind.

Ignoring the ringing of the phone as he showered and shaved, Bud realized he was no longer winging it, hoping some misunderstanding could be resolved so that he could get back to his life. Getting Rick off the hook turned out that what was truly in store was anybody's guess if you added the latest slipup, that Jack Reardon was just informed about the pilfered silver briefcase, it was a matter of a growing list that didn't quit. He'd narrowed it down to a touch of Method acting, locating and gaining Miss Amy's confidence and a quick solution. But, like everything else in this corner of the world, the realities were on a collision course and kept percolating and proliferating above, underneath, and beyond.

After a light breakfast of coffee and waffles in the café downstairs, Bud still had almost two hours to kill before attempting to sneak into Greta Hagen's final auditions some twenty-four blocks away on Bank Street. So he opted for a stroll down 8th Avenue to take in the sights and neighborhoods along the way and continue to get familiar with lower Manhattan's west side. A stroll intended to sweep away thoughts of impending lurking obstacles and get back to one task at a time, doing strictly what was doable.

But the sky remained ash-gray along with the chilly weather. And the acrid aroma seeping in from Union City, New Jersey wasn't suitable for any kind of stroll as well. Coupled with the remnants of the morning rush and running smack into Madison Square Garden where the congestion was the heaviest, along with the honking cabbies and people jostling one another, made even this simple venture all the more problematic. The thought of catching a bus the rest of the way occurred to him. But there was no bus in sight or any sign of a bus stop. By the time he reached 30th Street and couldn't take being hemmed in any longer, he cut over to 9th Avenue, which at least was more in line with the location of Greta Hagen's Studio H.

Turning down Ninth, he found the street was not only wider but there was space between passersby as box trucks joined the fray determined to beat out the cabbies servicing the Chelsea area. And still no sign of any bus service.

The bigger problem was the fact that the greater spacing between pedestrians allowed you to catch sight of anyone following you. A thought all the more plausible given the news that Jack Reardon was just informed and champing at the bit, doubtless vying for the silver case's recovery. By the time Bud reached 19th Street, he began to dawdle so that people could go by him, and then speed up in case he could throw off some burly figure in a trench coat he'd swear he'd gotten a glimpse of when he glanced over at a storefront window keeping pace and then slackening off again.

Getting more and more wary, he noted the Hudson River sign pointing west and a narrow one-lane street clogged with cars and trucks. All topped with overarching bare elms above the sidewalks, the walkway to his right blocked here and there by scaffolding, and fire escape ladders jutting out further down.

Still in shape thanks to all those tennis matches and pickup basketball games, with no actual justification for his concern, he cut to his right anyway, twisted around the scaffolding, sprinted for half a block, spun around another set of scaffolding, and spotted a dangling fire escape ladder some twenty yards away. In the back of his mind, he recalled the teenager racing past the tenements up on 44th Street by the Actors Studio heading toward the same river, climbing up a fire escape and ducking as a bunch of other teenagers appeared hell bent after him. Following suit, he reflexively climbed up to the first landing and lay prone against the pressure of the cold steel under his hips and thighs.

He lay there for a time, holding still, not daring to rise up or turn his head and look down. Not daring to take in the fact that not only was he hiding, he was a sitting duck should the burly guy in a trench coat spot him, climb up and nab him for whatever reason. He stayed that way amid the honking, intermittent shouts and revving engines down below feeling vulnerable, feeling scared. Which was a first. In his circle, among his acquaintances, this was unheard of. As a rule you were to keep your feelings to yourself, never let on you had weaknesses. Though it was never spelled out, it would make everyone uncomfortable. If fact, in grade school you were graded for self-control and could be sent down to see a guidance counselor. Moments passed, realizing he'd never been faced with any altercation whatsoever, until he heard someone yelling up at him.

"It's okay, mac, he took off. Hey, look, even if it's one of Gambino's or Genovese's crew, they ain't gonna hang around I'll tell you that. So you can get down now, you look ridiculous!"

Bud lifted his head, peered down and spotted a scruffy looking young guy astride a red Schwinn bike with saddle bags draped across the rear rack like a Miami Herald paper boy. Only this guy was at least twenty years old, had a mop of back hair, chiseled features, sported a black leather bomber jacket and jeans. He affected a cocky tilt of his head, and his saddle bags were tightly buckled.

"Come on, come on," the guy said. "What's the point? Where you from anyways, the sticks?"

At first Bud didn't answer, ashamed of his cowardice. Then, covering up, he said, "Miami, if it's any of your business."

"Figures. No wonder."

"What is that supposed to mean?" Glancing at his watch, realizing he was really going to be late, he clambered down, dusted himself off and said, "At any rate, I guess I owe you one monitoring the situation. Do you have any idea who the hoodlum tailing me was? Or if he really was a hoodlum?"

"'Hoodlum,' that's cute. Anyways, who knows? Like I said, could be one of Carlo Gambino's crew. Or even Reardon's judging from the word on the street."

"Reardon? You mean Jack Reardon?"

"Who else? Runs a bar down on Mott Street. I tell ya, you never know with that guy. He's another breed they say. So, tell me, when did you get in?"

"Sunday morning."

"Train, plane, or bus?"

"Train. What is this?"

"Considering the angles is all. I mean, who was it and why after some square like you?"

"Look, I've got to go. But, since you seem to know your way around, from the looks of things I very well might need somebody to point things out and take some soundings."

"Soundings?"

"Word on the street, things like that."

"Now you're talkin' if you need a guy keeping an eye out or putting his ear to the ground, I'm your man."

Reaching back and patting one of the saddle bags, he went on. "Just your luck I was only picking up betting slips but hey, a spooked square like you has no idea what I'm talking about, am I right? Which makes my services all the more needed."

"In all possibility. What's your name?"

"Make it Scooter. What's yours?"

"Bud."

"Miami, huh? Lost and spooked with a suntan to boot."

"Drop it, will you?"

"Okay okay. Just taking it all in, man."

Thinking it over a bit more, Bud said, "Anyway, I do owe you and actually should take you up on your offer."

"Then I'm gonna need a little more to go on. This your only hassle so far?"

"Unless you count the deadbeat who tried to swipe my duffle bag at the train station this Sunday morning."

"Okay, gotcha." Scooter pulled a card out of his leather jacket and handed it to him. "If I ain't finished collecting, one uncle's got a restaurant on Mulberry and the other's got a pinball arcade in Chinatown. Both numbers are on this card."

"Good," Bud said, turning back toward 9th Avenue. "I'll be in touch."

As Scooter peddled past him, it occurred to him he might very well need to know all about Jack Reardon and his territory. At the moment, though, he had over eight more blocks to cover, walking fast but trying not to draw any more attention to himself. Hoping that hood hadn't doubled back. Hoping there was still the chance of at least a glimpse of the fleeting Amy Evens.

Logically, it was still one step at a time. But apparently this town didn't run that way and perhaps never could.

Soon, he got lost as 9th Avenue broke off and became Hudson and broke off again and became Greenwich, splintering into side streets like Gansevoort. By the time he located Bank Street, passed the Viennese tea shop and snuck past the bespectacled receptionist, he was out of breath and completely rattled.

He did manage to find a seat on the first row of a set of risers. As near as he could make out, the place was pitch dark save for spotlights trained on a toy chest and a wooden nightstand resting on an empty playing area. Scattered about above and behind him were no more than twenty prospective students who'd achieved finalist status. Way over to his left stood a white desk with a green desk lamp illuminating a yellow legal pad and a glass ashtray. Holding forth behind the desk, waving a lit cigarette was a willowy figure with a blond pageboy hairstyle dressed in a full-sleeved blouse and charcoal-gray slacks. He was taken by her eyes, which seemed to be constantly searching things out, her husky voice, and the way she paused to take a deep drag on her cigarette as if it was soothing and medicinal.

As she went on about how everyone talks to themselves in private, it was all he could do to keep sitting there and stifle his dread of some guy in a trench coat busting in and dragging him out of there. Only one thing kept him stock still. It was the moment Greta Hagen took another deep drag and said, "Well, Amy, that brings us to your problem. Namely, what I take to be your ingrained habit of trying to please. As long as we have a little time left, would you like to try again and focus solely on your task? Allow yourself to become fully absorbed this time and never mind about us?"

CHAPTER TWENTY

For the next few minutes, Bud was struck by a few things. The first was actually seeing her in person as someone's notion of Marilyn Monroe's younger sister with that wistful, almost naïve look in her eyes. She also had what his sister Marge called "a nice wholesome appearance"—hardly any makeup, no lacquer spray stiffening her short honey-blond hair, wearing a white top with a Peter Pan collar and a light-gray flannel jumper. But even more than that, she seemed to have recalled what happened when she snuck into the Actors Studio and became mesmerized by some lady's private moment and was bound and determined to try and duplicate it now.

Staring at a prop rotary-dial phone she'd taken out of the toy chest and placed on the nightstand, she picked up the receiver. Then thought better of it, plunked it down and began talking to herself. Not acting it out, indicating how distressed she was for the benefit of Greta and the others. But working through it much like Constance had done at the police station during her live encounter on *Naked City*.

As near as Bud could make out, she was convincing herself how unfair it was to be typecast during her stint back in Chicago with an improv group called The Second City. Only allowed to do sendups of virginal girls on a first date, or ditzy nurses trying to fend off a randy patient, or at a loss deciphering her dad's explanations of the facts of life. Totally flustered, she began pacing around chiding herself.

"Come on, Amy, you can do it. Call your mom. It's been over a week since she's heard from you. You don't have to tell her everything except you're up here now not at the Second City workshop. Remember how she gave you that wish-upon-a-star charm bracelet? Well now's your chance. People drop out, alternates get called up at the Studio, Amy. Are you really going to mope around and worry yourself sick about that other awful stuff? Call her. Tell Mom your plans. Sweep everything else under the carpet."

But at that point Bud's fixation on Amy was short-lived as he thought he heard noises outside. It may have been his imagination or the fact the receptionist left the front door open. Whatever it was, he didn't really hear Greta Hagen's comments, only something about "having an honest moment." And looking for approval shortchanges everybody. He may have heard Ms. Hagen say "In that case, sorry, nothing here for you, folks." But mostly he recalled his fear and pictured some burly guy hell-bent after him.

Then everything drew still. Out of nowhere, Greta Hagen spotted him and came right over.

"And what have we here?" she said. "Don't tell me. You must be what Grace, my receptionist, called an eager young man who happened to drop by yesterday and wouldn't take no for an answer. And now, waiting till the very last minute, slipped in here trying to crash the party."

Bud had no answer. He couldn't pass himself off as a guy with a copy of *The Glass Menagerie* with an ulterior motive.

"But of course," she went on, "that's what it takes given the impossible odds in our profession to get your foot in the door. Brash, unadulterated nerve. May we have your name?"

"Bud. Bud Palmer," Bud said hesitantly.

Greta Hagen glanced up at the smattering of mostly young women and said, "What do you think? Never let it be said I put a damper on the spirit of the moment. Let's see a show of hands. How many are willing at the very last minute to let Bud show us what he's got?"

As far as Bud could tell, all the hands shot up.

He remained seated as Greta went on stage, replaced the rotary phone, opened the chest and beckoned to him. "Well? Come on, Bud. Let's see it."

He sprang up. It may have been exactly what his dad would've said to him. But mostly his twisty anxiety needed an outlet and any outlet would do.

The smattering of onlookers up on the risers seemed to sit up and take notice while she resumed her post up in the corner by the white desk.

With nothing else for it, he went over, peered in the trunk, took in all the stuff including a toy cowboy six-shooter, a baseball glove and bat, a jump rope, and a model sea plane. For no reason, he grabbed a teddy bear.

He stood motionless holding the stuffed animal and stared at the exit door, still hoping against hope some burly guy hadn't finally tracked him down and wanted a helluva lot more than a friendly chat.

"Come come," Greta said back in the shadows. "What are the previous circumstances? What do you need from Teddy? Why here? Why now?"

Bud plopped the teddy bear on the nightstand, walked away and pivoted sharply. "That's it, Teddy," Bud hollered. "You sit back and watch. After all, what's it to you? You haven't even been outside or had to face anything. You've been comfy in your toy chest waiting for some sweet little girl to come along, pluck you up, play with you, and put you back all snug in your nook."

Bud pointed in the direction of the exit door and strode up to a window shade and pointed. "Well I've got news, Teddy," he called back. "There's a real world out there. Guys in trench coats spooking you, making you climb up fire escapes, show your true colors, and duck." Hollering even louder, Bud said, "And then you've got to run down streets you don't know, with your heart beating like crazy. And where are you going to be when they finally catch up because you never know, kiddo. They could start whacking me with a rubber hose or God knows what."

Bud rushed down, grabbed the stuffed animal and shook it. "Turning a blind eye, isn't that right, Teddy? Like all those people who passed me by in the train station as some deadbeat ran off with my duffle bag. Minding their own business because once they step in or become a material witness guess what? That's right, how does that grab you? What are you going to do when you're in my shoes, when playtime is over and your days are numbered? Because maybe they don't listen to reason. Maybe because reason isn't worth diddly up here. Did you ever think of *that*? Huh? Did you ever think of anything? Answer me!"

Bud was shaking the teddy bear so hard, Greta had to come over and gently take it away from him. As she put it back in the toy box, he heard the murmuring up in the risers, as if they had been with him the whole time, identifying with his plight.

Greta Hagen glanced back and said, "Make an appointment with Grace. You and I need to talk. Perhaps there's a whole range of feelings percolating, begging to be released. Okay?"

Bud nodded, still at a loss. "Okay . . . yes, ma'am."

She went over to the others and said, "All right, that will do for now. Have to tell you, I've had a ball seeing you grow even in this incredibly short period of time. As I mentioned earlier, give it some real thought about preparing to play a character in a well-known play. What can you bring to spring it to life?"

She lit yet another cigarette, took a deep drag and moved in a little closer. "After all, that's what it's all about isn't it? People in the audience have spent their day going through the motions. Keeping what's really simmering under wraps, not daring to face the consequences. They need this vicarious release they can't get from safe and predictable entertainment."

She returned to her post and said, "Besides, the words themselves are, after all, dead on the page, just a lifeless script. Make it special, make it yours. Do an improv that'll set you off. Yes? Any questions?"

This time no one raised their hand.

"Fine," Greta Hagen said. "See you then."

She turned off the spotlights, flicked on the house lights, and she and the others filed out while some of the girls gave Bud a thumbs-up. It was only then that Bud noticed that Amy remained seated up in the far corner.

At first neither of them spoke until Bud, trying his best to compose himself, walked forward, gazed up and said, "Are you okay?"

"I guess. Greta talking about not keeping things under wraps . . . and you going on about what's waiting for you out there . . . I guess it's all starting to get to me."

"I can see that." Trying to slough it all off and make some connection, he said, "Oh, wow, can you beat it? I don't know how many times I heard some teacher in grade school tell us 'Don't you make a scene, you hear? and upset the apple cart. You need to practice some self-control. This country runs on self-control.' And here you get approval from Greta if, and only if, you *can* make a scene."

"And you did so well." Her face almost glowing now in utter amazement. In turn, Bud began to carry on, no longer guarded, as if finally confiding in a kindred spirit.

"Really? The truth is, I don't know what got into me. I got lost, was late, thought she might throw me out. Then she said the same exact thing my dad used to say to prod me at the swim meet at Venetian Pool, and I took it all out on the teddy bear. I call this whole episode a wonder."

"But how did you ever, on the spur of the moment like that?"

"It was a jumble of things. Including some deadbeat did try to glom my duffel bag like I said, plus, at the last minute, trying to take on this city for the past couple of days for reasons I won't go into. Just winging it under pressure."

Shrugging her shoulders after a moment of silence, she murmured, "I suppose it all depends on lots of things."

"I suppose." He paused. Then added, "I'm barely starting to get the hang of it while being light years behind."

He didn't know what else to say. During another awkward pause, he was still taken by her wistful sincerity. Worlds apart from the girls back in Miami and their feminine wiles. Even his sister Marge could be heard on the phone telling some unmarried friend, "Remember to let him do all the talking. You know, explaining things, though you know much more about it than he does. They always go for girls who listen."

Encouraged that she had stayed back and they were having this little exchange, he tried to keep it going a little while longer. "You see, I'm really new at all of it. Like fighting the crowds and constantly rushing around." Then, before he could stop himself, he did it again, came up with a ploy that was pure fabrication. "Came up from Miami and heard about Greta's teaching."

"Same with me, sort of. Was part of a troupe that kept me in my shell back in Chicago. And somebody put me on to Greta."

"I see."

Bud and Amy soon ran out of small talk. She gathered her things, put on a matching wool car coat, walked down the risers past Bud toward the exit, stopped, and turned back. "Well, it was nice talking to you and all."

Before she had a chance to exit, Bud caught up to her. "Wait. I know it must seem like some coincidence, but . . . " Realizing he was pushing it, but as Larkin intimated, he needed something to keep the connection going. "As it happens, I've been carrying around this Tennessee Williams play which I can easily relate to. And, as it also happens, you're perfect for Laura. And playing Jim . . . I mean anybody can play Jim during the gentleman caller scene. Especially a guy like me."

She waited for him to get to the point. Remembering Greta Hagan's next acting exercise he said, "Tell you what. You think about it. Given a shot in the dark she'll consider admitting me into the class . . . Anyway, I'll lend you my script and give you a call tomorrow and you'll let me know what you think. It could turn out to be something good for us both."

This time she seemed wary. Perhaps she thought it was one of those pickup ploys. Finally she said, "Okay" and took his paperback copy. "Hotel Chelsea. 243-3700. Call me around ten and we'll see how we both feel about it."

Another hesitation. He almost blew it about to add "Amy Evens, right?" but caught himself and said, "So that's your number, right?"

"No. There's a payphone in the hallway near my room where they can knock on my door. Us transients don't have our own phones like the long-term residents."

"I see. So I ask for . . . "

"Amy. Just ask for Amy." She walked away looking very much like a person who was having second thoughts, having revealed her whereabouts to a person she didn't know from Adam.

He stood there for a moment, not in the least having gotten over his dread over what might be waiting for him out there. He also wondered how in the world he'd managed to pull off that teddy bear scene and wound up shaking like that. And what possessed him to propose working on a play scene? He knew absolutely nothing about how to go about it. Moreover, how could he even conceive of getting Greta Hagen to accept him over a sudden fluke ploy to ease into Amy's good graces? Everything was becoming such a jumble he was beginning to wonder if somehow some spiritual ancestor of his had been a juggler.

At any rate, he walked into the front office and obtained an appointment from Grace for early Friday afternoon despite the quizzical look she gave him adding to his own wonderment over this charade. He walked out of her office and hesitated at the entranceway to the problematic outside world.

Consulting his sectional map for some non-threatening spot close by to hole up till he was sure the coast was clear, he noticed that not only were there a string of piers nearby, Pier #49 was only two blocks away—a cross over Washington Street and he was there. At the same time it came to him he had that mural at the hotel in mind, the one with the idyllic view of a New York harbor on the Hudson with tugboats and sailing vessels approaching the pristine docks, benign workers reaching into cargo holds unloading sacks of coffee beans and crates of bananas from the Caribbean. If the scene had any basis in fact, Bud could saunter over and while away the time till he got his bearings. But in truth there was nothing benign going on. Aside from the acrid aroma wafting across the Hudson, there was the racket from cranes and forklifts, hundreds of dock workers scurrying about yelling at each other, loading up awaiting trucks with all manner of seafood. The scene was in keeping with the helter-skelter of the rest of the city, including passengers getting on and off the ocean liners, buses and trains rushing to different points, crossing paths with those who knew exactly what they were getting into.

And if that wasn't enough, just the thought of crates of bananas and coffee beans being unloaded from the Caribbean led to Havana as a port of origin, Ed yelling at him over the phone that this caper had to be signed, sealed and delivered by Friday or there would be no Trafficante and Havana, whatever that was all about.

As if that wasn't enough, there was whatever Reardon was up to after learning the briefcase was suddenly in play. In addition to linking him to something across the waves to far off Belfast according to Reilly. Meaning Bud could be falling further behind a world of complications and had only a date to call Amy tomorrow to show for his efforts.

But all he could do at the moment was walk over the few blocks to the Sheridan Square book store and buy his own copy of *The Glass Menagerie* just in case Amy went along. Then cross the street to the diner, grateful that it seemed chock full of customers so that he could order some lunch and Larkin would be too busy to brush him off again. And, by chance, have cooled off by now so that Bud could broach the subject of mob elements on the prowl and if Larkin had anything to offer.

So he did just that. Bought another play script, walked back, entered the diner, and slipped into a nearby stool at the counter. Catching Larkin's eye, he held up a copy of the play as a half-hearted attempt to disarm him and ordered some lunch. Minutes later, catching his eye again, he said, "I just thought you might be interested in the latest episode of Chasing Amy. You see, there's a lot more to it."

"Oh, is there now?"

All of a sudden, Larkin came rushing around the counter, pulled Bud off his stool, and whisked him outside as though he were a trespasser. And then and there laid right into him.

"What is it? You've lost your memory, have you? Bits and bobs and you're to mail me the upshot with the stamped envelope I supplied."

"Yes, but I thought you might want to know I bought the

playscript as you suggested. Made contact but have run into another element and thought—"

"Well you thought wrong. At first I thought you were a godsend. Not to worry, offering a new wrinkle to my tales and me, of course, strictly the onlooker. Completely losing sight of only six degrees of separation between any one of us crammed cheek by jowl, constantly making entrances and exits in this port of call with the likes of seamen fresh off some freighter from the old sod amounting to just a drop in the bucket. At the same time, there's the worry over some slacker like Walt blabbing his mouth off, spreading lies. And Reilly tells me he let on about Reardon, which made your eyes light up whilst scribbling away on your note pad and on and on she goes."

"Not exactly in that order."

"Who cares? But close enough, which is far beyond only chasing after a girl as you said. Look to your multiplication tables. Only six degrees separation and the way things are going a hell of a lot less. So this is, was, and shall ever be the end of it. No more of you and me and this diner. I don't want to know you. Is that plain and simple enough?" For emphasis, Larkin pointed a finger directly in Bud's face and said, "Just a mailed coda, thank you very much, boyo whilst I beg the saints to preserve me!" With that, he barged right back into the diner as agitated as can be.

Left standing there, again Bud could only wonder how far this conundrum went if it set Larkin off like that. And added those selfsame criminal elements to the mix, possibly reaching far south to the Caribbean and across the Atlantic. Leaving Amy's flight and little hopes and dreams in the dust. All of it now simply unfathomable.

CHAPTER TWENTY-ONE

In contrast, Ed wasn't capable of taking in any of the slew of possibilities beyond recovering the pilfered briefcase and the Friday deadline. In fact, he gave himself credit for that song and dance telling Jack they just discovered the case was missing. He did it to cover for the fact this Bud character needed to quit dragging his feet and really get with it now. As always, Ed wasn't about to let anything get him down. He popped a stick of Wrigley's spearmint gum in his mouth and hunted around the pool area for Chip. Shielding his eyes from the steady glare of the sunlight, he drifted past the chaise lounges occupied by a handful of middle-aged women applying different kinds of face cream from a blue jar and spotted Chip slipping out of a cabana by the steps leading down to the beach. The way Ed saw it, he had four concerns on the back burner which included cousin Jack, Al, that weasel Rick, and Trafficante. And there was nothing stopping him right now from mixing business with pleasure.

At the same time, it wasn't lost on him that he pushed hiring this Bud character at the last minute because the last thing he needed was to be sent up to New York, a place he'd never been, under Jack Reardon's thumb, which alone would've driven him up the wall. Meaning the sooner all this hassle faded off the sooner he'd be on his permanent vacation. The payoff he was due after all these years keeping tabs on Al's windy city loansharking racket.

It was high time, baby. It was way past high time.

Standing by Chip's side, taking in the sand and surf, Ed said,

"She's classy and easygoing, right? Not your run of the mill call girl?"

"Like I told you, Ed. Just what the doctor ordered."

"And her name is Flo? She's got a great figure and no more than in her early thirties? Open to a touristy kind of arrangement, no surprises on that score? And the deal is, you get your finder's fee? Meaning she's a perfect companion, fits the bill, always on call if you get my meaning?"

"How many times, Ed? What does it take? You want me to draw you pictures, take you by the hand, introduce you and help you mingle? Two-thirty. She'll be out there on a thick beach towel, probably bright coral, almost bare skin in her top and bikini. Are we on or what?"

"We're on. Definitely on. You see, things have gotten a smidge out of hand here as you might have guessed, what with keeping that Rick character out of sight and under wraps. In the meantime, with Al Escobar otherwise engaged for the moment, it would be best all around if I was to be ship-shape in all departments, if you get me, fully rested and, not to put too fine a word on it, rejuvenated."

"Which is what we're all about at this place, making arrangements to suit our clientele's needs. You satisfied?"

"I'm planning I will be. Get it?"

"Got it."

"Good."

Feeling if he played it right he'd be all upbeat again, Ed made his way back, past the sun-tanning ladies into the lobby, took the elevator up to the suite, checked down the hall to make sure Al was getting dressed and they were on schedule. Nodding, he plucked a Heineken out of the ice bucket, snapped the cap and drained it. Then proceeded to the phone stand tucked away by the entrance and got ready to take the bull by the horns instead of all the time being on the receiving end of Al's moods and Jack's tirades. Careful not to reveal this Bud character sloughed off the per diem, making him less under their control. In fact, he couldn't say exactly what was making him play ball unless he really minded what they might do to that weasel Rick. Whatever. He was going through his paces, hooking up with luscious Flo and reaping his reward.

On time, the phone rang, Ed picked up the receiver but Jack was at it again.

"What do you think, Ed, I've got time for this? Got nothing better to do than keeping sure this leg man is on the job? And realizes we're on the clock here up against it? Besides leasing, financing, hiring, seeing to disposals, not to mention scheduling, and that's only for openers. Which calls for every bit of it to be signed, sealed and delivered in time. You read me, Ed? Even a go-fer like you from cheesy Chicago has to know we're up against it and the second I get a free minute—"

"I hear you, Jack, I hear you." But Ed barely had any notion what was underneath all the running around and was doing his best to slough Jack off. It was like Ed was some kind of sounding board and punching bag for Al and Jack no matter how he played it and it was getting worse. For a second they might listen to him for a change and not get PO'd when he wanted something explained or was trying to cool it down. Like telling him the exact casino in Havana and talking positive. Like letting him in on what all the running around up there was all about. Realizing Ed had only been to Havana for a couple of days while Al was checking some things out under Ed's nose. And Jack wasn't going to let the cat out of the bag providing details about the big deal he was hatching on his own, leaving Ed even more in the dark. Which was starting to get to him again.

"So?" Jack went on. "Where are we at?"

"The guy is closing in, I tell ya. She's about to make an appearance, I just checked back. Before you know it it'll be like this freakin hitch never happened."

"Tangibles, Ed. Tangibles means the goddamn silver case back in my hands in time or else. Tangibles means having this Bud character in tow."

"Of course and as soon as I hear from Trafficante, you'll get that much more assurance. You, of all people, got it coming to you, Jack."

But Jack was having none of it, punctuated by yet another "Or else" right before he hung up on him.

Getting more rattled again, Ed drifted back by the buttery leather furniture and waited for Al to reappear.

Which wasn't long as Al walked in needing help with his white-on-white skinny tie, and wanted to know if it went with his powder blue Cubavera jacket, white linen pants and penny loafers. Before Ed could reply, Al started muttering about how in the world he was going to pull this off, pretending he really cared about this Amy and what a pity it was she came down with the flu, when all he really wanted was to wring her thieving neck. And once more it was back to "How the hell do these things happen, I ask you? How?"

Al went over to the black marble coffee table, plucked a fresh Havana Panatela out of the cigar box, clipped the end, lit it, and kept working on it until the sweet-cedar aroma began to fill the room. Turning back to Ed, he said, "She was having second thoughts, did I tell you that? Getting depressed. If she hadn't wandered down to the cabana that night, she never would've run into that little creep, he never would've tried to weasel a tell out of her after filling her head with that Marilyn Monroe crap he got outta some Magazine. All because you said she was cute, eager, and easy to handle as a cocker spaniel."

"And that's how she came across every time. In skit after skit I saw, not too swift on the uptake, as gullible as they come and a believer. Plus she was laid off till the holidays. Talk about perfect timing. Talk about a perfect escort for your nephew's prenuptials or whatever. I tell ya, Al, all the elements are out there, if you play it right, which is what I did."

Pacing around, providing the air-cooling system with more cigar smoke aroma, Escobar suddenly held still. "But how can I go up to Boca Raton and pull this off with so much up in the air?"

"Because I just talked to Jack and everything's being handled. Because you need a break. We both need a timeout and you'll only be two hours from here. Hey, this ain't like you. You never give yourself away even when you're bluffing. Besides, what better gig for you than taking charge of a shindig? You're the man, Al. Before you know it, this hitch blows over, you'll be clear of Chicago, in the tropics for good and, night after night, raking it in. The big score, baby. What could be better?"

"You'll call the Hilton. You'll keep me in the know."

"You got it, I swear."

Escobar clamped down on the cigar, called for the bellboy to schlep his oversized leather suitcase to the awaiting rental Grand Prix, and soon was gone.

Ed went over to the balcony now more upset than ever. There the sparkling white sand, handful of sunbathing guests under their umbrellas, gently rolling waves, and lazy puffy clouds dotting the blue sky seemed to underscore the pep talk he'd given Al. And Jack. And above all, himself. As if a perfect day erased everything and a perfect future went hand in hand. Which was not at all the case and he needed to take it out on somebody.

He turned back, deposited his gum in the gold wastebasket, and went over to the phone stand. It was damn well his turn to go on the offense. The second Rick picked up, Ed started in on him.

"What's the routine, Rick?"

"Oh, come on, Ed, not again."

"You better believe it until that briefcase is smack back in Al's hands. Tell me you've been counting the hours. Tell me you've been counting the minutes. Tell me that leg man of yours is all he's cracked up to be and the sun will be shining even brighter Friday morning."

"Sure sure, what can I say?"

"You know the drill. Let's hear it."

Ed could hear Rick rattling around on his desk, fumbling for the proposition Ed forced him to type out on that manual typewriter. Back on the phone, reading the words out loud like a grade school kid in trouble, Rick said, "I understand if that silverline briefcase isn't returned forthwith, beside the gambling I.O.U. I signed, there are consequences according to Al Escobar's Chicago business practices which will commence forthwith."

Apart from the quiver in this loser Rick's voice, Ed had gotten some satisfaction out of using words like *forthwith* and *business practices*. He also got some satisfaction out of the next words out of Rick's mouth.

"Can't you back off a bit? I've hardly slept, there's my asthma and my nerves are shot."

"That's the ticket, pal. Keeps you on your toes. You'll be hearing from me and that's the one thing you can count on."

Ed hung up, glanced at his watch, walked out to the balcony and took in the scene once again. Waiting for Trafficante's call reminded him that all he knew of Trafficante was gotten secondhand. It seemed he had it set up in Tampa and Havana and partially with New York crime family acquaintances like the Lucchese and the Bonannos by that kingpin father of his who died only a couple of years ago. Where would Ed be today if he too had a mob boss for an old man who left him a legacy? If he'd been weaned and shown the ropes and been well-connected all these years he wouldn't be this anxious and beside himself despite all his efforts.

His pondering was cut short by the ringing phone. But when he rushed over and picked up there was no introduction, no how's it going? Not even a request to talk to Al. The tone was matter of fact coming from a guy who must have lots more besides this on his mind, which may be why he sounded like he was speaking into a Dictaphone.

From what Ed could make out, Trafficante was dealing with a hassle over his Yellow House Bar in the Ybor City section of Tampa and his Dream Bar had been gutted by some arsonist, all of which infringed on his bookmaking operation. And so he might be a little late Friday morning, wanted Al to know and that was that.

Left with the dial tone, Ed dialed the number of Al's hotel in Boca Raton and left the message that Trafficante got in touch, had a few business matters to take care of, would be a little late this Friday but all systems were go.

Wondering if he'd ever be let in on the exact three-way deal, needing something to calm himself down, Ed walked back onto the balcony again and in practically no time spotted Flo carrying the oversized beach towel Chip spoke of. She was wearing a leopard skin bikini and moved like she was in slow motion. She stretched out the towel in that same way, reached up and waved her arms slowly like some exotic dancer.

Ed left the suite, took the elevator to the lobby, and made his way across the pool area. He stopped to give Chip a high sign and continued down to the beach. As he weaved around the sprinkling of sunbathers, he told himself to appear nonchalant as though he might be interested in hooking up with her but not eager like some jerk with nothing else going for him.

As he reached her, blocking her view of the rolling surf, he looked down and said, "Hey, I'm Ed. I take it you're Flo."

As casual as can be, she turned on her side, gazed up, studied him for a few seconds and said, "You got it."

Unsure of his next move, he was relieved when she said, "You're just in time to do my back. The coconut oil's in the beach bag."

He went over to the yellow canvas bag, pulled out the glass vial, and nodded when she rolled over onto her stomach while undoing her halter. "Okay, Ed," she said. "You're on."

Though he realized she was calling the shots, he unscrewed the cap, knelt down, sprinkled some oil on her upper back, and went to work trying to match her easy tone. "You're probably wondering about the proposition I got in mind."

She murmured, "Maybe . . . you might say that."

For the next couple of minutes he tried to sell her on Havana, careful not to push it and keep matching her casualness. He mentioned the long legged showgirls at the Tropicana, practically naked underneath, headdresses like lit chandeliers, ostrich feathers on their arms. He added conga drums, palm trees going through the roof, other dancers up on the catwalks in their voodoo costumes. When she still didn't bite except for an occasional "Mmm," he listed all the socialites, night clubs, casinos, and celebrities like Ava Gardner, Frank Sinatra, and Ginger Rogers. He tossed in a quote from The Cabaret Quarterly he'd practically memorized: "A goddess of pleasure and delights . . . replete with tropical beauty and beauties . . . " After yet another "Mmm" he came up with the Hotel Nacional with its seven roulette wheels, twenty-one slot machines, ten gambling tables and so forth.

When he wasn't sure if she was still awake, he stopped massaging her back. He put away the suntan oil and couldn't help recalling how this Amy chick was the exact opposite. The way her eyes opened wide when the plane from Chicago began its descent and she took in the sight of the skyscrapers. And the way her eyes locked in the travelers' lounge at the sight of Cousin Jack and turned away the second he slipped Al the silver briefcase while looking her up and down. And less than twenty-four hours later she was at it, on board the Orange Blossom Special, heading back to the Big Apple, a place she never knew. Where she was at this very minute, up to God knows what, a complete mystery as to her plans.

And here he was, trying to get a rise out of a sleepy call girl. Hanging around at the beach, feeling like her houseboy while she offered nothing enticing, not even able to string a couple of sentences together so they could have a conversation.

Getting depressed as well as besides himself—left holding the fort, holding the bag—he wanted to know how much more it took. How much more do you have to put up with? Do you just have to wait until the smoke clears and help pick up the pieces?

He spent the next few minutes conjuring up the perfect ending worth all this grief. But there were way too many holes, too many loose ends.

CHAPTER TWENTY-TWO

For his part, Bud was up in his hotel room still thrown by his run-in with Larkin. Feeling totally on his own now, in well over his head, still with only an iffy date to call Amy going for him. And what was in the silverline briefcase that was so valuable in the first place? Added to Ed's tossing in "there goes Trafficante and Havana" coupled with Larkin's loopy six degrees of separation running through his mind, he was in danger of literally overloading the circuit.

Simmering down, he told himself he was still an observer on assignment no matter how you looked at it. When you're on assignment you have to delimit the subject and determine what it would take to fill in specific gaps. So you dig deeper, consult experts, do some research. Go out there and experience the realities firsthand if needs be, but never confuse pondering with understanding what was actually going on. Which, in the scheme of things, left Scooter as an accessible go-between who knew the territory and could put his finger on the true nature of the given circumstances.

Instinctively, Bud got out his notepad and began to sketch in what little he knew about these dangling matters. By extension, he recalled glancing at a few glaring sidebars in the *Miami Herald* the other week. The island of Cuba was shaped like a saw palmetto frond lying on its side surrounded by the Gulfstream and the Caribbean. Looking from left to right, at the tip end was rebel Fidel Castro's stronghold up in the Sierra Maestra mountains.

Way over on the opposite end was Havana and the short ocean gateway across to the Keys up to Miami Beach. Thus a link to this guy Trafficante and some impending meeting. Thus also the link to where Ed and Escobar presently had their base of operations.

There was also another item Bud recalled. Recently, Howard, the current affairs editor, had called Bud over to his desk in his never ending quest to get Bud to consider switching from mere sports reporting. As usual, Bud had to wait until Howard tamped down the tobacco in his briar pipe, struck a march and got it going again. Then, as if relaying a juicy state secret, he said, "Yaguajay will be next, Bud, mark my words. And Che Guevara is bound to take Santa Clara."

"I see," Bud had murmured, nodding, gaining interest.

Scratching his cropped salt-and-pepper hair, Howard peered over his bifocals, employing his firm word-to-the-wise tone. "What's the watchword, Bud?"

"Perspective," Bud said. "Intrepid in the news gathering business but, at the same time, seeing things evolve from a remove."

"Relying on and citing credible sources. Deciphering the fact that Yaguajay and Santa Clara are well within reach. Moreover, reports show the rebels have joined forces with other resistance groups. What we've got here is a combined insurgent army on the offensive."

"So there's no doubt things are happening, picking up steam."

"And you know what that could very well mean? Nationalization. You can trace it back to Batista's corrupt dictatorship and Fidel Castro's clamoring for justice. Cubans everywhere clamoring for reform."

"Looks like everything is on the verge," Bud had concurred. Which, doubtless prompted him to note the protests of a young lady named Kathleen at the White Horse Tavern this past Sunday, intent on joining the Cuban rebel forces. Not to mention the barkeep Reilly cajoling him with talk of terrorist machinations across the sea. And pigeon-holing Larkin as a guy who did his best to cast a blind eye.

Which brought on that same apprehension that overtook him during that teddy bear stint over all manner of things in motion, including some burly figure tailing him, including Larkin's "only six degrees of separation between him and God knows what out there." Keeping him from going out there again until he had a handle on what was possibly awaiting him.

He left his room and took the elevator down to the lobby. He noticed that Claire, the perky receptionist in the maroon glasses that matched her uniform, was unoccupied. He went over to the front desk and tried to casually ask her if anyone had come by wanting to glance at the latest entries in her reservations log.

Giving him a mischievous look, she said, "Despite what you've seen on the silver screen, that's strictly against the rules. Company policy."

"How about asking if I was in or inquiring about some guy from Miami who might have recently booked a room?"

"I would have called you or left a note in your box."

"I see. Good to know."

Going over to the rack with the sightseeing pamphlets, playbills, maps and brochures, she said, "If you're hung up or looking for something to do, here's the program at Radio City Music Hall, the movie times for *Bridge on the River Kwai* at the Roxy, which I hear is quite a spectacle starring William Holden. And here's a brochure for *West Side Story*. A chance to see it with the original cast while it's still fresh, way before the road company goes on tour."

And there it was, that same, recurring black-and-white image. The last time it was dwarfed by a giant Pepsi and bottle cap on the rooftops of Times Square in competition with Canadian Club whiskey, Chevrolet cars, etc. All the humongous competing imagery in vibrant color making a tucked away shot of a young carefree couple running down the streets of New York seem irrelevant. Except for someone like Bud, who was starting to wonder about everything that was impinging on him.

Bud gave Claire a thanks-but-no-thanks. She nodded and gave him a conspiratorial wink as if she realized something had him unnerved.

He took the elevator back to his room. Unable to take his apprehension any longer, he decided to get in touch with Scooter forthwith. If he didn't start to nail things down, he'd be of no good to anyone.

The first phone number Scooter gave him got him nowhere. Amid the ringing and pinging of pinball machines, the irritable guy on the other end informed him Scooter hadn't been around all day and hung up on him, not even offering to take a message. The other number connecting him with a restaurant in the Little Italy section was more promising. With the faint recorded sounds of a soprano opera soloist in the background, Bud was told that Scooter should be by any minute to make his delivery (whatever that meant) and for Bud to leave his name and number where he could be reached. Bud quickly complied.

He got out his notepad again and began jotting down names like the starting lineup of a ball game: Reardon, Trafficante, Carlo Gambino, Vito Genovese, and Crazy Joe Gallo.

Minutes went by. He checked out the national and international news section of the Tribune on the off-chance he might have missed something. He came up empty and was depositing the paper in the trash can when the phone rang. Picking up the receiver he was greeted by that same cocky tone that belonged to Scooter.

"Right, let's have it, Mac. Are we in or out?"

"We're in if you can get me a bead on five characters."

"I thought I only told you three?"

"Well it's five if you include Vito Genovese and Crazy Joe Gallo, names I got from another source. And leaves me still in the dark in view of an impending time frame and the game clock."

"Game clock … time frame? What is this? What are we talkin' here?"

"Never mind. I need to know how many mobster families are in play and possibly after me. One would be hard enough to shake off. More than that and my whole juggling act would be problematic."

"In English. What's with problematic? Give it all to me straight in plain English."

"Fine. Reardon, Carlo Gambino, and Trafficante', plus Vito Genovese and Crazy Joe Gallo. According to the word on the street, what are they individually or collectively up to? That's your job as my proxy, that's what you've got to come up with. Call it the process of elimination so I can take it from there."

For the longest time there was only the muted sound of the soprano singing another aria that sounded vaguely familiar, the occasional rattle of dishes and the clink of glasses. Then Scooter came right back with, "It's gonna cost you, man. So this is the way I figure it. Twenty-five dollars an hour starting from about thirty minutes from now after my uncle Guido finishes chewing my ear off about something like always. That should cover the wear and tear from Mulberry up to Cooper Union and Chooch the deadbeat's home turf."

"Chooch?" Bud asked, recalling the duffle bag incident at Penn Station. "Straggly, wiry little guy like I told you?"

"Deadbeat, okay? Then up and over to the pool hall around Stuyvesant Square."

"Fine, okay okay. Whatever it takes."

Then he came right back with, "So I make it at least three hours, give or take, plus a bonus for each time I hit the bullseye. If I come up empty, you leave what you owe me in your mail slot at the hotel and I'll pick it up when I get to it."

Bud wondered how he knew what hotel he was staying at but let it go.

"But if I score all across the board," he went on, "I'll tip you off, you'll buy me supper in one of those fancy little dives you got. We'll meet around six-thirty. I'll give you the skinny and you'll divvy up. Too much for you or what?"

"No no. Supper in the smaller spot called The Mezzanine. Casual, cozy with no dress code where we can have a chat."

"Chat huh?"

"Talk casually without having to watch your manners."

"I gotcha. What you're giving me is an out-of-towner getting real antsy over his head. And what I'm offering here is what you do or don't have to be climbing the walls about. Correct?"

"You got it."

As they hung up, Bud couldn't help worrying what Scooter would come up against in Bud's place. How far would he get in the next three hours? What would it be like to actually put something on the line, streetwise, acting as his alter ego? As a real deal leg man checking out the priceless realities?

CHAPTER TWENTY-THREE

T he way Scooter saw it, filling in for this guy Bud for a few hours was a cinch. All it took was three stopovers paying off, ending with a free supper at a pricey midtown hotel, a quick report and then collecting some needed coin. What's to worry?

All set, he left the two bags of cash wagers upstairs with the accountants in the numbers bank room. Then went back downstairs and waited for the waiter to return from the kitchen for Uncle Guido's chilled cannoli, Tiramisu, and a bottle of Chianti. With the opera music seeping through the speakers above the gilded photos of Verona, Scooter thought things over. First of all, he never understood how Uncle Guido could keep this up with his numbers racket operation upstairs and his restaurant down here, which was only a front, which only did good business on Friday and Saturday nights. How could he keep it going, especially lately, unless he was still paying off the beat cop and/or somebody new like Vito Genovese, whom he now had to please?

Next, not of course nearly as important, how a daily round of deep fried pastry shells and ricotta, plus coffee cannoli, plus Tiramisu with its heavy whipped cream, mascarpone cheese, lady fingers, and liqueur washed down by the Chianti, plus no exercise, wouldn't clog up your veins and do you in? These matters crossed his mind lately, considering his future, and he didn't want to wind up anything like Guido. But, at the same time, he kept his hand in without rocking the boat. So, concentrating right this minute, for openers, how was he going to dig up any information from his set-in-his-ways uncle without giving himself away?

Anyways, he put aside thoughts of cannoli, Tiramisu, and no exercise 'cause no matter how he bragged about the shape he was in thanks to the miles he put on with his bike was never going to make a dent in Guido's habits. And how Guido kept going was beside the point. As for the main thing right now, he had to come at it from left field. The second you ask a direct question or in any way tip your hand, you've had it. As long as Guido was munching and slurping and groaning about something or other, Scooter could gauge how things were going up to the minute and come away with something to build on.

Soon enough, Aldo the waiter returned, Scooter took the tray, made the usual wisecrack as a warmup—"Hope you didn't stint on the calories, Aldo"—and took off up the winding staircase. Careful not to spill anything, he pried open the heavy wooden door, slipped past the glassy-eyed accountants clicking their registers and adding to their tallies, and brushed by the round cage with its shiny numbered white balls. He eased through the second door, which was partially open, and plunked the tray on the mahogany desk in front of Guido's seated bulk. Dressed as usual in his double-breasted pin-striped suit, weariness written all over his jowly face, Guido made quick work of a cannoli, uncorked the Chianti bottle and filled a wine glass to the brim. He snatched a white handkerchief from his breast pocket, gulped down the red wine as if he was parched, filled the goblet again, and wiped his lips.

After still getting no recognition (which was par for the course), Scooter jumped right in. "Hey, Uncle. Have you heard the one about the rat-fink's tombstone? 'Here lies Ray, the snitch, Zitti, born such-and-such a date, whacked New Year's Eve.'"

"Not funny," Uncle Guido said in that same old wheezy tone as he finally looked up. "You better watch your mouth if you should find yourself around any wiseguys who are in no mood."

"I save the jokes special for you."

"So next time don't bother. Okay?"

"Okay, I hear you."

"So how goes it?"

"Much better than the Lower East Side and Chinatown with all those clinking coins. The Chelsea beat gives us crisp tens and twenty dollar bills. Like we hit the Dow Jones market on the upswing."

"Don't count on it."

Pushing it, Scooter said, "Why not? Say, you know what would be cool? If, in competition with the Dow Jones, there was an under the radar, syndicate market. Can't you see it? This week Trafficante and Gambino holding steady along with Genovese. But Reardon starting to inch ahead of the pack."

Sitting up straight, Guido said, "Who told you? Where you getting this?"

"Where am I getting what?"

"Knock it off," Guido said, tearing into the Tiramisu. "That's how rumors get started. Some smart-ass starts poking around, raking up the coals, trying it on for size. Pretty soon word gets around and then what happens?"

"What do you mean?"

"Don't act stupid. What I tell you so you would keep your nose clean? Because everything is out of joint lately. Because I promised your mother I'd look out for you."

"Hey, what are you getting all serious about?"

"What are you, dense? We got Anastasia out to get Genovese because he hears Genovese rubbed out Frank Costello, his ally in the Syndicate. Gambino hears Anastasia was jealous of his wealth and power and out to ice him. Next thing we got a hit man from Joe Profaci's crew. Which leaves Crazy Joe Gallo still out there on a short leash."

"Oh, yeah," Scooter said, as if he was just remembering. "Crazy Joe."

"So what happened at Grasso's barbershop at the Park Sheraton? And who is still bragging about what a perfect job he done spreading more goddamn rumors? And now you want to start something with this Jack Reardon, up to something, getting everything totally out of joint?" Swinging his beefy arms wildly, he sent the plate of Cannelloni flying off the desk onto the rug.

Scooter held up his hands in mock surrender and quickly backed-up toward the door.

"Where you going?"

"Got some things I gotta do."

"You hear what I'm telling you? I finally struck brain? Nowadays you got to really keep an eye out. Count on nothing!"

"Hey, take it easy will you? What you want to get, an ulcer?" Scooter made his way past the accountants shuffling through the pile of betting slips, unable to stop grinning. Jerking his uncle around was such a blast. He rushed down the stairs and out the front door. Back on his bike, he checked his watch and nodded to himself. All things being equal, Chooch should be casing his turf around Cooper Square around this time, with or without a partner. From what little Scooter knew, if Chooch was doing his thing with another guy, he relieves the mark of his wallet bumping into him and slips it to his teammate coming from the other direction reading a newspaper. That way, Chooch is never holding. But if he was on his own, Scooter had no idea what his play would be.

But at least it was something Scooter could easily handle as long as Chooch showed up. With Scooter top dog instead of putting up with his uncle to get the green light how things stood.

He got set for his second stop and peddled over to 4th Avenue, dodging the mid-afternoon traffic, exhaust fumes, and the same cruddy gray smog that seemed it would never lift. He maneuvered around between the cabs and finally covered the six blocks or so to Cooper Square, turned right, and pulled in at the bike racks. As he chain-locked his front wheel on the side of Cooper Union, he still never could get over this rusty-brick five-story cube with its shrine-like black marble statue of some bearded guy named Peter Cooper seated across the entrance. Flanked by two ancient-looking columns, Cooper seemed to be looking down like Moses at the bums, panhandlers, bag ladies, and winos milling around the gated park wondering what the hell happened to his place. Here lowlifes could cadge handouts from passersby on their way to the crosswalks. And it was around this busy scene, even alone, Chooch could do his thing, hit and run in all directions.

But there was no sign of him yet, alone or with a partner, so Scooter made do hanging around by the bike racks at the side of Cooper Union. As a cover-up, he reached for a pack and lighter in his zipper pocket, lit up, and began smoking a Lucky Strike as if he was on a break like a Western Union messenger boy.

All the while, given all the noise and traffic, it struck him that once upon a time it wasn't like this. Nothing was like this. The East Village wasn't the East Village, only a little spot east. Old-timey builders had no idea what they were putting up would get torn down or get dwarfed. Grassy squares would give way to avenues like 4th cutting through everything on a slant, humongous glass shapes would take over, people rushing by not even noticing some statue doing its best to lord over them. Architecture students were strolling inside Cooper Union for free back in the old-timey days probably with no scroungers like Chooch on the prowl and mob outfits never leaving well enough alone.

But what was the use of bothering his head about it? It is what it is.

Just then, some lady screaming above all the noise got his attention. He flicked his cigarette into the gutter, got set taking in the commotion somewhere by the Peter Cooper statue, spotted the ragged raincoat and tried to guess which direction Chooch was heading and the best way to cut him off.

Next thing, Chooch came busting out behind the statue, a red kerchief tied around his mouth, darting away, switching course and crossing over in Scooter's direction. The second Chooch reached the edge of the humongous building, Scooter grabbed his shoulder and sent Chooch and a lady's straw handbag flying. Like playing fetch with a hound dog, Scooter picked up the handbag and flung it further down. Chooch no sooner scrambled back onto his feet when Scooter flung it even further, keeping the game up till they were around the corner sandwiched between the back of the building and a brick wall.

"Jeez, Scooter," Chooch moaned, tearing off the bandana, his bloodshot eyes tearing up. "Whaddayou doing? Give it back. This ain't funny."

Scooter couldn't help laughing at him. Besides not being the sharpest crayon in the box, Chooch was always aware of Scooter's connection with the five crime families through his uncle Guido and just stood there shaking.

"This is so lame," Scooter said, "I could puke. Snatching purses now, bandana around your mouth like a train robber in some western flick. And before that, a duffle bag at Penn station which you couldn't even pull off. That does it, man. You are drawing no more attention and drawing in the cops. You've had it!"

"Don't please," Chooch cried, shoving the kerchief into his raincoat pocket. "What can I do? What can I say?"

Swinging the handbag back and forth like he was thinking it over, Scooter began toying with him as Chooch desperately tried to finagle his way out. Some five or so minutes of this and Scooter had the information he was after. He began walking back toward the bike rack, still swinging the handbag with Chooch scurrying behind him.

Getting even more desperate, Chooch jumped in front of him. "Give me at least a fiver or ten to tide me over till tomorrow. Things ain't been going too good. Come on, divvy up something till my partner Gyp gets over his cold and we can operate together. Okay, man, whuddayou say? Come on, please?"

After another fake thinking-things-over, Scooter reached inside the handbag, slipped out a few bills and no sooner handed them over when Scooter sprinted away and was swallowed up by a gaggle of passersby causing a new commotion.

Scooter left the handbag on the stone front steps of the college figuring either some do-gooder would try to return the driver's license and all to the owner, or a bag lady would toss it into her shopping cart and wheel it away. In any case, what difference would it make?

Scooter walked back, removed the lock and chain, and tossed it in his saddle bag. Ready to roll again, he figured one more stop and he should have a story to tell.

Though it was only eight blocks up 3rd Avenue to Stuyvesant Square and the pool hall where Stash hung out, at this late afternoon the traffic was stop and go forcing Scooter to do a lot of jockeying between cars and cabs. At the same time, he thought about owning one of the big Oldsmobiles or the hardtop Pontiac Grand Prix he passed, picturing himself sitting back in the plush leather seats, enjoying the Hydra-Matic auto shift, listening to tunes on the radio. Enjoying being in a totally different class. Someday maybe. Someday soon.

Once he finally got to Stuyvesant and went through the same chain-locking routine at a bike rack, he entered the smoke-filled pool hall. Right off, he spotted Stash's lanky frame, shock of red hair, and that laid-back look on his hawkish face. Scooter took a ring-side seat in a folding chair that gave him a perfect view of the table where Stash was dispatching some dumpy-looking mark. The thing Scooter had to keep in mind was the fact Stash had no patience with small talk. Which, like Uncle Guido indicated, led to rumors. "Never give yourself away" was Stash's strict motto echoed by everybody else who knew the score.

Along these same lines, he and Stash had worked out a quick exchange like spies in the movies. Scooter would take a piece of slate out of his leather jacket along with a piece of chalk and a sponge to wipe the slate clean.

The way things were going, Stash would be running the table in no time flat relieving this patsy of a hunk of cash and leaving a temporary lull in the action. Then Scooter could slip over and get an okay to his poking around. Sure enough, Stash chalked the end of his cue stick one last time, leaned over, and with the smoothest stroke as if automatically seeing each shooting line, he went through a series of combination shots off the rail. Like hitting the target ball and sending the four ball into the corner pocket, the eight ball off the rail into the side pocket, and like that.

In no time, the dumpy mark was handing Stash his winnings and shuffling out the building like some greenhorn who'd lost his way in the cigar and cigarette smoke. Stash pocketed the cash and had the piece of slate, chalk, and sponge Scooter had handed him at the ready. They both positioned themselves leaning up against the central pool table side by side facing a blank wall. Scooter asked "What's the good word?" which meant was Stash onto anything that was going down? Stash made a check mark on the piece of slate.

"Who's got the hot hand?"

Stash scribbled an S.

"Anybody in on it?"

Stash scribbled a T and erased them both.

"Anybody else who'd want in on the action?"

Stash scribbled a VG, a CG and a JG, erased it all and handed the piece of slate, chalk, and sponge back to Scooter.

"Well?" Stash asked, glancing directly at Scooter.

"Thanks. I owe you."

"Damn straight."

Stash turned around and eyed an approaching heavy-set guy with a walrus moustache. As soon as the guy reached him, he said, "Hey, man, you game?"

"You bet," was the answer.

"Then let's get it on."

Stash draped his lanky body over the central table and began collecting and racking up the balls. Not even bothering to nod goodbye to Scooter which, as always, would be a waste of energy.

Scooter was both satisfied and put-out having to now trek uptown to the New Yorker hotel. Which would be a hassle for a guy on a bike to face the traffic and pedestrian after-five crunch around Herald Square, Macy's, Madison Square Garden, Penn Station, and all the rest of it. Not to mention the white-collar types scrambling for the subways and Yellow cabs clogging things up even more. He'd be lucky to find a bike rack anywhere near the hotel and arrive on time.

Truth to tell, he'd much rather meander back down for some jazz at the Five Spot with Dizzy Gillespie or Sonny Rollins wailing away. Where he'd be running into pushers and guys who were well-connected, working his way up to being a standup guy with a sharp eye and his ear to the ground, taking it all in. Anything to be shed of this damn bicycle running errands.

But right this minute, he'd at least be getting a good meal and a big tip for digging up what was going down at this very moment. Totally unlike Stash, Scooter got a kick out of connecting the dots, crossing the Ts, and being on top of things. As for this Bud character, the guy probably wouldn't know what to make of anything Scooter ran by him. Which was good. When you're dealing with an out of town spotter you slip him a little taste while still leaving him in the dark. Which put Scooter in the same league as Stash.

CHAPTER TWENTY-FOUR

Not long afterwards, Bud was back in action seated in a booth in the far corner of the smaller hotel restaurant wondering if Scooter would show up. A middle-aged couple, also seated in a booth a short distance away, were the only other occupants, which accounted for the blank-faced waiter in a maroon vest doting on him, continuing to refresh his cup of coffee. The wife of the touristy duo lowered her menu from time to time checking up on Bud. Now and then she would make comments like, "Well, dear, you never know what you're going to find. Greatly overcrowded or practically vacant. Unlike Ohio, constant surprise, surprise." Comments that certainly didn't help his growing anxiety, needing some idea what he was up against with that impending deadline Ed had underscored.

Another ten minutes went by until Scooter finally appeared bursting through the glass doors with his stringy black hair disheveled, his leather jacket askew and a scowl on his face. Spotting Bud as he strode past the couple who joined forces hiding behind their menus, Scooter hollered, "I tell ya, at this hour, traffic is a bitch!"

Plunking himself down in the curved banquette directly opposite Bud, he continued to carry on.

"What is this?" Scooter asked, looking all around. "You call this cozy? I'm sitting on a shiny bench here, we got a glass table between us on metal legs. Everywhere the lights are bouncing off chrome and black mirrors. Even the chairs are curved and shiny, plus the chandeliers are wrapped in chrome, which makes everything worse on the eyes. What's the story here?"

"If you'd keep your voice down," Bud murmured, "I'll explain."

"Okay, so tell me,"

"It's called Art Deco."

"Oh, yeah? Meaning?"

"I asked you to keep it down."

"It's down, it's down. Talk to me."

"As far as I know, it started in Paris. To reflect the modern age. Make things sleek and streamlined using modern materials like aluminum, chrome, and stainless steel. Can we get off this and get right down to it?"

"Come on, come on. I want to know who I'm dealing with here. How do you know all this?"

"Because lots of Miami Beach hotels like the Sans Souci and the Sherry Frontenac feature it as a draw. Okay? Like I told you, I need some answers before carrying on."

"Yeah, all right, keep your shirt on."

But the next hurdle was ordering supper. Brushing the hair out of his eyes, Scooter had trouble with the menu. He wanted to know what a Waldorf salad was, a seafood casserole, and filet of sole. This led to, "Where's the pasta? Where's something that sticks to the ribs for a guy who's had a hard day?" Bud quickly recommended a pot roast platter with all the trimmings.

The addition of a bottle of Rhinegold beer enabled Scooter to pull back a notch as Bud simply ordered a BLT, French Fries, and yet another cup of coffee. As the waiter scurried off to the kitchen, Scooter began looking around again, spotted the husband ordering for his wife, and wanted to know what her problem was. Was she shy, unused to eating out? Bud tried to slough this off as well but to no avail. Countering, Scooter claimed that any broad he took out knew how to handle herself. "Matter of fact, Donna D'Onofrio always asks *me* out and afterwards wants to go to a jazz joint. A real chick, you get my meaning? Or else why bother?"

"Enough," Bud said. "Look, as long as I'm paying for it, plus a bonus, otherwise you wouldn't be here unless you had something to offer. So, can you quit messing around and give me the upshot?"

Scooter gave him a thumbs-up. "All right, at least we know you got a little spunk, which means laying it out for you won't be a total waste."

Another interruption as the waiter came by with the beer, coaster, and a tall glass on a silver tray. The waiter started to pour the beer in the glass when Scooter stopped him. "Hey, what are you doing? Do I look helpless? I'm a guy, not some prissy wimp."

The waiter's blank look held steady as he left Scooter to his own devices and exited once again. Scooter downed half a glass of the chilled Rhinegold, put the glass aside, and acted as if it was Bud who'd been stalling all this while.

"So, what do you say we tell it like it is? For starters, what's with a guy who winds up ducking for cover on a fire escape in Chelsea because some mob foot soldier's been tailing him?"

"That's my business and beside the point."

Scooter guzzled some more beer and said, "Not exactly. I says to myself, maybe he stumbled onto something. Then maybe he has no idea about loan sharks, card sharks, pool sharks, and all kinds. Multiply that with the five crime families running the five boroughs on the lookout. 'Cause I got it from the horse's mouth everything's one big crapshoot these days."

"Changing times, right? I get it, I get it."

"Bingo. Then you also must know you are goddamn just asking for it."

That was the last straw for the out of town couple. Scooter's tone and what he was insinuating was apparently more than enough for the husband to rise up, leave a tip, and escort his spouse away from this unpleasantness.

Oblivious of the departing couple, Scooter went on. "What I'm saying is, they're all licking their chops over new territory, a new angle that'll put them in the catbird seat."

As Scooter punctuated the silence by guzzling the rest of his beer, Bud couldn't help thinking of the irony. Here was Rick, a certified P.I. who would never think of investigating who he'd be dealing with before latching onto an illicit high stakes poker game, and here was Bud with no credentials, doing his damnedest to get the picture."

"Hey," Scooter hollered, "you getting this? I'm talking a new front for the regular narcotics, extortion; Uncle Guido's numbers racket in Little Italy and harping on me to watch my back. I am running this by you so's maybe you can get wise that something's up and heads may roll."

"Come on, come on. Meaning what exactly?"

Scooter shook his head, spied the waiter and motioned. The waiter replaced the empty beer bottle and left. Scooter poured the beer slowly in his glass as the waiter returned and served their food. Though it was all he could do to hold his temper, Bud waited Scooter out, ate half his BLT and a few fries as Scooter dug into the pot roast platter. The moment Scooter paused, milking this for all it was worth and wiped his mouth with a napkin, Bud leaned forward and said, "Now? Can you spell it out? I know something imminent is going on spearheaded by this guy Reardon. Besides these other sharks' interest, what specifically is Reardon up to?"

"Let me think how to break it to you. Then add up your IOU and split before somebody snaps my bike chain and I'm totally screwed."

While Bud finished his BLT, Scooter made quick work of the rest of his meal and came right out with it.

"Okay, this is the skinny as far as I know. This Jack Reardon got hold of your photo, don't trust you maybe as far as he can throw you, and got Liam—big guy, flat-top crew cut, right hand man—to tail you, which is the first of the tail jobs. To keep a low profile, Liam got Chooch the deadbeat to snatch your bag the second you appeared on the main concourse at Penn station. So's Liam couldn't help spying you playing tug of war with Chooch and some idea what you're made of. From there it was a piece of cake to keep track till you wound up in the lobby of this here hotel. So now Reardon had your whereabouts and style nailed down for openers. Got it so far?"

All Bud could do was nod.

"At the same time word got out that Reardon is on the move, 'cause Vito Genovese and Carlo Gambino's outfits are in play, maybe Crazy Joe Gallo and even Trafficante. But Crazy Joe is strictly a hit man and Trafficante flits in and out of here from Tampa, so go figure. I tell ya, it never ends." Scooter reached into his bomber jacket, pulled out a piece of slate and chalk, and began marking the slate.

"What are you doing?"

"Figuring the tab, what else? So, taking in the mileage and the grief . . . subtracting the time at the pool hall while I sat around waiting . . . this should do the trick."

Still thrown by Scooter's mobster tally, Bud paid him off.

While pocketing the cash and rising up to go, Scooter said, "Nice doing business with you." Then he was almost out the glass doors when he turned back. Pointing his forefinger, he said, "Wake-up, man. You are a fish out of water strictly on your own. They're coming at you from all sides. When I say Reardon is on the move sudden like, that's what I meant. Go back to your palm trees while you're still in one piece." Then he was gone.

Bud forced himself to hold still and take stock. Reardon's presence somewhere nearby had become self-evident given the fact he'd employed his henchman and the deadbeat to make sure Bud had shown up. Add the fact Reardon just learned Amy snatched the attache` case which was now in play. The outfits of Carlo Gambino and Vito Genovese were also engaged, plus Crazy Joe the hit man in some capacity. This Trafficante person seemed to have had his hand in everything while, according to Ed, was primed for a meeting down at the Tropic Isle this Friday morning to clinch the deal, whatever it was. Meaning Bud was really up against it and the clock was ticking away.

An involuntary shudder ran up his spine as it all fully registered with Havana and who knew what-all resonating in the background, hinging somehow on that elusive silver briefcase.

CHAPTER TWENTY-FIVE

Rubbing his sleepy eyes, recalling grade school platitudes like "Discretion is the better part of valor," Bud entered his hotel room. He turned on some lights and, with nothing else for it, got ready for bed. The encounter with Scooter not only clarified the mounting pressure he was under, but listed the players engaged out there contemplating their next move.

Back in Miami, when you'd taken on too much all you had to do was break the routine—go for a long walk or a swim, take in a movie. Then return with a fresh outlook. If nothing else, an old black-and-white Humphrey Bogart movie at the Royal Theater downtown was always showing: *The Maltese Falcon* or *To Have and Have Not*, *The Big Sleep*, or *Casablanca*. In the dark, cooling off, looking up at the silver screen, you could always escape to a world where everything was simply black and white. Reassured, recalling the fanciful plot, practically nodding as Bogart spouted lines like "I don't mind a reasonable amount of trouble . . . Things are never so bad they can't be made worse." Returning to the sunshiny light of day, Bud would return to his problems and take care of them. Once, in a more lighthearted frame of mind, he even repeated a bit of movie dialogue that was more witty than anything you could devise yourself: "The problem with the world, sweetheart, is everyone's a few drinks behind."

But none of this was apt when you were up against it at this time and place. To still his sleepy, worrisome thoughts he turned on the little TV set to see what was playing in this big town of many channels.

But he quickly discovered everything broadcast at this hour was sugarcoated and more or less mindless. Lifelike crime dramas like *Naked City* filmed on the spot apparently were shown earlier and only once a week. And they themselves dispensed with any lingering danger by showing episodes sandwiched between commercials of Westinghouse products for the home like refrigerators and freezers. Bud kept switching the dial between *Perry Mason, Donna Reed, Dragnet,* and *The Honeymooners* and stopped trying. Nothing helped.

Getting as overtired as can be, he opted for the radio once again and the show tunes station. Within minutes another song from *West Side Story* came filtering into his room. This time the star-crossed lovers put the images on the poster to words, yearning for "a special place," claiming if they held on tight they could take each other there. *Somehow, some day, somewhere.*

Even after he switched the radio off, the sweet melody and yearning lyrics stayed with him. But soon faded and dovetailed into the dread of what might await him under these pressing circumstances. He finally let go of it all and sank into a fitful sleep.

———

In the dream, the sky was not only steel-gray and overcast but became so foggy he could barely see where he was going. If only there were signposts instead of endless brownstones and row houses as tall as the skyscrapers obliterating everything. If only he had taken that tourist map with him. But more importantly, if only he had a distinct destination. If only, like Scooter, he had some big city credentials.

Out of the fog, Scooter suddenly appeared on his gearless, red

Schwinn bike, circling around him, and shooting forward. "Best all around if you just beat it," he cried out. "Go home. You don't know what you're doing. Didn't I make it plain enough for you? You're way too square. I am talkin' real pathetic, man."

Trying to flag him down, Bud began traipsing after him. "But you don't understand. I'm close. I'm this close, really I am. All I need is the right shove in the right direction. Or the streets to avoid. Once given the chance, I can come through. Can't you see that? Why can't you see that?"

"No way. Forget about it."

"But I can't forget about it," Bud said, slowing down to catch his breath. "I always finish my assignments. Ask Russ Hodges, my managing editor or Howard at Current Affairs. I'm very dependable that way."

"What are you talkin'? Do you see any palm trees? Do you see any flamingos? Take a hike. Take a plane. Just take off, will ya and get outta my hair."

"Wait! Wait! What do you want? Toughness, right? Bud affected a tough world-weary look. Then repeated one of Bogie's lines: *If I let you get away with it, sweetheart, it's bad for business, bad all the way around.*

But there was no response. He thought of Greta Hagen. She saw he'd stuck his neck out. He didn't fake it at all. But she was nowhere to be found.

He opened his eyes wider to get his bearings. Scooter had to be headed east toward Little Italy where he said his uncle Guido had his restaurant, engaged in his racket, where Jack Reardon's pub was located, or so Reilly had told him.

There was a hazy camera shot of mobsters in a smoke filled arena including Ed and Escobar . . . shades of Reardon, Vito Genovese, Carlo Gambino, and Crazy Joe Gallo. And Trafficante, a vague slick figure in a dark blue, double-breasted suit, much further away, circling New York and past the Miami Beach skyline. In an instant the apparitions dissolved.

A half turn and Bud was headed in a southerly direction where Stella Parsons could be reached to back him up. But he still couldn't see in the haze. Still no street-signs, only noise, heavy traffic, and gaggles of people rushing here and there. Only the gauzy outline of brownstones and row houses as high as the sky. Plus the outline of fire escapes and alleyways. And added to it all, padded footsteps trailing behind him.

He spotted the dim lights of Larkin's diner. But Larkin was miles away over at the other side of the counter at the flat-top grill, scraping the grease with his spatula. The scraping getting louder and louder. "You owe me, boyo," he shouted. "Grand possibilities, if you please. Boy keeps chasing after her. Nothing slamming shut. Nothing over for keeps. None of that now. It'll do me in. Do us all in!"

And so Bud was at it again moving west this time. The footsteps trailing him. Inside Greta Hagen's dimly lit studio Amy's face was out of focus . . . no sign of a briefcase anywhere . . . his hands shaking as he grasped a Teddy bear. Darting out of alleyways, he knocked over a newsboy who was hollering, "Extra, extra, read all about it, rebels getting closer to Havana, get a load of Belfast too!" Up a fire escape ladder, he flopped onto the grate hoping everything would just stop.

Then trying to rise up, straining, slipping back down, and at long last found himself holding still, sitting up in bed.

The room was pitch dark, sounds of rushing traffic out the window below, and the incessant beeping horns of cabbies telling him it was all much more than just a dream.

CHAPTER TWENTY-SIX

Early that Wednesday morning Bud awoke, grateful for a few hours of mindless sleep but still unable to get over the dream. He never had dreams worth thinking about. And if he ever remotely had dreamy notions, he'd stick to current affairs editor Howard's rule of thumb: "Stay in the here and now, discard all diversions and decide on the most productive course of action." Along these same lines, his dad's once upon a time prodding crossed his mind: "Come on, Bud, don't dawdle. Rise and shine and get cracking. You are what you do." More to the point, he could just hear Ed snapping at him this very minute: "Your lookout is strictly to find the girl and close this out like it never happened. Like everything is running on time, in place where it should be with no one the wiser. We then all get what's coming to us, Rick's gotta pay his dues and the slate is wiped clean. End of story."

And so, accepting the pressure of this looming deadline and putting aside his incessant misgivings, Bud once again resorted to that old truism: *First things first*. On today's agenda was a call to Amy Evens finalizing a meeting early this afternoon using the scene from *The Glass Menagerie* as a pretext. His goal, to uncover her part in this conundrum and why. Seguing to the issue of the silverline briefcase. Onto some kind of resolution before things got totally out of hand.

"Right," he muttered aloud. "Get a grip. Play it by ear. If something crops up, handle it as best you can and stay on track. Being edgy is a good thing. It makes you keep a sharp eye out. It keeps you going." He told himself these things until he almost believed it.

He got dressed and snatched today's *Herald Tribune* left outside his door as a matter of course and took the elevator down to the little café that doubled as a breakfast nook. He ordered the standard bacon, eggs, hash browns, and coffee and perused the running sidebar on the Cuban Revolution while waiting to be served. Today's dispatch focused on the movements of Castro's and Che Guevara's forces as they pressed on. As best he could make out, that was the scope of the news on that front. Still killing time, he turned next to the general election in Cuba and the odds Andres Aguero would become president elect. However, it turned out, Aguero called Castro a sick man and declared it would be impossible to reach a settlement. Leaving the distinct possibility that Aguero may very well not be able to take office in the next few weeks. Also, reflecting back to the day's skirmishes, the news columnist surmised that dictator Batista's fate hung on a certain outcome: whether the rebel forces took Santa Clara and continued on, or got stalled, or retreated.

Which may have something to do with Ed, Trafficante, and Havana. Or just whether or not both the briefcase and Trafficante showed up on time on Friday. Or whatever.

Bud put away the paper. Continuing to guess what Ed meant or didn't mean about anything was not in the realm of getting somewhere. Ed had proved himself to be both as feckless as they come and on the ball, depending on which way the wind was blowing. Which prompted that phone call to Miss Amy. Because her going along with his ploy and recovering the briefcase were as good as one and the same in his quest to resolve this conundrum as far as he was concerned and cross the finish line unscathed.

Oddly enough, the couple from Ohio was seated only a few

tables away. They lowered their menus simultaneously and gave him one of those disparaging looks which, like everything else at this point, could mean anything, perhaps a concern Scooter might come barging in again. More guesswork he definitely had no time for.

Back once more in his room, he rang the Hotel Chelsea, asked to speak to Miss Amy Evens. Then asked the young lady who picked up the community phone to go to the end of the hall and tell Amy there was a gentleman calling for her at the appointed time.

The young lady said, "You mean a guy just touching base, right?"

"Whatever."

After a short wait, Amy got on the line and began to have second thoughts over the plan to meet early this afternoon. "I don't know, Bud. I mean, not to hurt your feelings, but I hardly know you. Don't really know you at all."

Reaching for some way to get beyond this, Bud said, "It's okay. You didn't think I meant we would meet up in your room. Oh no, that wouldn't be right. Especially when, as you said, we've barely met. Look, all we're doing is going over a famous scene, trying to find a way to make it work given the fact the two of us are veritable strangers, exactly like the circumstances in the play. Except that our getting together wasn't set up by your mother and brother in their seedy Saint Louis apartment way back then. So we have to find a way and a spot to approach this awkward situation given our separate circumstances during the present day. I mean, isn't that the gist of what Greta would say?"

It was a stretch, but Greta Hagen did intimate that's how the so-called Method worked. In playing a scene you weren't pretending. You were bringing your own reality to it so it seemed to be actually happening. At least that's what Bud got out of it so far.

When Amy kept hesitating, Bud pressed a little harder. "Listen, isn't there a lounge somewhere where it's quiet and perfectly respectable? Where we can tap this built-in awkwardness that's already there and you can have an escape hatch at the ready, like close to the lobby or the elevator or something like it. If you were uncomfortable at all."

"Well . . . yes . . . As a matter of fact there's a kind of lounge at the far end of the main floor which would do. Except . . . except . . . "

Bud couldn't get over the fact he was trying to talk a girl into simply meeting and going over a play. After all, he was used to being part of the in-crowd since high school. In fact, girls tried to wangle some way to meet up with him and get in with his same upscale bunch. And besides, Ed pointed out to Escobar that he was the perfect front given his clean-cut appearance. Unless it was the way he started coming apart, thrown out there on stage latching onto a teddy bear. Maybe he unwittingly revealed some latent volatile part of himself. And Amy naturally saw herself now as a fugitive and had to stay as secluded as possible while pursuing her stage dreams and keeping the attache` case under wraps. Maybe that was what this hemming and hawing was all about.

Really pushing it this time, Bud said, "Look, Amy, what you saw on stage was a guy who'd never been thrown out there before. Greta Hagen must have seen something in me otherwise she wouldn't have suggested I make an appointment. Which I did. Made it for this Friday afternoon. But what good is it if I can't be a plain ole nice guy as well? And had this *Glass Menagerie* improv under my belt to talk about before I see her? What I'm saying is, you'd be helping me out and you'd be helping yourself out too, completing her assignment. Can't you see? It's all harmless, perfectly above board."

"Well . . ."

"Besides, you admitted you were trying to get into the Actors Studio. What better preparation than playing Laura? Somebody fragile instead of fake like you did back in Chicago. Look, like I said, if at any time you're at all uncomfortable we can call it quits. Just give it a chance."

Amid the sound of the girl's voice who answered the phone now pestering her, asking how much longer she was going to tie up the line, Amy seemed to be giving Bud's sales pitch some thought. Under both pressures, she said, "Well, I guess it can't do any harm. And everyone is out and about by early afternoon anyways, even the jazz musicians who stay up late."

"Two o'clock then? On the main floor back in the lounge?"

"I guess. We can try it, see how it goes."

"That's the ticket. Thanks. Terrific. See you then."

Hanging up, he was taken by the way he carried on. As if he really wanted to try his hand as the gentleman caller and go on from there to impress Greta Hagen and be admitted to her advanced class. It wasn't lost on him that getting real through some subterfuge was a total contradiction. As flawed as Amy being sweet and vulnerable like the character of Laura while covering up her crime or whatever she was really up to. At this point, Bud could only hope the masks would start coming off and this twisty game of charades would completely wind down in just a few hours time.

Later this same morning, Ed too found himself dickering over the phone. But in contrast to Bud's ploy, he was trying to get rid of

Escobar, cut the conversation short, take the elevator back down and meet up with Flo on the beach and come to terms. He wasn't trying to talk somebody in to something but finally, for crissakes, get him off it.

Getting more and more frustrated, Ed said, "You were supposed to get this screw-up off your mind, Al. Clear your head, take in the sights in Boca, and smooth things over with your sister. Meet your nephew's fiancé, mingle with the church crowd, and make like you're legit, remember? "

"Oh sure," Al shot back. "Except this Amy you saddled me with was supposed to take the lead. All I had to do was hang back and see to the details of this shindig. But what if the whole time it was just an act, which is her stock in trade, right? What if she always was in cahoots or something like you said?"

Shaking his head, Ed countered with, "Like Jack, my cousin said. Meaning being PO'd over some airheaded chick showing up at the airport lounge that ain't supposed to be there. Which is only natural in all the rush right before he slips you the briefcase. Meaning throwing another monkey wrench into something. Enough already, so can we just drop it? Look, in less than forty-eight hours, if everybody cools it down and lets this guy Bud do his job, we can sweep it all under the rug and get this show on the road. We can goddamn forget about all this hassle."

By this point, Ed was really starting to lose it. He'd almost made some headway with Flo about the Havana night life, hobnobbing with celebrities, riding around in a pink Caddy with the top down and all. And here was Al handing him another load of what-ifs. Ed took a deep breath and said, "Al, she ain't no mystery. Both times I saw the improv back in Chicago she was agreeable like putty in your hands. The show was closing, she was hung up, couldn't bear going back to Podunk and throw in the towel. You met her and gave her the green light. So give it a rest, will ya? Give me a break and let it ride."

"Yeah, but still dammit—"

"Enough!"

Ed wanted more than anything to remind him he brought this all on himself. Smacking her around, yanking out his .38 and all the rest of it. But all Ed could bring himself to say like he was talking to a little kid was, "Like I said, only less than two days when we seal the deal, whatever it is. Like I said, this Bud character is closing in, almost there."

"You swear? And Reardon is cool with it?"

"It's a lock, Al. Take it from me," Ed said, lying through his teeth. "Go back to the church people. Just what the doctor ordered. As added insurance, just know whatever this chick is up to, Jack won't stand for any delay."

Running out of arguments, Al finally got off the phone when Ed swore on his mother's life it was all in hand and he'd keep Al in the picture.

Ed let out a deep sigh. Being the go-between, nursemaid, fixer, and flunky was really doing him in. He shuffled over to the balcony, got out a stick of gum, and looked down for any sign of that slinky form coming this way. He hoped Jack had everything in hand by now and crossed off working on Bud anymore. Just leave it to Jack and this Bud character, he told himself. Let it be and play it by ear.

CHAPTER TWENTY-SEVEN

For his part, Bud didn't have the luxury of going along come what may. In fact, Bud had to try extra hard to keep any hint of anxiety in check if he hoped to put this escapade behind him as soon as possible. And so he spent time in his hotel room coming up with a progression that not only would disarm Amy but put her at ease.

Which meant some initial small talk with no apparent hurry to get things going. No indication he might have some ulterior motive in insisting on going over the gentleman caller scene today. Rather, as he'd indicated, it was a stepping stone to putting himself at ease as a wannabe actor for their mutual benefit.

For openers, taking his clue from the gentleman caller scene itself, he could gently skirt around it to draw her out given her reluctance. By, say, asking about the Actors Studio, wondering what possessed Marilyn Monroe to forsake her flourishing Hollywood career in order to marry a New York playwright and come all the way east to study at the Studio or do scenes or whatever it is they do. Perhaps (he could chime in) she'd been inspired by the work of actresses like Constance and wanted to try her hand as well. By the same token, he could offer his encounter with Stella Parsons, her guidance, and how taken he was by Constance's lifelike approach. In this way, they would have even more in common and could segue naturally to the improv.

But then he had no idea how he could broach the subject of

the stolen attache` case. At any rate he had time to come up with something that wouldn't duly upset the apple cart and keep things somewhat on an even keel. Hopefully. Possibly.

Doubling back, recalling Greta Hagen's assignment, they were to go from a read-through first and then do an improv based on their own experience. To bring their personal underlying motives to bear. Which could get tricky. He'd have to really work on that in the meantime. And go over the whole scene to be so well acquainted with the lines he could retain eye contact so that his head wouldn't be buried in the script the whole time.

Needless to say, he definitely had his work cut out for him if he was to go through the motions without a hitch, without this whole ploy blowing up in his face.

Just then the phone rang. It was the front desk, a male voice he didn't recognize telling him somebody was waiting to see him in the lobby. And all this person would say was that it was strictly business. Assuming it had to be Scooter who had news, was playing it close to the vest, and had second thoughts about telling him to pack it in, Bud said he'd be right down. He slipped on his corduroy jacket, left his room, and took the nearby elevator down. But he no sooner got out onto the lobby when a large man with close-set eyes, flat-top haircut, dressed in a wool topcoat that barely fit accosted him and began ushering him toward the front door and out onto the street.

Totally thrown, all Bud could say was, "Hold it, this must be some mistake." And then, "Look, as it happens, I've got a very important appointment in less than two hours and can't afford to be late."

"Oh yeah?" the guy said shoving him even harder, "well you got an appointment with Jack Reardon right now."

"Not that I know of. Tell me you're kidding."

"Jack don't kid. Jack don't mess around."

Then it came to him. "Wait a minute, will you? You're Liam, right? Reardon's right hand man? I'm sure it's all a misunderstanding and we can surely work something out."

But Liam didn't answer this time. Before Bud knew it, they came upon a dark-green Olds 88 parked at the curb. Liam forced him into the passenger seat and, in relatively no time, Liam hit the ignition and Bud found himself being driven amid the honking yellow cabs as Liam was fully intent on keeping up with the traffic.

With no other option and a chill running up his spine, Bud paid close attention, pulled out his notepad, and began jotting things down. All he could think of was to mark the route Liam was taking, get this encounter with Jack Reardon over with, look for a cab and make it back to the Chelsea section of town in plenty of time to meet up with Amy. He hadn't had a chance to grab his playscript but they could still engage in some small talk and, providing that Bud could pull himself together, slip into the improv and just wing it.

Bud rolled up the passenger side window to muffle the traffic noise and said, "Did Jack Reardon give you any idea what this was all about?"

At first Liam still paid no attention to him. Then he said, "Remember what Chooch told you?"

"Chooch? That deadbeat you mean? I've never spoken to him."

"When he grabbed your bag," Liam hollered over to him. "He told you the way I said to tell you. Gave you the message. He swears he did."

"What message?"

"'A couple of days is all you're good for,' that's what message. Meaning Jack don't have the time to mess with you."

Bud did recall Chooch yelling at him right before he took off into the crowded main concourse. "But I thought he was commenting on the way I was dressed in my tennis sweater. That I was completely out of my element. Which was perfectly understandable."

"No," Liam said making a sharp turn. "Jack was trying to get across he had his eye out and you were on a short leash. And that was before he finds out about you giving his cousin Ed the runaround. Then he finds out it's even a thousand times worse, the broad has gone and swiped the silver case, you keep talking a good game and up till now come up with zilch. So no more runaround, no more jerking Jack's chain, your time is up."

That said, Liam went back to concentrating on his driving and Bud had no inkling what to do. He went back to looking out the window and jotting down the landmarks. Consulting his folded map of lower Manhattan, as best as he could figure out they had been traveling east, then south down Broadway, then east again across a wide congested corner on Lafayette. They zipped past scaffolding covering the sidewalks, overflowing dumpsters, abandoned storefronts, and fire escapes. This soon was followed by a series of squat weathered-brick buildings and storefronts covered with steel rollup shutters. A few minutes later, he found himself traveling down Houston Street and crossing Mulberry, Mott, and Elizabeth when it dawned on him they were in a section marked Little Italy. Which was Scooter's uncle's territory and little wonder Scooter was well acquainted with Mister Reardon.

Slowing almost to a crawl, Liam drove by a faded *Gino's Accessories* sign plastered on a store window on Broome that intersected Elizabeth. Bud spotted a neon *Reardon's Pub* sign past the abandoned accessories shop, across the street and sandwiched between more abandoned storefronts. There was no way he'd be able to backtrack from here. He had no idea if cabs even came across this isolated neighborhood.

Which must be the way Reardon wanted it: an obscure Irish pub with an unlit neon sign catering to a highly limited clientele. A front for some much more lucrative or nefarious operation.

Liam parked in an empty lot diagonally across from the pub, grabbed hold of Bud and, dodging an old produce truck headed down Broome, ushered Bud inside. He told him not to move "or else" and proceeded past a heavy curtain to a dimly lit back room.

Bud felt himself getting more and more unnerved as he tried to steady himself and take in his surroundings.

Apparently, this setup was a smaller version of the White Horse Tavern located somewhere west of here in the Village. There was the same dark-wooden bar ahead to his right capped by a bronze railing, the same copper tower in the center propping up draft beer tap handles, and the same chalk board hanging above the bar noting New Castle brown ale as a specialty. There was also an array of bottles of whiskey perched on a shelf behind the railing earmarked, no doubt, for Reardon's cronies and regulars, the usual assortment of dangling beer mugs, and the identical White Horse burgundy stools fronting the bar. At the far end of the bar sat a greenish bottle of Jameson Irish whiskey, a double-shot glass and a beer pitcher.

In addition, there was a duplicate of the old pendulum clock above the heavy curtain to the dimly lit back room and a set of framed bronze swans on either side. All that was missing were garrulous men in cable-knit white sweaters toasting the romantic Irish who wanted all of Ireland united—Protestants and Catholics, with scrawny Kathleen yelling above the din she was going off to join the Cuban women recruits coming down from the mountains instead.

But as he looked more closely, he could see this was truly all a front. Because there, tucked away high up in the far corner to the left of the curtain, was a green banner featuring a golden ploughshare and a sword serving as the plough's blade. Just below it was a green raised fist in the center of a smaller white banner. Across the way, tucked up in the opposite corner, was a green, white, and orange banner with the words "Freedom first, Brit's out!" in black block letters. As he stood there almost transfixed, there was little doubt he was smack inside the murky alternative pub Reilly the bartender alluded to. The very hangout for supporters of IRA terrorists across the waters who, in contrast to the romantics at the White Horse yearning for harmony, wanted nothing better than to drive the Brits out of Northern Ireland employing any means necessary.

Bud tried to shake this off. He certainly didn't want to think about terrorist's activity he had the vaguest notion of in far off Belfast, wherever that was, any more than he wanted to concern himself with rebels coming down from the Cuban mountains. But that, then again, would put him in the same class as Larkin, seeking refuge, solely focused on running his diner and an equally cozy wrap-up for his Greenwich Village tales. Which, at the moment, was no worse than Bud's hankering for an easygoing wrap-up for his dubious assignment so he could get back on board the train to his safe and predictable life among the sheltering palms.

All of this anxious musing was cut short when a muscular figure wearing a sweatshirt with the sleeves rolled up displaying bulging biceps came bursting out of the back room. His craggy face, broken nose, and salt-and-pepper crewcut added to the picture. His raspy Brooklyn accent clinched it as he said, "So, what we got here?" All told, there was nothing subtle about Jack Reardon. In combination, the expression of disdain on his face said it all.

In tow, Liam came shambling out of the back room as well, took his place by Bud's side, and guarded the front door. "I don't know, Jack. So far he's some slick guy from out of town like the photo your cousin sent. And trying to talk his way out of this like you figured."

Reardon positioned himself at the far end of the bar near the fifth of John Jameson whiskey and looked Bud up and down. "Which fits this whole mess. I mean, you got a hitch, you call on a fixer. Somebody you know and used before with what they call a track record. But this ain't any normal operation. This is made of separate pieces, one-of-a-kind special, which is the whole point so nobody has a clue. But there can't be no right hand, which is mine, don't know what the left hand is doing. No way Ed calls and says it's even worse while I'm up to my ears in logistics. No way in hell!"

Unable to follow any of this without some kind of access code, resorting to glancing over his shoulder at the front door, Bud said, "Would you mind if we talked this over later? As I told your associate here, I have a pressing engagement with a contact which, if met, will finally go a long way towards resolving the hitch in question of your dubious dealings."

Bud started to turn away but Liam shoved Bud further away from the door.

"Associate, huh?" Reardon said. "Pressing engagement . . . contact. Is that how what Ed calls a bona fide leg man operates? At the same time keeping me in the dark, handing me the East Side while you do the real thing west of Broadway?"

"I needed time to get my bearings, that's all. And didn't want to work at cross purposes."

"Bull." Reardon said, slamming his fist on the bar. "Not coming clean is not working through me, Mac. And passing up your per-diem? And then the crap hits the fan with the big news about the missing silver case? I mean, what the cockamamie hell is this? Crazy town?"

Unable to hold back any longer, Bud said, "Look, there's no

way I can deal with this with Ed pestering me over the phone, then relaying things to some third party who may not like the way I do things. Especially after promising what a lark it's going to be. So, if we can cut this short and allow me to get on with it apart from anything else you've got up your sleeve."

With that sorry attempt all he could muster, Bud tried to get by Liam and reach for the door knob. Liam spun him around, pulled down the shade, and shoved him against the front window. Liam's fist slammed into Bud's midsection, fear and pain catching up to him, taking control, doubling him over. Then Liam jerked him upright as he cried out gasping, leaving him no option but to clutch his ribs and hold still, trying to catch his breath.

"Hold it," Reardon called out. "Look, fella, I can have Liam work you over, but where would that get me? The second she spots you hobbling around, she flies the coop again."

Echoing Reardon's frustration, Liam slammed Bud against the front window again.

Shaken, never having been hit or shoved around before, Bud held onto his solar plexus even tighter and continued to try and catch his breath.

"So" Reardon said, "we are going to take all the loose pieces, straighten things up, sweep what's broken under the rug, and get everything under control. Call a spade a spade. We're gonna communicate real good so there's no chance for no miscom-munication and get things back running in the nick of time. You read me, fella? Your dangling days are done. Your word contact gotta mean Amy, the mousy type I ran into at the airport who, it looks like you goddamn finally located. And you're right, counting on Ed as go-between while I have to strike while the iron is hot don't cut it. Ed leaving out the skinny till the last minute, like nobody'll be the wiser is as lame as it gets.

Are you getting my meaning? Am I coming through loud and clear?"

Bud could do nothing but nod as Reardon, so wound up at this point, continued to vent.

"But what really sticks in my craw are the bonehead moves by Escobar, which as far as I can see started it all off, which can drive anybody outta their skull!"

Reardon reached for the bottle, poured himself a double shot of Irish whiskey, and downed it as Bud glanced at his watch.

"That's right, pal. The clock is ticking and once you lose the handle in this business, you've had it. So I got to know I got you by the scruff of your neck, you are gonna cut the tap dance and get this show back on track like your life depended on it, which it does."

Another large slug of whiskey and Reardon began snapping his fingers. "This is where it all went wrong and this is who she is. At the handoff at LaGuardia, Escobar shows up with this extra baggage in tow, does it behind my back. She's gonna be a believer at his nephew's engagement party in Boca. 'Cause the bride is from this born-again bunch from the boonies, which is where the wide-eyed chick is from. Which Escobar's sister will go for and get off his back for all his sins. So we got religion, oil, and water that don't mix."

Snapping his fingers again, Reardon went on. "Plus this chick is giving me looks like I'm in with the devil. Which, later I learn, Ed tells her I'm just passing through. Which gives her a free pass to come back up here like Marilyn Monroe, like your boss at the detective agency cons her whilst trying to get her to fork over Escobar's tells for some cockamamie card game. Which is bonehead moves numbers two and three. Plus whatever in hell got her to swipe the case under Escobar's nose, making it bonehead move number four!"

Reardon was so agitated, he reached behind the bar, pulled out a wooden-handled grip-strengthener, and began squeezing it as if squeezing the life out of someone.

Again, Bud looked at his watch but was relieved that the pain had subsided a notch, enabling him to just wince off and on.

Reardon slid the grip strengthener away. "So we got the picture now chapter and verse? This Rick Ellis on ice with no phone or car and only you between him and getting deep-sixed in Biscayne Bay. Correct?"

"I guess. That's my understanding."

"And though I made sure to underwrite this operation with out-of-towners and clinch it in Miami Beach, something went screwy. Why would I want to keep an eye out so you could nab her and get her back for this dumb engagement party when I was glad to get rid of her? And how could it take a couple of days till Escobar discovered she also snatched the silver case from the wall safe? Huh, huh? Answer me that."

"I couldn't tell you. I don't rightly know."

"You don't have to know. You have to step in, sweep up, and clear out. We struck brain, on the same page now or what?"

Bud nodded again, groping for something to say but absolutely coming up empty. He was still in pain, fearful, and no longer in charge.

"So I ordered you a cab. Not any cab but Seamus' who's one of my boys, who I was filling in as much as he needs to know. Who will mark exactly where you get let off 'cause you don't have time to fake him out. 'Cause if you're late trying to cover the rest of the distance, this Amy chick will sure as hell cut out."

"Fine," Bud said. "I get it, I get it. As long as he gets me there before it's too late."

"Bingo. The way I see it, this nervous little broad is dying to confess. 'Cause anybody hard-up enough to go along with Escobar to some churchy thing down in Boca with an eye on making it in show biz up here, you got guilt tacked on big time. So, first off, she's got to do an out-of-sight, out-of-mind and stash the silver case across the bridge and over the river in some church vestry but close enough by. After she spent the past couple of days covering the scene, the guilt over what she done has to be getting to her real bad. And that's where you freakin come in. Yes?"

"Whatever you say."

"Whatever I say is the way it shakes out. Like Ed said—which is the only thing he got right—a clean-cut type like you is the only foot in the door. You get the confession before she runs back to the church. Now you're the bag man instead of some pastor or priest. You slip off and go to Gimbels or Macy's and get one of them flight bags—not from Pam Am, TWA, Eastern or National that goes direct to Miami and gives the game away. You get one that says Northwest that'll throw anybody and everybody off."

Bud kept nodding.

"Speaking of which," Reardon went on, "you're up at the crack of dawn. You got the flight bag plus the exact spot she stashed the case planted in your brain. You got a map, right?"

"I do."

"You catch a cab heading south and stop off before the Brooklyn Bridge at a Rikers diner for a cup of coffee. If the coast is clear, you get another cab over to Flatbush. A lost birdbrain like her could only come up with some simple spot over the East River out of the way. If she says she stashed it in Flushing Meadows, you go the other way, stop off at a Rikers before crossing over the Queensboro Bridge and like that. Whatever it takes for you to throw anybody off and get back with the goods all zippered up to hand off to Liam in your lobby by eleven-thirty in the morning. That's so's he can check it out. With Seamus' cab gassed-up and ready exactly at noon, the Northwest bag should throw off any torpedo laying in wait. So we got you hoping like hell the papers are as untouched as the day they left here, back in the Tropic Isle wall safe where they belong, ready for a certain party who will arrive first thing the next morning as freakin planned. Repeat."

Stifling another wince, Bud said, "Has to be back there for the deadline early Friday morning."

"You better believe it."

Despite the pain it caused, Bud fumbled for his notepad and scribbled a few notes. At the same time, Reardon said, "This here is your only chance. Coming through, leaving Liam plenty of time to get to LaGuardia, hop a plane, take a limo over the Miami causeway. I'm talking goddam signed, sealed, and delivered like this screw-up never happened."

Returning to the bar, Reardon helped himself to another double shot of whiskey and paused. "So why in hell should I leave all this up to you?"

"Because I'm the clean-cut type and won't spook her," Bud said winging it. "Am not in it for the money, even refused a per-diem. My record is clean, I'm dying to get back to Miami and a life of ease, and the last thing I need is any association with the rackets."

"For starters," Reardon said, pointing a finger straight at him. "But the kicker is 'cause you don't want the fallout. 'Cause if you blow it, it's the girl's neck, your neck and your loser of a boss's neck. You got the whole picture? Am I coming in loud and clear?"

"Crystal. But if I come through with this like you said, we're square, right?"

Reardon grabbed the beer pitcher and hurled it against the door jam and the wall, the shattered glass just missing Bud's head. "Get him out of here before I lose it altogether!"

As Liam was hustling him out the door, Bud glanced back for a second and could swear Reardon was raising a mug to the golden ploughshare up in the corner. And was saying, "Now's the time, boys. You can bank on it, so help me."

CHAPTER TWENTY-EIGHT

While approaching the awaiting cab, still dealing with his aching midsection, Bud sensed he'd shifted into a different gear. It was not unlike what happened when Greta Hagen egged him to go on stage for the first time in his life. The tension, ache, and edginess held steady and he had no idea what he might say or do.

He no sooner eased into the cab and said, "Chelsea," when Seamus, Reardon's chubby flunky, turned into an extension of Reardon himself. Wearing a New York Yankees cap, plaid flannel shirt, and a frayed Kelly-green scarf, Seamus was quick to lay into Bud as he revved up the motor and made a quick turn up 3rd Avenue, barely missing an elderly man with a push cart. In that same nervy way, he cut across 13th street and yelled over, "Who you think you're jerking around? What you mean is Hotel Chelsea, right? Not just Chelsea, which could mean anywheres around here."

"I was getting to it."

"Like hell. Reardon said you might pull something. And here you go trying to throw me."

"Not true. Can you back off for a second while I try to take this all in?"

"Back off? In this town? What are you, kidding? You hesitate and right off you're behind the eight ball."

Another swerve while leaning on his horn and they became stuck behind a file of box trucks and a half dozen more yellow cabs waiting for the light to change up ahead at 6th Avenue. In the meantime, with a fixed scowl on his scrunched-up face, Seamus kept hollering, this time about how Bud brought this on himself instead of coming clean in the first place.

Having had quite enough of this, Bud hollered back over the din of the idling engines. "Oh, that's cute, tell me about it. Did you get dragooned to take the train all the way up here? And then get jerked around every minute?"

"What does that have to do with anything? You should've checked with Jack right off and kept in touch."

"How? And no clue how he fit in?"

"Not your business. Not your department. That's between you and your handler, the middleman Ed. What do you think you're getting paid for?"

"Not by Jack Reardon, a person I never met. This whole arrangement is totally convoluted."

Another lurch as the traffic got moving again, another sharp turn and they were careening up 6th which was exacerbating Bud's aches and mood that much more. And still Seamus wouldn't let go. "Yeah yeah, yatata yatata. You think Jack's got nothing better to do?"

"Do you think I've got nothing better to do? Hauled down to his pub in the middle of nowhere, shoving me around, giving me a lecture and my marching orders, holding an axe over my head? And, on top of it, I've got to put up with you?"

"Damn straight," Seamus countered again. "'Course now you're gonna get it done."

Bud let it go. What was the use? Before he knew it, Seamus slammed on the brakes somewhere on 23rd Street and pointed out the windshield. Gazing directly across, Bud took in a looming twelve-story building that seemed to take up an entire city block. On each floor, eight sets of gray windows bordered in brick were bracketed by a wrought iron balcony. The balconies in turn stretched across until they ran into a bulging vertical strip with its own set of windows cascading straight down from the top of the building to just above the street; the pattern continuing from floor to floor, each set of windows running into the next bulging vertical strip; the entire structure was massive and overwhelming. An illuminated *Hotel Chelsea* sign above a welcoming red awning leading to the entrance was the only break in the building's seemingly endless configuration.

"Okay," Seamus said, still hollering as usual, "what we got here is over two-hundred–and-fifty units, plus single rooms, parlors, kitchens, and who knows what. Characters coming out of the woodwork, apart from longtime apartment residents, including drifters, wannabes, beatniks with beards and bongos, hoofers, hookers, old vaudeville comics—you name it. If this chick is as antsy as Jack says, you got your work cut out for you. Push it, she'll slip off into one of those zillion cubby holes where you'll never find her. For my money you're dealing with a little broad who passes herself off as an angel from the boonies who's really pulled a heist, out to make the big time and bright lights. Take it from me, pal, take it from me."

"I'll play it by ear if you don't mind." Bud got out and reached for his wallet. Seamus stopped him.

"You see any meter running? Wise up, will ya? And how about a little gratitude?"

"For what, the ride? All the put-downs?"

"Hell no. What, Jack didn't tell you? As soon as you let on where she was holed up, Jack wanted me to beat it out of her. But I said it could get messy. Besides, like I've been telling you, she spots a guy like me, she'll take off before I can get hold of her. Or hide out in one of them zillion cubby holes. You get it?"

"I get it. You had the right idea."

"So? So move it. Deliver. That's the password, Buddy boy."

As Seamus' cab peeled off into the bumper-to-bumper traffic, Bud held stock still for a minute. He'd have to come up with some excuse why he might involuntarily wince now and then and why he didn't bring his copy of the play-script. Matter of fact, he'd have to chuck his tack of a gradual progression altogether. How he made some headway or what became of his efforts was purely up for grabs.

He made his way carefully across the wide street, raising his hand and dodging a few cars. He passed under the hotel awning and entered the glass front door. And there, despite Seamus's sketchy intro, Bud was thrown once again.

Glancing to his right, judging from the huge fireplace framed by carved wooden figures and the cluster of dark leather club chairs, the lobby apparently was once a gentleman's smoking lounge during a bygone era. But the walls and high ceiling were painted a filmy yellow. Vagrant artists must have taken over for a time and dashed off mismatched paintings instead of paying rent and hung their work helter-skelter. As a result, there was no room to hang any more renderings of horse's heads, hazy pastel couples lounging on a hazy pastel beach, a floating umbrella, and garden flowers suspended over a lopsided vase. Sculptors must have gotten on a ladder and dangled cherubs on a swing and whatnot from the ceiling. And no one ever thought of taking any of this hodgepodge down.

Soon, Bud heard voices and caught a glimpse of three fleshy girls descending a broad staircase. Their frizzy hair dyed different shades of red; each wearing fur jackets, ropes of glass beads, short skirts, and high-heels as they giggled past him out the door.

The creaking sound of an elevator caught his attention further ahead as another gaggle of girls dressed in purple-velvet pants suits disembarked, whispering in hush tones, drifted by him and also made their exit out under the awning onto the busy street.

He kept moving forward beyond the creaking elevator as it worked its way higher, perhaps all the way up to the twelfth floor as the sound continued to trail off. He then came to a cozy nook that passed for a reception desk with a short wooden counter. Behind the counter was an old-fashioned roll-top desk and a bulletin board perched above, strewn with thumbtacked notes and notices. Perhaps deeper inside there was a manager's quarters but from this angle it was hard to tell.

What caught his eye next was that same poster from *West Side Story*, blown up and prominently displayed on the wall at the beginning of the next aisle. The black-and-white photograph serving as the only reflection of the real world, the couple caught in suspension. The girl always in freeze-frame tugging her sweetheart down the city street, both yearning for closure just around the corner.

In Bud's distraught mind, the image was a crossroad. In his case, there was a line between the romantic yearnings at the White Horse Tavern and the nefarious goings-on hidden down in Reardon's pub. Perhaps less than six degrees of separation between all the moving parts.

He looked back, half expecting her to come down from the elevator or the broad stairway by the glass front doors. But the hotel had become still. There was only one answer. Either she had changed her mind or she was early, waiting for him up ahead in a parlor.

Wincing, he hesitated at the brink of the long musty hallway. He only had a vague notion of the beginning of their encounter in mind. If she was there, for openers he primed himself for only some brief small talk. To use Greta Hagen's idea of an improv to start right in to at least get the ball rolling. At the same time, he couldn't help hoping that certain vulnerability he'd found in the photo, on stage in person, and over the phone that had carried him this far was worth staking everything on. Regardless of the disparaging remarks from Reardon, Ed, and Escobar.

He moved on, passing more mismatched pastel renderings of beach figures, far-off watercolor vistas, and abstract shapes fighting for attention. He drifted through an alcove into a parlor and there she was.

At first glance, her presence seemed totally out of place. Standing there, dressed demurely in a white blouse with a Peter Pan collar, light-gray wool jumper, and saddle shoes juxtaposed against a rolled-arm brocaded sofa covered with fringed, mauve throw pillows. The huge sofa sat awkwardly next to a sagging love seat upholstered in gold. The mix-match continued with dusty hanging tapestries of embroidered oriental landscapes. A faded woolen rug ran the length of the parlor, scuffed on so many times you could hardly tell it had ever been an illustrated fairytale with Persian motifs. It was one more item that had long since outworn its usefulness.

Bud stepped forward between her and a smudged window far over to his left overlooking the street and said, "Hi. Hope I'm not late."

"Oh no," Amy said. "I got here early. It's a habit, making sure I wasn't tardy."

"Right. Being tardy was letting somebody down." Cutting through an awkward pause he added, "One more in a barrel of truisms and hand-me-downs. Like don't make a scene."

"Uh-huh."

Another involuntary wince on his part despite his effort to cover it up.

"Are you okay?"

"It's nothing really." Then concocting some excuse, he added, "So dumb. I started reaching for the back seat in the cab—for my play-script I mean, when the cabbie lurched forward, door handle or something must have grazed me. So I'll keep the wincing down and, if you don't mind, we can get right to the improv."

"Oh?"

"Like I said, the cabbie took off before I could retrieve my play-script. Anyways, we can at least give it a try if you're game. In the scene we're doing, we've got Jim, the gentleman caller, saying it's all a matter of self-confidence. One more of those standby truisms."

Another uneasy pause. Nevertheless, Bud kept pressing on. "So, that's a given, right? So what can I myself bring to it right now, if I've got the assignment correct. That's the key, isn't it? Me in my way, you in yours."

"You mean skip reading the scene first? Not even share my copy somehow?"

"Which would be awkward at best. Look, we know the scene, how it works from the first beat to the next. But can we bring it to life, moment to moment, like it's actually happening? Can we at least share what we each really have to bring to it?"

Again she didn't respond. Then, ever so slowly, she reached into her handbag and pulled out a charm bracelet. "Well, anyways, I brought that charm bracelet I was pretend talking to my mom about on stage, remember?"

Bud said, "Sort of," though he'd been distracted by noises outside the studio door and must have missed that part.

"Isn't it perfect for Laura?" she asked. "See, here's a little star you wish upon. And a rainbow for somewhere over the rainbow. The charms slip on these little hooks. A substitute for Laura's glass figurines. Imaginary but real, tapping into something personal."

"I see. You bet."

But despite himself, he just stood there. It may have been the resumption of noises back down the hallway where the creaking elevator had landed. It may have been people rushing down the wide staircase out into the street. People rushing around reminded him it was getting later and he had get somewhere with this.

"What's the matter?" she asked.

"Well, Greta said to bring what was happening to us now to the scene. Something that would generate that same kind of immediacy."

"Uh-huh," she said, fumbling with her bracelet, eyeing the alcove behind him, perhaps having second thoughts and regarding it as an escape route he'd promised her.

"Well, for openers," Bud went on, really pushing it this time, "this is a memory play. Looking back when things were a lot simpler. Sure, Jim was only hiding the fact he was already engaged and didn't want to hurt Laura's feelings. And Laura was only hiding the fact the workaday world was too much for her and she'd much rather slip away into her fantasies. But in the here and now, trying it out for starters, maybe you could talk about what you yourself are trying to slip away from?"

"What do you mean?"

Then it finally came to him. The perfect ploy to get to the heart of the matter. To get on with his so-called charge from Reardon or else.

Doing his best not to seem too eager, Bud said, "During your private moment on the toy phone you said you could get around what really happened. You could sweep it all under the carpet. But truthfully you really can't, can you? As much as I can't slough any of what's going on with me."

As she eyed her escape route more obviously this time, Bud said, "Tell you what. I'll break the ice. All you have to do is sit on the couch and hear me out. This is mister most-likely-to-succeed Jim in the flesh. Except there's a helluva lot more at stake."

"But can't we do the sequence as written? Once we get that down... can actually work together, I mean... then maybe we can get into the personal stuff."

"Except there isn't time."

"What do you mean?"

"I mean the really personal stuff. I planned for us to take our time, get to know one another, do an improv and then get into what's troubling you akin to what Laura is really afraid of. But guess what? Reardon, remember him? He wasn't just a business associate, making a handoff, passing through on the way to a connecting flight. He hardly knew Escobar but needed someone outside the New York syndicate I guess. Reardon is the ringleader, with his dingy headquarters close by on the fringes of Little Italy."

Amy suddenly grew still, her eyes wide open in disbelief.

"That's right," Bud went on. "His henchman intercepted me an hour or two ago, shoved me into his car, hauled me down to Reardon's pub, punched me in the stomach, which is really why I'm still in pain. Reardon proceeded to hold an axe over my head. However, as an alternative to really roughing me up, spooking you and doing it the hard way, he gave me till just before noon tomorrow to untangle this major glitch you caused."

Amy turned back, almost in a daze, and settled into the brocaded sofa between the fringed pillows. It took a while before she said, "But why you? Unless you're mixed up in it too or something. Unless you're not at all what you seem. Not at all honest, not aspiring to be—"

Bud held up his hands like a traffic cop and pressed on. "How about yes and no and somewhere in between? How about how I wound up here on Sunday on the train from Miami? How about my scam artist uncle Rick getting in way over his head at an all-night poker game on Miami Beach and losing his shirt? That's right, the very same Rick Ellis who put you on to Marilyn Monroe and tried to wheedle Escobar's poker tricks out of you?"

Shaking her head in disbelief, Amy reached for a throw pillow and clutched it as hard as she could.

"Look," Bud said, unable to stop himself. "I just want you to know I was caught in a bind. From time to time, my mom asked me to check on her baby brother, make sure he wasn't getting into any more trouble because she claimed I'm the only one Rick would listen to. Set to go off on a cruise last week, she begged me to look after him because she sensed he was surely up to something iffy."

"What are you saying, for pity sake?"

"I'm saying what he was up to spilled over and was all mixed up with shady characters. I'm saying I did my best to look into it without having anything to do with Reardon, getting hold of you, working something out. But Reardon cut in anyways and just now gave me an ultimatum. Meaning, it's your turn. Help me out here. You're not what you seem either. How in the world did you wind up some kind of thief on the run? What is really going on here?"

She let go of the pillow and pressed her fingers against her temples as if trying to figure some way out of this. Finally she blurted out, "Well it certainly wasn't my intention, I can tell you that. How many times can you hear your old drama teacher tell you it takes years to be discovered overnight? And hear your mom say God has a plan for you? If I have a calling, if I really do . . . "

"And so?"

"And so there was only the same old, same old. The lead in that silly show *Little Mary Sunshine*. Back to the improv group in

Chicago for another season doing the same takeoffs on Cinderella and Snow White and the virgin on a blind date."

"But this time?"

"Yes, this time. The cast was breaking up. Wanted me to go with them to Hollywood and get into sitcoms doing even more of the same. So I got to the point . . . looking for signals, maybe a blessing in disguise . . ."

Then she began to ramble. All Bud could make of it was at the last minute Ed came backstage. There was the hook of an engagement party featuring a preacher's daughter and all expenses paid in sunny Florida. A guy she was told was a little rough around the edges who only needed an escort, a nice, sweet buffer between him and an angelic prospective bride for a shindig in Boca Raton; a guy who had connections in show business in New York in exchange for only a couple of days and she'd be on her way.

As gently as he could, Bud asked, "And how did it come apart? Was it down at the pool area Friday night or something immediately afterwards?"

Almost as if walking in her sleep, Amy rose up and drifted across the faded Persian rug to the window overlooking the late afternoon traffic.

In turn, Bud drifted over as well, standing close enough by so he could hear what she was saying.

"I felt so lost," she murmured. "Sitting out there on the patio with everyone else as happy as can be. When he came over. He was drunk but . . ."

Bud moved in even closer, realized at the rate she kept faltering, he'd have to prod her. "Right, good ol' Rick seemed to be answering your prayers. After all, if Marilyn Monroe could get a jumpstart from being stuck in the throes of naïveté, why couldn't you?"

"But, like you said, he wanted Escobar's card tricks." Looking at Bud almost imploringly, she began blurting everything out. "And Escobar came rushing over, dragged me to the elevator . . . back to the suite, told me I'd be on a short leash from here on in. Right after the engagement party I'd be shipped back to the boonies, out of the way."

Then she stopped. Then Bud pressed on even harder.

"Next," Bud said, taking a complete stab at it, "in such a rush to get to the card game, he admitted he lied about having show biz connections. Are we close to it? The clincher, I mean?"

"Yes. Then . . . then . . ."

"It's all right, Amy," Bud said, almost hovering over her. "I'm listening. I'm trying to understand."

She looked out the window as if peering through a fog. "Rushing around in his bedroom, tying his tie, telling me the silver briefcase was everything, I was nothing, good for only one thing . . . Ed came bursting into the room, something about a telegram."

"And?"

"Escobar was yelling, 'I'll watch out for Crazy Joe all right.' He pulled a gun out of his shoulder holster screaming 'The second he shows up and goes for the case, there'll be blood on the rug and a hole between his eyes!' I tried to stop him, told him to put the gun away."

Amy began to shake. He wanted to comfort her, put his arms around her. But all at once she turned toward him, tears streaming down her face. "He flung me so hard against the wall I hit my head and thought I'd pass out. He left me there, saying I would keep and to stay out of his way. They both hurried off. I was so groggy, I got his keys off the nightstand, staggered out into the hall, opened the wall safe, thought if I got my travelers checks and took the silver case out of there, there'd be no bloodshed . . . God would like that . . . leave all the evil behind me. But didn't really know what I was doing my head hurt so much. I remember returning his key ring to the nightstand in his room but . . . but . . . ”

She was crying and shaking so hard, Bud reached out and held her. They stayed that way until he gingerly led her back to the sofa. Soon she continued to let it all spill out. “On the train, I still had this lucky charm bracelet on, hoped I had done the right thing and kept the evil at bay. But as my head began to clear, I realized I wasn't at all prepared for New York, and the charm bracelet wasn't going to ward off a blessed thing.”

Sitting up, she said, “And now you say this Reardon person is nearby and a ringleader. And you? Who are you? What are you really?”

Reflexively, Bud started to scuff around like he really didn't have a good answer.

“This past Saturday I was a seasoned, carefree Miami sports reporter about to take my niece to the Parrot Jungle. Next thing I know, I'm roped into tracking you down under false pretenses with Rick's welfare hanging in the balance. But now there's you. At this point, I'd do anything to turn things around.”

At an impasse, they both fell silent until Amy finally spoke. “After all this, I didn't stop anything, did I? Didn't sweep it all under the carpet. You said at Greta's workshop you were pretending someone was tailing you. But you acted it out so well because it was true, wasn't it? And now you say Reardon called you in and gave you an ultimatum. Which means I can't sweep anything under the rug any more.”

When Bud didn't reply, she went on. “And I can't get by playing little Miss Innocent even though I want to believe. Even though, groggy as can be, I thought I was avoiding some bloodshed and, at the same time, like Marilyn, on my way about to learn how to get real.”

She stood up and started rummaging in her purse and came up

with an index card. "Soon as I got off the train I put the silver case in a locker, went into a phone booth, looked through the yellow pages and jotted down the address of a couple of police precincts. Let them handle it, I thought. But I still felt woozy, wondered what they'd make of some gullible ninny who'd made off with the silver case over something she'd overheard in Miami Beach. What would happen then if Al Escobar decided to press charges? Or track me down? I'm telling you I didn't know what in the world to do."

Handing the card over to Bud, she said, "Here. That's the answer. You can explain things."

Turning sharply, Bud said, "Terrific. Except you're forgetting Reardon has me under the gun."

"But he's a culprit and you'd be aiding and abetting. And all of this would be for nothing, this Crazy Joe will still be out there somewhere and awful things will happen."

"So?"

"So somebody has got to step in who knows exactly what to do. We're not cut out for any of this."

"You mean play it both ends against the middle?"

"Call it what you like. It can't end like this. You said yourself this Reardon person was up to something dreadful. And in cahoots with Escobar and Ed. Something has to be done."

Index card in hand, Bud slipped out into the alcove and thought it over for the longest time. The lead up to Amy's confession didn't take that long. He didn't have to spend any more time on that score and then struggle through that whole rigmarole to retrieve the silver case, dodging mob guys who might be tailing him, going all the way over the East River to the wilds of Brooklyn or Long Island and back again. Only someone fixated over rivals like Reardon could come up with a loopy set of maneuvers like that. Though he knew next to nothing about Manhattan police procedures, Bud could use the time to confer with an NYPD precinct close by. They'd be bound to be familiar with Reardon's exploits, would want to know what he's up to, and could put the whole conundrum in perspective. Come up with some way to play it Reardon's way while, in some way, having him in their sights.

Turning back, with nothing else for it, he said, "Okay, missy, you're on. Worth a try. I'm sure the police have their ways and I'll have to go through channels. But maybe I'll be able to set something up in just a couple of hours, swing by here while we go over some story that eliminates Escobar and you from the equation and just focus on the briefcase. If it all works out, that'll leave me most of the morning to rest up before I'll need to come down to the lobby and deal with Reardon's henchman before noon, briefcase in hand. Okay? Make sense?"

Unable to follow this but registering a glimmer of hope, she gave him a wistful, "I guess."

"In the meantime don't go anywhere. Don't do anything. I'll call and let you know the verdict."

In reply, she nodded and held onto that wistful look.

"Fine. You got it."

As he left the Chelsea, at least he was no longer on his own. Apparently the purely vulnerable side of Laura had materialized, giving him someone to care about and look after. A prospect a lot more engaging than solely trying to get a grifter uncle out from under it.

CHAPTER TWENTY-NINE

By the time a cabbie left him off at the NYPD 5th Precinct, it wasn't lost on Bud that even though it was broadcast live, the show he'd watched the other night on *Naked City* was a showcase for the acting talents of Stella's friend Constance. And it was shot on a set designer's replica of the first and second floors of a station house. It served as a layout, a semblance of what took place when you climbed the front stone steps and entered a real precinct.

And so, counting the dank, chilly mist during this late Wednesday afternoon, Bud stayed strictly with the realities, including his abiding ache and edginess. Whatever was going on inside the first floor was amplified by the traffic and street noises outside on Elizabeth Street. The rough ambiance was augmented by the goings-on below Hester Street and Chinatown to the south and the Bowery to the east bordering on Jack Reardon's territory. It was no surprise when Bud entered the station doors to be confronted by the hullabaloo emanating from protesting gang members with flat-top haircuts who'd been run-in after a knife fight. Added to the fray were carjackers, street walkers, derelicts who'd tried to pass off counterfeit bills, dope dealers, etc. Plus people harassing the duty officer to file a complaint against noisy neighbors, a heavyset woman with a black eye who wanted to get back at her boyfriend and so forth.

Bud bypassed the first floor and made his way up the stairway to the door marked Detective Division and the actual plainclothes detectives squad room. Instead of coming upon three men in suits and ties seated at their desks typing reports like the TV drama, he encountered a smoke-filled world occupied by a half dozen men puffing away on their cigarettes, answering phones, penciling-in notes, and shouting over one another. Saying things like "But why is he threatening you, lady? . . . Hey, talk to me. Is this a domestic dispute or what?"

The plainclothesmen glanced over now and then at a closed door marked *Lieutenant Burns* way over to the left side as though making sure they appeared busy if their boss suddenly burst out of his office and caught them slacking off.

Bud stood there by the low-slung wooden gate at the entrance, looking for an opening in the action so he could proceed with his proposition. However, it took some fifteen minutes for all but one of the detectives to stop what they were doing or passing him by—one hauling off a nearsighted little man who'd been sitting in a corner the whole time, now pleading against being dragged downstairs to be booked on charges. All of which left a harassed looking detective with red-rimmed eyes seated at a desk to Bud's right wearing a rumpled plaid cardigan that had seen better days and a polka-dot bowtie he'd all but given up on trying to tie. Brushing a shock of wispy, sandy hair off his forehead, he got back on the phone. Partially acknowledging Bud's presence this time with a glance and a roll of his eyes, he reached for a corn-cob pipe and barely gave the caller the time of day.

"Yes, ma'am, this *is* detective Steve Cordera. How many times have we been through this? It has to be tangible. How do you know he was a prowler? Did you have your glasses on? How do you know what you heard were gunshots? These are the basics if you want to be taken seriously."

Still barely listening to her, he reached for a pouch of tobacco and proceeded to pack the pipe bowl a pinch at a time. Then he cut her off, telling the woman to please stop calling until she got her story straight.

While Cordera finished packing his pipe, Bud thought of Scooter. He thought of his run-in with Reardon and other inklings he'd gleaned so far. As Amy had indicated, these detectives had seen it all and the last thing Bud needed was to be given the brush-off.

When Cordera motioned him to pass through the low-slung wooden gate and state his business, Bud decided to take his cue from Howard, his erstwhile mentor back at the *Miami Herald*, and come right to the point. He waited a few seconds until Cordera tamped down the tobacco in the bowl of his pipe, struck a match, and got the corn cob going as the aromatic smoke overtook the odor of stubbed-out cigarettes emanating from the vacant desks. And then Cordera said, "So, fella, what's on your mind?"

"Bud. Just make it Bud. "

"All right, Bud, make it snappy. As you can see, we're really up to our ears right about now."

"Would you mind if I left out all the twists and turns?"

"That's the ticket. Give it to me plain while I have a little smoke before running off to take a witness' statement."

Cordera leaned back, the pipe stem clutched in his teeth, slowly releasing more maple-scented aroma into the squad room.

Stepping forward, Bud said, "I assume you're acquainted with Jack Reardon. Well, it seems he's up to something imminent."

"So what else is new? You should have gotten here earlier when agent Dugan makes his rounds. You could compare notes. That is, if it's about something beyond our jurisdiction. What is it? Maybe I'll check it out or pass it on."

For a second Bud was thrown. He was reminded of Reardon's IRA regalia and salute to the "boys." But what did that have to do with a silverline briefcase and an impending meeting down at the Tropic Isle hotel?

"Hey, don't just stand there, Bud. What have you got?"

Bud moved closer to the side of Cordera's desk. "Okay, this is it on the face of it. My uncle in Miami Beach is in a jam over Reardon's missing attache` case. To bail him out I agreed to come up here and zero in on its recovery."

"Go on."

"For openers, I've been tailed by at least one mob type."

"What gives you the idea you were being tailed?"

"One of my contacts advised me that since the guy was playing it cagey, keeping pace, easing back, and slipping off, it easily could be someone from Carlo Gambino or Vito Genovese's outfit or even Crazy Joe Gallo if he's around."

Removing the pipe stem from his clenched teeth, Cordera said, "That's it? And it connects somehow with Reardon's attache` case? And this contact . . . ?"

"Happens to be a numbers runner who works for his uncle here in your vicinity."

Cordera pulled back, got out a long legal pad, scribbled a few things down, and glanced at it. In turn, Bud had second thoughts about exposing Scooter. But he was forced to connect the dots if he wanted to get anywhere.

Cordera gave Bud another of those leery looks. "How long did you say you were in town?"

"I didn't say. But I've only got till noon tomorrow."

"So, maybe you catch on fast and picked up on some word on the street. And maybe Gambino or Genovese or both are after what's in Reardon's case. But why you of all people?"

"Because I've been poking around for four days now. Because

I know for a fact Reardon is up to something big. Because Reardon just had me hauled down to his pub and gave me a final notice regarding the attachè case."

"You mean Liam O'Connell hauled you down. Big guy driving a green Olds 98, right?"

"You got it. Reardon spelled out my marching orders. I certainly don't know what's in this silver case and don't want to become an accessory to whatever he's got in mind. I assumed this precinct wouldn't want some hoods out there trying to bump each other off and would rather beat Reardon to it whatever it is he's got in mind. I only want some way out of this, not just for me but for someone else who's inadvertently concerned."

Cordera put his pipe aside, seemed to be thinking long, and hard and finally scribbled something else on his legal pad.

Bud then pushed it even harder. "Look, the upshot is I've got to have the case untouched, ready to hand off to Liam in the lobby of the New Yorker Hotel before noon tomorrow."

Cordera sat up straight. "What you're saying, if we cut the bull, is somehow you located it and want me to examine the case beforehand and determine what to do, if anything. Plus leave some party who's indirectly involved but knows the whereabouts of the item out of it."

"Exactly."

Bud was straining so hard now he agitated his aching midsection. Grimacing, he couldn't help nodding as Cordera guessed Reardon had Liam work him over a bit to make his point. In fact it was Bud's pain that seemed to clinch the deal.

Cordera glanced at the oversized Benrus clock hanging on the wall and rose up. "Tell you what. Check back first thing in the morning, say around eight-thirty with the case in hand and we shall see what we shall see."

"But isn't that cutting it a little close?"

"Everything in this town is cutting it close. And even then, it's always a big fat maybe."

Cordera pocketed his pipe and was about to slip past the gate when Bud said, "Mind if I use the phone? Have to check back with that same person who can end this scavenger hunt. Only take a second."

Cordera gave him another of his signature looks, started to leave, and turned back. "Say, tell me, given all you've been through, how come you don't smoke? You should be smoking up a storm by now."

Bud shook his head. He couldn't remember where he left his pack of Lucky Strikes and hadn't given it a second thought.

"Terrific," Cordera muttered to himself as his voice trailed off. "A missing briefcase, Reardon and the mob. Does it ever end?"

Bud made another mental note about Reardon and the IRA, despite the fact Cordera was having enough trouble dealing with what Bud had told him so far.

———————

While waiting for Amy in the parlor of the Hotel Chelsea, there was the added factor of his growing fatigue. He'd always managed to get about eight hours sleep, but the effects of the recent fretful days and nights were catching up to him. Sitting in the sagging love seat next to the oversized sofa and throw pillows, it was all he could do to keep from yawning.

Presently, Amy came hurrying in and immediately noticed how tired he was. "Are you all right? Guess it's all been too much, hasn't it?" She was still dressed in the light-wool jumper with a white blouse and Peter Pan collar. And that worrisome look in her blue eyes, after becoming suddenly aware Reardon was close by, had returned.

"It's okay," Bud said. "Just need to stop for a minute. Then, if you'll kindly hand me the locker key, I'll get cracking. Only good thing, Cordera doesn't seem at all concerned about what finally put me on to the whereabouts of the silver case, so we can skip coming up with a story to cover your involvement."

"But maybe we should think this over some more," she said, still standing there at the parlor entrance clutching her purse. "When you called me just now, you said the detective didn't have time to question how the briefcase slipped through Reardon's fingers in the first place. And could only manage to fit you in early tomorrow. Like he was in a rush."

"And only interested in the briefcase. Because there's no way to know what's at stake until someone can decipher the contents without leaving a trace. Which, as far as the police are concerned, is all they're possibly concerned with."

"So he didn't just dismiss it out of hand?"

"He penciled it in right before he had to run out to check on a hold-up."

Amy mulled it all over. "At this point I don't know what to think. You know what I was doing," she said, gazing out the window at the early evening traffic. "Starting another letter to my mom. Explaining she was right about putting my faith in tomorrow. But left out that the cast members at the improv troupe said you need an edge. And I went along with this Ed person who claimed he liked my work. I also left out their promises and lies were all part of it. No mention Al turned out to be some kind of mobster who suddenly flies off the handle. No mention of some killer coming down there in all that sunshine and blue skies after some darned briefcase who might even be here out there now. No dark side of things at all."

She stopped speaking and continued gazing out the window. Which told Bud it would take hardly anything for her to become disheartened and pack it in. A prospect he had to do his damnedest to avert. So it all came down to something coming of his appointment with Cordera early the following morning. Something truly positive.

"Okay," Bud said getting back on his feet. "That does it. 'Everybody up, rise and shine.' That's a line from the play and good as any cheer from the grandstands."

Going over to her, gently turning her around, he said, "The locker key, please."

"You haven't heard a word I said, have you?"

"I certainly have. And I mean it about you staying put."

"I was leveling with you."

"Fine. You want it plain? How do you think I got back here from Reardon's pub? Seamus, Reardon's cabbie henchman drove me. He now has a bead on where you live and I, for one, can't live with the thought of any thugs tracking you down. Your idea of getting the attache` case to the police, even for a little while tomorrow morning, is the only chance we've got short of throwing in the towel. So please give me the locker key."

At first she didn't move. Then she asked, "But if they know where I am?"

"We've got a grace period as long as I get cracking."

As hesitant as can be, she reached into her purse and handed it to him.

"Location of the locker? Penn station, as soon as you got off the train, am I right?"

"Yes."

"All right. I'll call you by noon tomorrow and tell you how it all worked out. Remember, you're going to keep a low profile."

He kept wishing there was some way he could get her to perk up. But he had to settle for a gentle pat on the shoulder and a soft, murmuring, "Guess there's nothing else that can be done but hope this Cordera comes up with something."

He left her looking more unsure than ever. But knowing at least Reardon had given him this block of time. And if there was anything like a mobster's word, she'd be free of any unwelcome visitors for now.

CHAPTER THIRTY

At first Bud was relieved that the intermittent spasms in his midsection had subsided leaving only a slight ache that didn't impede his movements. However, as he walked up 7th Avenue toward Herald Square and Macy's Department Store the chill in the air coupled with a misty drizzle this early Wednesday evening seemed to make the crowds more restless. So he had to contend with their jostling and dashing ahead to get inside where it was warmer and take advantage of the stores that kept open late. Plus the sports fans were bound and determined to get the best seats for a New York Knicks game at Madison Square Garden adding to the fray. And when he did manage to go through the doors of Macy's out of the inclement weather, he found himself elbow to elbow with the throngs vying for sales items everywhere you looked. It was as if just about everything was subject to a challenge.

The only good thing so far was the fact no one was trailing after him. Moreover, he'd learned the hard way that obviously being under pressure only drew attention to himself. Which was why Chooch, the deadbeat, had spotted him right off at the train station. And trying to ditch the guy in the trench coat caused him to break into a sprint, clambering up the fire escape, so Scooter couldn't help stopping by and offering his services. But at this point, having tried his hand at Method acting thanks to Greta Hagen, he learned that to play a part convincingly you make a personal adjustment. As in what would he do in this particular situation to blend in? The only thing he could relate to were those times on an off day when he might meander around Coconut Grove, peek inside the quaint shops, sit among the bamboo benches and hibiscus bushes, and casually eye the pretty girls in their sun dresses as they sauntered by.

And so he took his time to take it all in.

When he casually reached the luggage department and discovered all the flight bags were embossed in white letters for Pan Am, TWA, Eastern and National and there were no Northwest Airlines carry-ons, it was no problem. In his Coconut Grove mode, he asked the petite perky clerk if she wouldn't mind peeking around the stock room and see if she could find some other flight bags, perhaps one that had been left over. Returning minutes later, all she could come up with was a pale blue KLM Royal Dutch item that was a little dusty. No problem. He bought it anyway. Even though the prospect of Liam catching a flight to Holland tomorrow toting a KLM bag was too preposterous for any of Genovese or Gambino's outfit to swallow, it was the only non-flight-to-Miami option.

Regardless of the fact it was getting later and his aching eyes and fatigue were starting to catch up to him, he kept up his nonchalant pace. Out the door at Macy's, accepting the damp chill, sloughing off the passersby who brushed by him down the tunnel-like passageway into the Penn Station main concourse. Flight bag in hand, he drifted by the bank of lockers. He spotted the one he was looking for and paid it no mind. Practically starving, he went over to the Chock full o'Nuts booth, ordered two helpings of date-nut bread and a large Styrofoam cup of regular coffee, added cream and sugar and perched himself on the end of one of the long wooden benches. There he downed his snack while seemingly waiting patiently for the arrival of a later train, fitting in with a dozen lounging others.

A few minutes later, he spotted the latest edition of *Life Magazine* prominently displayed on the newsstand across the way. The very issue his uncle had used to cozy up to Amy in an attempt to ply Escobar's poker ploys from her, having no clue she didn't know what he was talking about.

Bud got up, bought a copy, returned to the bench riffling past Marilyn's color photo on the cover, and read the text. In her interview she declared she was leaving Hollywood to learn how to get real at the Actors Studio thanks to the auspices of her new famous New York playwright husband. Bud couldn't get over the fact if Rick hadn't read this, hadn't had it displayed prominently on the magazine rack in his bungalow, if he wasn't such a hapless con artist, if the Shriners hadn't been in town who were an easy mark. Add on, if Escobar hadn't arrived a few days early for an engagement party in honor of his nephew's betrothal to a Midwest preacher's daughter, if only . . .

But Bud might as well dismiss coincidences, chance, and bad luck as total flukes and not part of the natural order of things. He might as well believe everything depended on whoever was in charge. That only guys like Reardon could pick up the pieces and force the issue. That no one else had a chance.

Rubbing his sleepy eyes, unable to put it off any longer, he left the slick issue of *Life* on the bench for some other patiently waiting traveler, discarded his coffee cup and napkin, and got back to the business at hand. No one of those mingling around seemed the least bit interested in his activities, and neither Chooch nor anyone else was in position to monitor his movements.

He ambled over to the locker, inserted the key and deposited the slim silver case in the KLM bag. For all intents and purposes he was another well-traveled salesman about to make his way into the adjoining passageway to the New Yorker hotel. Continuing to take his old sweet time, he drifted down the passageway, checked the bag with the night clerk, underscoring that he'd have to retrieve it first thing tomorrow and needed it handy.

There was another reason he checked the bag. It would be close to impossible to keep from opening the latches to get a peek at what all this trouble was about. It was late enough and the last thing he needed was to get even more sleep-deprived pondering over the case's contents Reardon explicitly said couldn't be touched, when he had to spring up bright and early and grab a cab down to the Little Italy precinct. If he was lucky, Detective Steve Cordera would show some interest. All would be revealed and left to the devices of law enforcement before having to rush back in time to hand the case back to the waiting arms of henchman Liam O'Connell.

However, back in his room, try as he might, he couldn't fall asleep. Couldn't keep from likening this venture to the luck of the draw and roll of the dice. He turned on the clock radio and soon after the late-night station played the best of the sleepy time melodies like Debussy's *Claire de Lune*. The selections gradually segued to "Somewhere A Place For Us" from *West Side Story*. Though he didn't believe in signs and signals, there it was yet again.

A little after midnight he tried other stations and paused at WOR as someone named Jean Shepard was reminiscing about the good ole days in small town Indiana. And how terrific it felt to take his Red Rider BB-gun rifle atop the hill and lie in wait to protect the imaginary herd against rustlers. Yawning away, Bud couldn't help thinking of Amy and her own Midwestern small town where she too once had hopeful daydreams. And how he wanted to do all he could to rekindle her hopes before she sank irretrievably into disenchantment and despair.

CHAPTER THIRTY-ONE

Clutching the KLM bag, more sleep-deprived than ever, Bud barely had time that early Thursday morning to scarf down a Danish pastry and cup of coffee at a nearby doughnut shop, hail a cab—with the disgruntled cabbie doing all he could to maneuver through the clogged traffic—get off at the 5th Precinct, but still wound up climbing the stairs to the squad room ten minutes late. Adding to the frustration, Cordera didn't appear at his desk until another ten minutes had gone by. And even then, Cordera put on his horn-rimmed glasses and began typing away, giving the excuse he had to put in the finishing touches and turn in his full report vis-à-vis the Chinatown robbery the evening before.

Actually, Bud was grateful for the opportunity to rest as the other plainclothesmen were busy on the phone, or typing away like Cordero, or flitting in and out of the lieutenant's office. In the interim, Bud closed his eyes and fought off sleep-deprived woozy fatigue, hoping he could get through this session with Cordera and all the way back to the hotel to complete the handoff in plenty of time. He could then take the elevator up to his room and sack out for a little while after reporting back to Amy with news what this hassle over a briefcase was all about and how law enforcement would step in.

A few minutes later, Cordera yanked his report out of his typewriter and headed over to the lieutenant's office.

A few minutes after that, Cordera hurried back to his desk,

moved the typewriter aside, and plunked the silver briefcase down in its place. The snap of the latches caused Bud to sit up and stop Cordera just as he reached inside.

"What is it?" Cordera asked.

"Reardon warned me I better hope there was no sign anybody got there first. Nothing out of place, tampered with, or even handled. Or else there would be hell to pay."

Evidently given up on the corn-cob pipe experiment, Cordera dug into his blazer pocket, came up with a pack of Chesterfields, lit one, inhaled, and gave Bud a long-suffering look.

"All right, tell you what. I'll go down to the basement, slip on a pair of rubber gloves, and feed these papers into a Xerox machine. I'll bring the copies up, put the untouched case back in the flight bag, shuffle the damn papers to my heart's content and hope the phone doesn't ring. Will that do it for you?"

"You bet."

"Friend, this better be worth the candle."

As Cordera closed the case and was about to take off down the stairs, a heavyset man whom Bud assumed was agent Dugan appeared through the doorway making his customary rounds— blue suit, curly red hair, lantern jaw, a glint in his eyes. Cordera muttered a few things to Dugan and motioned back in Bud's direction. Whatever Cordera said caused Dugan to reply, "I hear you, believe me. Which reminds me what my informant just regaled me with." Cordera exited and Dugan entered the squad room, whisked by Bud like someone with a dicey story to tell. He greeted a couple of plainclothesmen in the back with a juicy opening remark. "Now here's the latest from Reardon's pub I don't at all mind sharing strictly on the Q.T."

Bud got out his note pad as Dugan's voice rose and fell interspersed with periods of laughter. The few things Bud gleaned sounded like ". . . of course it'll take a goodly amount of cash . . ."

And a little later on ". . . the topper was the detonators labs . . . All malarkey mind, to be taken with a grain of salt."

Soon after, Cordera reappeared with another lit cigarette dangling from his lips. He placed the silver case back in the flight bag, scattered the Xeroxed copies on his desk, and pulled up a chair. Dugan continued to carry on in the back of the room as Cordera rubbed his palms like a tout examining a horse racing form. "Five gets you ten," Cordera said, "it all comes down to Reardon pulling a fast one leaving the others in the lurch."

Cordera paused, seemed to be focusing on what looked like a memo from City Hall, and said, "Wait a second, hold the phone." He got up, memo in hand, and hurried to the back of the room where Dugan continued to hold forth.

Bud reached into the pile of papers and noticed that though Reardon and Escobar had affixed their signatures, Trafficante hadn't signed his part of the bargain whatever it was. Bud scribbled down another note and Trafficante's phone number and address as Dugan let out a, "Well, there, then, now" in the background. Yawning, Bud tried to get a handle on the three-way agreement. But he lost his train of thought when Dugan blurted out, "Like some radio serial, I tell you. Highlighted by car-bombing in Belfast, perhaps moving on to Derry and Omagh. Have you ever?"

Next, Dugan and Cordera had a brief exchange, Dugan waved to the others, strode up to Bud and patted him on the shoulder. "Got to hand it to you, fella. Tossing the Reardon papers in Steve Cordera's hot little hands."

"Yes, but what's all that about a car-bombing?"

"Listening in were you? What can you say, I ask you? That's what comes of a bunch of drunken louts staying up past midnight. My informant among them in Reardon's dingy pub, egging them on. But not above cluing me in first thing once he got his head on straight."

"But—"

"Listen, if it goes any further I'll be the first one hoisting it up the flag pole to see who salutes it. Never let it be said grass ever grew beneath Dugan's feet when the situation called for it."

With that, Dugan moved past the low-slung wooden gate and out the door before Bud could come up with any way to stop him. Bud added to his notes anyway.

Presently, Cordera left the other plainclothesmen, returned and began shuffling through the Xeroxed papers, sorting them this way and that. The other plainclothesmen were back to work as well, on their phones or typing away. Perusing his legal pad, Cordera said, "Let's see . . . taking into account what I've picked up here and there . . . and now this. What've we got?"

Bud glanced at his watch and said, "Can you distill it down for me? I have to hail a cab, get back to the hotel in time, and deliver, remember?"

"And I've got to get on the stick before the lieutenant wants to know what all has thrown a monkey wrench in the works around here."

Cordera plucked out yet another Chesterfield, lit it, took a deep drag and tossed off the gist of the matter. "Okay, here it is. It starts with the city's sanitation department cutting its budget, no longer providing trash removal for nonresidential swanky stores on Fifth Avenue and the like. Sanitation should let carters know and open the stops for bids. But, since it hasn't been made public, if Reardon gets his bid in by Friday at noon, those juicy stops are all his. And guess what?" Cordera handed over the memo. "According to Dugan, the sanitation head happens to be Flanagan. Flanagan and Reardon are related."

"Wait a minute," Bud said, shoving the paper toward him. "Look at that scrawl. If I'm not mistaken it says 'Up the rebels.'"

"Which is a cheer," Cordera said, snatching it back. "Ever hear of it? From fans, which is short for fanatics."

"I know what fans are. Nevertheless this could mean—"

"Enough, dammit. Are you interested in the contents of this briefcase or not? I've got better things to do. And you are running out of time if you want to hand this thing off and cool things down."

Cordera took another deep drag, eyeing the door to the lieutenant's office as if concerned he might come bursting out any second. "So, let's run the possibles. Let's say Reardon gets the jump on everybody and bilks those fancy shops like Tiffany's and Saks Fifth Avenue for whatever he wants to cart their trash. As for the deal between the three partners, the contracts indicate Reardon runs the show, Escobar forks over a haul from his money laundering in Chicago, flees the coop, and runs one of Trafficante's Havana casinos. In turn, Trafficante gets his foot in the door up here thanks to Reardon's connections. Leaving the Gambinos and Genoveses out in the cold."

"Okay, but think of the aftereffect. Think overseas. Think—"

Eyeing the door to the lieutenant's office again, Cordera said, "Not your problem, not your place, none of it." Shuffling the papers, putting them in some kind of order, he reached down, yanked a manila folder out of a drawer, labeled it, inserted the papers and slapped the folder into a bin on top of the desk.

He stood abruptly, still eyeing the door, and broke into what sounded like standard procedure for the lieutenant's benefit. "All right. You handed the material over. We made copies so that you can return the briefcase intact. What we subsequently do with the material or file it away for future reference is not your concern. In other words, your business with this precinct has concluded. Have I made myself clear?"

Doing his best to fight off a wave of fatigue, Bud said, "Okay, all right, I get it."

"Terrific. Not that we don't appreciate all the effort you've put into this." Cordera stubbed out his cigarette, plunked the flight bag on the desk and said, "So finish your errand and get some sleep. God knows you need it."

The ticking Benrus clock on the wall seconded the motion. Bud snatched up the bag and hurried past the gate. He exited, hurried down the steps, and left the station looking here and there for an empty cab. His fatigue made it that much more difficult as he traipsed west past Mott and Mulberry Street, over to Lafayette, and further still till he hit Broadway. And even then, the constant gunmetal gray of the sky, dank, misty chill and the acrid odor wafting in from the river seemed to be mocking him, telling him he only stirred things up a bit but not enough to make any difference.

It was only until he flagged an empty cab after a couple of men in business suits and an elderly couple all beat him out that he got going again. By the time the ill-tempered lady cabbie weaved, stalled, and worked her way through the snarled traffic and discarded Bud at the hotel entrance, yet another twenty minutes or so had passed. It was all he could do to shuffle in, plop down on one of the leather club chairs in the lobby, and concentrate on one simple task: stay alert and hand over the flight bag. But even that was no go as he sensed the lumbering form of Liam O'Connell hovering over him a few minutes early. The next thing he knew, Liam was un-zippering the bag, peering inside and zippering it back up. Then he said, "What's with this Dutch bag? Jack said to get a Northwestern."

"They didn't have a Northwestern flight bag. The clerk rummaged all around the stock room and this was the best she could do, indicating a flight far removed from service to Miami."

"Oh yeah? What'll some certain guys think?"

"They'll think you really get around. A world traveler."

"What are you, a wiseguy?"

"Just completely out of it as you can imagine."

"Hold it before you conk out on me, I gotta ask two questions. You run into any trouble getting ahold of this? Guys following you, guys maybe gotten to it first?"

"Not that I know of."

"So no sign of anybody messing with it?"

"Not on my end or the girl's for that matter. See for yourself."

Liam placed the case on a coffee table, was about to snap the latches and thought better of it, perhaps because he himself could mess things up. "Okay, never mind. We are quits. And Jack ain't paying you a cent 'cause of all the grief you give him, then making me track you down and haul you to his place and get you on the stick. You get my drift? Huh? Yeah? Do ya?"

"Fine, yes, I get it, I get it."

Still unsure, Liam lingered a little while longer and then shambled away muttering to himself.

Barely keeping his eyes open, Bud watched Liam get into Seamus' awaiting cab and drive off like the last shot of a movie. But the credits didn't roll, the theme music didn't play, and nothing had drawn to a close.

CHAPTER THIRTY-TWO

Bud shuffled over to the elevator, got off on his floor, and absent-mindedly scooped up today's edition of the *Herald Tribune* lying by his door. He entered his room, thought of glancing at the headline above the fold, thought of Liam catching the flight to Miami, thought of lots of things. But mostly realized anything he had to tell Amy would be so hazy and jumbled she'd be a lot better off if he called back in a little while. He left a message at the front desk at the Hotel Chelsea that his mission was accomplished but he was so sleep-deprived he'd have to get back in touch soon after he took a nap.

As it happens though, it wasn't just a little nap. And all the tossing and turning only made things worse. All told, he'd only succeeded in adding a pounding headache to the state he was in.

A few hours later and he still didn't know what to tell her. He couldn't slough off the fact the attache' case contained a three-way contract hinging on cornering the market on garbage removal on 5th Avenue. And that wasn't all, especially on Reardon's end. He also couldn't say the case was on its way back in Escobar's hands so that her efforts to avert any bloodshed vis-à-vis Crazy Joe Gallo were all for naught. For all Bud knew, Crazy Joe could still be waiting in the wings up here or down there.

Nevertheless, he had to get in touch. She'd been waiting all this while to find out what happened. But try as he may, the only tack he could think of was to pass it off onto Cordera and Dugan.

Despite the headache, he rang the Chelsea's number again. In a few seconds she apparently got to the phone on her floor right away and answered hurriedly. There was an opening concern over his loss of sleep, which he tried to casually brush off.

"I'm fine under the circumstances," he said. "Look, you were right about turning the briefcase in. You'll be happy to know that not only did I spark detective Steve Cordera's interest but I touched base with a federal agent named Dugan as well. As a result, Cordera examined the contents and was able to spot Reardon's shady dealings right away, Xeroxed the pages linking Reardon, Escobar, and some other gangster figure named Trafficante, and put it on file."

"On file? And what does this other gangster have to do with anything?"

"That's the catch. He's the silent partner and the only one of the three who hasn't signed the contract. That's why everybody's going around the bend. He's due Friday morning to show up at the Tropic Isle and complete the deal. In other words, I returned the case to Reardon's henchman and the precinct can handle the aftermath."

"You returned it? And that's it?"

"Not really. Reardon and Escobar will think they're back on track but are not at all out of the woods."

"But how? And what about this Crazy Joe person? And what's being done about this someone named Trafficante?"

Stumped for a reply, he could have told her the ball was strictly in Cordera's court now and/or Dugan's. But that wouldn't allay her concerns. Instead, really reaching, he said, "While the long arm of the law is considering the options, in addition, if I can look into some alternative tack . . . "

"What options? What alternatives?"

Bud tried to shake off the headache and clear his mind but to no avail. What could he do about it? What could any of us do?

"Truthfully," he said, "at the moment, I have no idea."

Luckily, as if alleviating some of the pressure, she said, "It's all too much, I know. And my insistence on an immediate solution isn't helping any."

"But there's still time before tomorrow morning. Before Trafficante has to sign. After I take everything under consideration and go over my notes, I'll call you back. Given a little more time, I'll be a lot more clearheaded. I mean, you never know."

A soft, almost resigned "Okay, of course" on her part, they said their goodbyes and Bud was back on his own. At first, he just sat there. For the life of him he couldn't come up with any way to stop this thing in its tracks. There were too many moving parts, too many variables.

The old standby crossed his mind again. "Walk away and it will come to you." It circulated in the back of his mind and gave way to his gnawing hunger.

He chose the smallish Art Deco restaurant downstairs, which once again was nearly deserted. Ensconced in a similar curved banquette he'd shared with Scooter, he contended with the glass table and fluorescent lights reflecting off the chrome and silver and black mirrors. Even as he dug into his New York strip steak with all the trimmings, it reminded him of Scooter's revelations about the local crime families looking for a cover-up and the impending fallout. This timeout offered no relief and only reminded him of all that was at stake.

He finished his meal and washed everything down with cold, sparkling mineral water with only his hunger abated. The need to accomplish something and for some doable solution persisted. He returned to his room and had the operator dial his sister's number back in Miami. It had been days since he'd been in touch.

A few minutes of normal patter might do the trick in freeing his mind toward some elusive remedy.

Katie picked up the phone, announced "It's about time," and informed him "Mom's at a meeting, I'm with the babysitter. Got to do this stupid homework before supper and then after I get to watch *The Colgate Comedy Hour* on the new television set."

"That's great. I only wanted everyone to know there's nothing to worry about."

"Oh no, not so fast, not so fast. You were supposed to take on the mob and report back. What happened? How did it go?"

"Katie, I only called to let your mom know Uncle Rick is off the hook. Not entirely but as soon as a certain lost item has been retrieved and back in the owner's hands, it's down to a gambling debt which Rick can work off. So, would you tell her after a lot of poking around on my part, everything's more or less square?"

"Wrong-o. Everything is not square. You were supposed to have stood up to the bad guys, which is what Scout in the story did. So I could forgive you for not taking me to the Parrot Jungle and breaking your promise. So I could learn that sometimes you have to put aside your selfish stuff for something bigger."

"Right you are, kiddo. But first you have to check things out before you can make your move."

After thinking that one over, Katie said, "You mean like checking out this girl at recess who's always trying to start a fight? Seeing how tall she is and stuff and then you maybe take her on?"

"Can we get off taking someone on? And will you please pass along the message?"

"Except what's gonna be done about getting mister Rick to behave? Big trouble he was in and now much smaller trouble is still trouble. And he should learn you don't throw my uncle Bud out there. You get off your rear end and take care of it yourself."

"Absolutely, I hear you."

"'Cause it's not fair. An older person cannot all the time expect a younger person to fix things he's caused. That older person should by now stop misbehaving and doing dumb things and learn his lesson. And that younger person should tell him no more of this so he can keep his promises and that's what I'm going to tell mom. Gotta go. Nice talking to you and getting the scoop. Finally!"

It may have been the sense the afternoon was winding down and his little chat with Katie. Something was altering his view of things. Absentmindedly, he scanned his recent notes. Nothing clicked. He recalled Reilly the bartender's notion that momentous things were on the verge. And Larkin, though he himself was keeping a low profile, was insistent that Bud's quest come to something. Which reminded him that he still owed Larkin a final report. Which he began to view in terms of a reckoning.

He sat at the desk, got out some hotel stationary and the stamped envelope, grabbed his pen, and dashed off his reply:

For Conor,

I can only assume you'd be perfectly happy if I ended our association by thanking you for the tips during my chase after Amy. To relate, as far as I know, she's downhearted but still has the dream of Broadway in mind. In this way, I'd just be some lovesick out-of-towner who briefly flitted through your diner after my dream girl and left you with another footnote in the merry-go-round of those who touched base while passing through your colorful Greenwich Village stopover.

But let's drop the charade and tell it like it is. No doubt each of us, in our own way, was trying to skirt around Reardon. You because of your checkered past and me because initially I was chasing after Amy to save my hapless uncle's skin back home.

But nothing holds still in this town. You can't draw a line in the sand and cordon yourself off from the Lower East Side any more than I can avoid being dragged down there and shoved around. Which, let's face it, is the very thing you want no part of. I'm talking mostly about his funding of terrorists across the ocean in your old stamping grounds; reminiscent of your dicey days linked to the I.R.A.

As for myself, I am unable to turn a blind eye. Though it may be futile, I'm scouring around for some last ditch ploy. Taking a shot in the dark. Words like that.

And so, you can wind things up by saying alas the poor soul then went off on a tangent and I couldn't make heads or tails of it. I can only guess he ran into too many distractions while he was up here. Too much jazz, too many colorful people, too much of the new wave. And so it goes in this madcap town.

Or you can work-in Amy, the poor man's Laura, and/or use any of this as a springboard for that final yarn. It's your call. Again, you in your way, me in mine.

Best, Bud

Bud folded the note, inserted it in the envelope, sealed it, hurried out into the hallway, and dropped it down the mail slot. The note succeeded in getting him back into gear as he returned to his room. Aware the news was waiting there atop the nightstand keeping track of the latest developments, backing up Reilly's thesis and countering Cordera's declaration that Bud's involvement was over. If nothing else, it was Bud's move.

Soon enough, the latest *Herald Tribune* headlines told him Castro and the combined revolutionary forces were proceeding as planned. They had Santa Clara firmly in their sights, former supporters of the dictator Batista had joined the revolutionaries, and it wouldn't be long until they were on their way to Havana.

What was surprising was the fact Andres Aguero, the president elect, declared there was no way he could take office and work with Castro, as if the overthrow of the dictator Batista was already a fete accompli. In addition, the C.I.A. had it on the best authority if Castro continued unimpeded heading for nearby Santiago de Cuba, Batista planned to flee to the Dominican Republic.

With his thoughts spinning like mad, Bud recalled Trafficante's part of the bargain as outlined in the contracts. It all hinged on Trafficante to cinch the deal and time was running out. Which led to the notion Trafficante may not be up on these latest developments. And it was then that old standby came into play: "A chain is only as strong as its weakest link."

This led Bud to the realization Howard, his quasi mentor at the *Miami Herald*, was doubtless putting the finishing touches on his current affairs section of the next edition. Bud considered Howard's unspoken expectation that Bud was a primary candidate to move up the ladder from the sports section to Howard's unit. He also reminded himself not to be put off by Howard's habit of toying with his briar pipe as he thought things over. So, prodded by the way things were going on the Cuba scene, he had the operator dial the news room extension. Almost immediately Bud was back in touch, not at all certain if he could pull this off..

"Bud, my boy, how are you faring?" Howard asked. "Still in the wilds of Manhattan playing Galahad in pursuit of some runaway? But not getting overly involved I hope."

Bud sidestepped this one. The last thing he needed was another constant reminder to see everything from a cool remove.

"As it happens, by extension, that's what I'm calling about," Bud said. "You always reminded me not to confuse motion with action. To get my facts straight first and fill in any gaps before proceeding."

"Now hold on. Let's not get ahead of ourselves. It's my understanding you left here suddenly over a family matter. I fail to see how the pursuit of a runaway would have anything to do with something I'd be commenting on."

"Except that a racketeer my runaway got involved with is about to invest in casinos in Havana. If I could cast a shadow on this venture, I could step in and straighten things out."

Another delay, this one much longer. Howard then came back on the line still hesitant as ever. "Bud, I simply still don't see what any of this has to do with anything I could provide. Plus, as you may recall, at present I am on deadline."

"I know, exactly, I realize that. You have to keep up with the news. That's your charge. The second anything comes over the wire, it's generated by a credible source. You are my credible source. And I only need your take, short and sweet, on a certain procedural matter. So I can take it from there."

Bud had no idea how he could keep this up. All he could do was hope Howard was more interested in his own deadline than continuing to try to make any sense of this. And, sure enough, he said, "Well, I'm sure someday when we both have the time, we will sit down quietly and revisit this whole matter logically from the beginning. In the meantime, what information do you need exactly?"

"Last time we talked, you mentioned something about nationalization. How would it affect the holdings of, say, a guy named Trafficante?"

"You mean Trafficante is involved in all this?"

"The guy she inadvertently got hooked up with is involved with Trafficante."

"I see. All right, give me a minute and I'll consult my files. Trafficante, you say?"

"Yes. Trafficante and nationalization."

"Hold on."

With the soft patter of IBM Selectric typewriters in the background, other thoughts crossed Bud's mind, including the odds of Howard providing something apt and, if so, getting Trafficante on the phone.

Presently, Howard was back on the line, as if he already knew the answer and only wanted to make sure the language was precise.

"All right," Howard said, "Given the current trajectory, taking into account the nefarious Trafficante was operating under Batista's Hotel Law 2074 offering tax incentives and casinos licenses etc. for a notable sum . . ."

"Yes yes, go on."

"According to my sources, a certain Resolution 3-Law 851 will go into effect, nationalizing all businesses owned by Mob investors prior to the revolution. Including Trafficante's casinos and newly constructed Hotel Deauville."

"Will go into effect, you're saying, as soon as Castro takes over?"

"That's exactly what I'm saying. Given the current projections, as soon as Castro and the revolutionary forces approach Havana and the moment Batista makes a getaway, Trafficante and any past, present, or future partners will be out in the cold. "

"Beautiful. Thanks, Howard, that helps. That helps a lot."

"Now now, my boy, as the old saying goes, discretion is the better part of valor."

"I'll be sure to keep that in mind."

Bud hung up. He was so beat and wound up he had no idea how to handle this next call or even if there was any chance someone would actually come on the line. He went over to his jacket, thumbed through his notepad, found the Tampa phone number of Trafficante's home base, and braced himself. If he did get in touch, as long as he cut it short, maybe he could pull it off.

The operator dialed the number he gave, a gruff voice picked up, and Bud went right into it. "Got a message for Mister Trafficante. If you could relay it on to him, I'm sure he'd appreciate it."

"Message? Mister Trafficante? Relay? What is this, Western Union? Some kind of gag? Who is this anyways?"

"That's not important. What is important is—"

"Hey, I ain't doing nothin till I know what this is, fella."

"Don't."

"Don't what?"

Bud could feel he was about to lose it but couldn't help himself. "Look, just cut the tap dance, okay? I've been duped, punched, and jerked around long enough and it's got to end. As far as I can tell, everybody has been running around playing hide-and-go-seek, keep away, and get him before he gets you. Just too damn busy and that probably goes double for Trafficante. So, instead of giving me a hard time, would it kill you to run something by him? Things aren't what they seem. Like everybody else, he has no idea there's a catch, and Trafficante's glory days in Havana are numbered."

"Oh yeah?"

"That's right. And if he arrives at the meeting tomorrow morning wearing blinders, the fallout will be on your head not mine."

"Hold it, hold it. What fallout? What catch? What the hell you getting at?"

"I'm saying unless he's got some secret loophole up his sleeve, he's on shaky ground. I'm saying, Batista only seems to have everything under control and unless Trafficante checks it out, he has had it"

"Checks what out? Are you gonna spit it out or what?"

"Have you got a pencil and a piece of paper? I'll make it short. "

There was a delay, sounds of rummaging around, and then

the guy was back on the line. "Okay, wise guy, let's have it. What the hell is going on?"

"Batista holding out, staying in power, or throwing in the towel any day now is what's going on. What are the odds with Castro and his rebel forces zeroing in on Santiago de Cuba is the kicker."

"Look, you gonna make it short or what? I ain't giving Trafficante no message from no cold caller full of doubletalk about odds, Castro, and maybe this or maybe that. Make sense will ya for crissakes?"

"Resolution three, Cuban law 851."

"Okay . . . number eight-fifty-one. Meaning?"

"Meaning, this whole three-way deal is hanging by a thread. Meaning, it's Trafficante's move, he hasn't signed on, and he'd better think twice before—"

"Yeah yeah yeah. Enough already!"

Before Bud could utter another word, Trifficante's henchman hung up on him. Bud's hands were shaking like crazy. He'd never confronted anyone before, not really, let alone a mob figure. Never floated anything that had dire consequences. Sports were sports, not the end of the world. How many hundreds of times had coaches, fans, and players shouted "Wait till next year"? With this game there would be no second chances, no annual competition. What was done was done.

He tried to tell himself he gave it a good try, but it didn't help. In the meantime, he could at least call Amy back. Level with her short of mentioning Reardon's support of I.R.A terrorists or anything else remotely harrowing. She'd gone through enough. In some way, he had to make her see there wasn't any more to be done. Hold his anxiety and fatigue in check for another minute or so and call it a night. But, like everything else, even this task was up for grabs.

He reached the Hotel Chelsea. Someone down the hall close to the phone on her floor was able to pick up and knock on Amy's door. In short order, she was on the line.

"Hi," Bud said, "just wanted you to know I tried a last ditch ploy. Let's just say it's all up to Trafficante now."

When she didn't respond, he pressed on. "Trafficante. You remember, the silent partner. Call it the third link in the chain. I thought if I could pry this connection loose it might all unravel. No more stake in the action for Trafficante up here, no more Havana incentive for Escobar, and there goes Reardon's whole three-way game plan."

When Amy still didn't respond, he pushed it even harder. "Depending, of course, on whether Trafficante's henchman passed on the message. Then, whether or not Trafficante is in possession of some iron clad exempt clause. In short, all we can do is wait and see."

With a tone that sounded completely dejected, she asked, "And that Crazy Joe person?"

"Just another fuzzy link in the chain."

Another hesitation until Amy sighed and said, "Bud . . ."

"Yes?"

"I'm sorry I put you through all this. But I've been so scared and alone this whole time. Getting all teary and vulnerable. Hoping someone or something would come along. That's one of my major shortcomings. Which is what drew your uncle in in the first place and made things a hundred times worse."

"Not your fault, Amy. Besides, I'm glad I found you. Glad you pushed me to go out there, to the police. Glad I was no longer on my own."

"But still and all look at us."

Her spirits seemed to be sinking even lower. And he was at a loss as his fatigue began taking over and he was running out of things to say.

"You know what?" she said. "A short while ago, a pair of older show biz ladies invited me over for tea in their cozy apartment. Told me about how they first broke in with their song and dance act. Picked up bit parts on radio soap operas like *Mary Noble, Backstage Wife,* and *Stella Dallas*, anything to make both ends meet, wherever they could find work."

"That's nice."

"Not really, not when I didn't back them up. At first they tried to humor me. But then they lost patience. I'm no Marilyn Monroe, they said. Don't be foolish. Once you get your foot in the door, you don't squander the opportunity. How many people would give anything to find a niche in this world? It was about time I woke up. Went back, stopped daydreaming, and made the best of it. "

"Now don't do that. Take what they said with a grain of salt and sleep on it, okay?"

"Nothing to sleep on, Bud, as soon as you stop kidding yourself too."

There were a few more sputtering attempts on Bud's part that got him nowhere. Which left them with the understanding he'd call back in the morning after he checked up on things in case. But she wasn't buying it, wasn't buying any of it, and ended the call.

It was getting late and all he could do to crawl into bed. The fatigue was so pervasive it overshadowed everything—all he'd gone through, the notes he'd taken, even the throbbing headache. Before he knew it he was fast asleep.

In Bud's dream, Cordera ambled over to a blackboard, crossed off *Hauling and Crating on Fifth Avenue* and returned to his desk. In turn, Dugan appeared, shouted, "Put it out of your minds, fellas, forget I was even here!" Dugan pivoted and hurried down the stairs, out of the precinct under skies so overcast they hovered like rippling sheets of metal over the piers and extended far out to sea. The sea itself began to roll and crash till it finally washed ashore and transformed into a smoky haze. The haze settled on a weathered wooden sign that said *Belfast* which, in no time, led to a hidden munitions lab.

Two technicians wearing white smocks emerged from the lab and edged down a dingy cobbled street to a main square. The wiry one of the pair halted and held a walkie-talkie to his ear. Reardon's crackling voice could be heard saying, "Tell me you got the funds I wired and you're set to get cracking."

"That we did," the wiry one replied, "and yes we surely are."

"And you understand there's plenty more where that came from?"

"Understood and isn't that grand?"

"So, tell me, will the new gizmo work like you said?"

"You just wait and see."

"Okay then. Now's the time, boys. From now on, day or night, you can bank on it, so help me."

Reardon's voice trailed off. The wiry one put away the walkie-talkie, the heavier one of the two nodded. Shrugging off the storm clouds and drops of rain, the pair of them finished placing plastic explosives into the side door panels of a British armored vehicle and slipped off into the mist. The heavier one got out a hand-held device with a toggle switch and paused for a second as a group of schoolchildren approached skipping and singing.

Both terrorists nodded anyway as the wiry one played lookout and the heavier one flipped the switch. The blast caused a hail of granite and debris to come raining down on the children, smashing the armored vehicle and everything in sight leaving nothing but the hovering storm clouds drifting on.

Bud woke with a start, so shaken it took a minute to realize where he was. The honking outside his window and the late-night darkness helped to snap him out of it but not quite. He didn't want it all to come undone. Didn't want anything to happen to the children across the sea or Amy to leave the city in despair. He wanted to come to her and ease her pain and make all of it go away.

But the dream seemed to prove it wasn't just a bunch of drunken rebels the night before letting off steam in Reardon's pub. In fact, Bud had caught Reardon stone cold sober a few hours earlier primed to rouse his followers. All set no doubt to wire the racketeering funds from Escobar to support a munitions lab overseas. Then keep things rolling through the profits from his new carting service up and down Fifth Avenue. In a sense, the dream laid it all out plain as day.

But the dream was only a dream not an actual harbinger of things to come. Then again was it a premonition? Or as good as a warranty?

CHAPTER THIRTY-THREE

Bud overslept. Still groggy that fateful Friday morning, he got up and gazed out the window. The furled skyline hovered overhead as if something was on the brink.

He got dressed as fast as he could and thumbed through his notepad for the number of the Tropic Isle hotel. He had the operator dial. However, due to an influx of arrivals and departures, the woman at the front desk had her hands full and the best she could do was put him through to the pool and patio manager. The very same Chip who had served as a reluctant confidant and was now more harried than ever.

"Chip, it's me, Rick's nephew," Bud said. "Remember? Calling from New York. Can you spare a minute?"

"What is that, a joke? This place is coming apart at the seams."

"I know, I heard. Listen, I only want to know if someone named Trafficante checked in yet?"

"Right. Tell me about it. More headaches."

"What do you mean?"

"Never mind. What do think, I got nothing better to do?"

"Come on, just give me a hint."

"Just give me a hint, he says. For openers, I hear all this racket out back. I come across Escobar losing it by the dumpster, cursing to beat the band, slamming this silver briefcase against the lid. If that's not enough, he flips it open and sets fire to the papers inside like some kind of arsonist. By the time I get back there with a hose, it's nothing but a smoky mess. Next thing I know, not more than ten minutes later, they checked out."

"Who? Escobar and Ed?"

"Who else? Plus some big guy named Liam." Chip was so agitated by this point, Bud heard the flick of a lighter as Chip took a deep drag."

"Trafficante," Bud said. "What about him?"

"Right. Cancelled his reservation. Taking off to Havana and from now on would be incommuni—"

"Incommunicado?"

"You got it."

A few more drags and a slew of hems and haws before Chip said, "And if that ain't enough, Rick gets wind of it all, calls muttering about locating his spare car keys, whatever the hell that means, and races over.

"Which," Chip said, "is the only reason I'm putting up with you. On top of everything, he's putting the bite on me about some new development going up on Sanibel Island. On the West Coast near Naples, he says. What do I say? What do I tell him? At the same time, he's working on a widow in the far cabana as we speak. Nice bod, coral bikini, flushed with dough. I sent him over to her but can't stall much longer. I tell ya, I can't work at this pace, can't even think."

"Would you put him on?"

"That's your answer? I'm talking quid pro quo here."

"If you don't know Rick by now, what can I say? Just do it, will you please?"

"Oh sure, that's par for the course today, what the hell?"

Within seconds, Rick was on the line, yelling at the top of his lungs. "Bud, buddy boy! Where are you? I don't know what you did but I owe you big time. Name it. Name the price, anything and it's yours!"

"Cross me off your list."

"Very funny."

"You're not listening, Rick. And while we're at it, you should know Katie is on to you, relayed it all to Marge, who will doubtless relay it to my mom and your big sister as soon as she gets back from the Caribbean."

"Oh no. And you put her up to it? No way, Bud. No way."

"Didn't have to. She's a sharp kid, got your number right off. In case you need it spelled out for you, give her a call." Bud hung up before Rick could get in another word.

He dialed the Hotel Chelsea. But after a number of attempts, the phone on Amy's floor was still busy. He could have kept trying. Instead, he dialed one last time and left word at the manager's office that Bud Palmer was on his way.

He left the New Yorker hotel, hailed a cab and, as luck would have it, encountered little traffic as the lady cabbie covered the ten blocks down 7th Avenue in relatively no time. He rushed through the Chelsea lobby and was about to hit the elevator button when he spotted her descending the curved staircase by the front entrance. Before he could utter a word, she ran over to him and began escorting him back out again.

"Wait a minute, Amy," Bud said, stopping in his tracks. "I tried calling you. I've got news. Good news."

"Wonderful. Come on, you can tell me along the way."

"On the way to where? What are you doing?"

"Oh, didn't I say? I signed up as an alternate. That was the Actors Studio I was on the phone with. There was a cancelation. We're on."

"What do you mean *we*? What do you mean *on*?

Grabbing his hand and tugging him out the door, she said, "Doing our gentleman caller improv at last. I told them I have a partner, we'll have to wing it and they said it was okay."

"But—"

"Don't you see? Things have come full circle. Now you can call on me for real."

Still hesitant, Bud glanced up. Seemingly all at once, as if hearkening to some long lonesome wail of a jazz clarinet, things began to change. The air felt crisp, shafts of sunlight glinted across the looming buildings, and the skyline above became a bright, iridescent blue. At the same time, there was a look of wonder in Amy's eyes as she tugged a bit harder, taking him down the teeming sidewalks, past a number of brownstone row houses, leading him on.

The city was a lady. She was calling. There was always a chance and anything was possible.

ABOUT THE AUTHOR

Shelly Frome is a member of Mystery Writers of America, a professor of dramatic arts emeritus at UConn, a former professional actor, and a writer of crime novels and books on theater and film. He also is a features writer for Gannett Publications. His fiction includes *Sun Dance for Andy Horn; Lilac Moon; Twilight of the Drifter; Tinseltown Riff; Murder Run; Moon Games; The Secluded Village Murders; Miranda and the D-Day Caper; and Shadow of the Gypsy*. Among his works of non-fiction are *The Actors Studio; A History,* a guide to playwriting and one on screenwriting.

   Fast Times, Big City is his latest foray into the world of crime and the amateur sleuth.

   He lives in Black Mountain, North Carolina.

OTHER BQB PUBLISHING BOOKS
BY SHELLY FROME

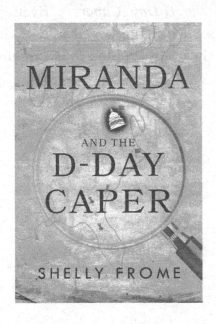

Small town realtor, Miranda Davis, never expected to uncover a terrorist plot. But when her cousin, Skip, playfully broadcasts some intercepted code messages like "Countdown to D Day" on his radio show, he begins to receive threatening anonymous messages leaving Miranda to wonder if he's stumbled into something much more sinister. After Skip's beloved cat, Duffy, is snatched as a warning, Miranda finds herself roped into a dangerous mission to decipher a conspiracy that threatens to tip a crucial senatorial vote.

As they're forced into a race against time to unmask the

perpetrators and prevent a disaster, Miranda must somehow decipher the use of old timey WWII tactics to bring the terrorists' shadowy plot to light. But, the clock is ticking.

Miranda and Skip will have to act fast if they want to prevent innocent blood from being spilled and keep themselves alive in the process. Can Miranda crack the code and stop the terrorists? Or will she be too late?

Miranda and the D-Day Caper, a riveting contemporary mystery that mixes modern political intrigue, old time heroes and values, and life in the beautiful Blue Ridge Mountains.

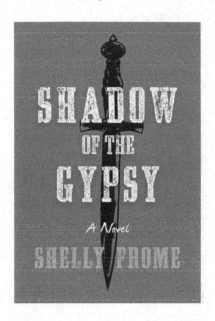

Josh Bartlett had figured all the angles, changed his name, holed up as a small-town features writer in the seclusion of the Blue Ridge. Only a few weeks more and he'd begin anew, return to the Litchfield Hills of Connecticut and Molly (if she'd have him) and, at long last, live a normal life.

After all, it was a matter of record that Zharko had been deported well over a year ago. The shadowy form Josh had glimpsed yesterday at the lake was only that—a hazy shadow under the eaves of the activities building. It stood to reason his old nemesis was still ensconced overseas in Bucharest or there-abouts well out of the way.

And no matter where he was, he wouldn't travel thousands of miles to track Josh down. Surely that couldn't be, not now, not after all this.

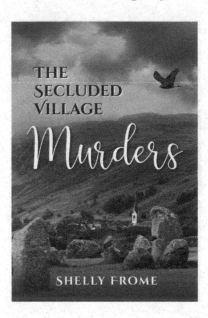

Written in the style of a classic British Mystery with a contemporary young American woman as the amateur sleuth. Entertaining. Keeps you guessing until the end.

From a small secluded village in Connecticut to the English Countryside, readers are taken on a roller coaster of events and quirky characters as amateur sleuth Emily Ryder tries to solve a murder that everyone thinks was an accident.

For tour guide Emily Ryder, the turning point came on that fateful early morning when her beloved mentor met an untimely death. It's labeled as an accident and Trooper Dave Roberts is more interested in Emily than in any suspicions around Chris Cooper's death. For Emily, if Chris hadn't been the Village Planner and the only man standing in the way of the development of an apartment and entertainment complex in their quaint village of Lydfield, Connecticut, she might have believed it was an accident, but too many pieces didn't fit.

As Emily heads across the pond for a scheduled tour of Lydfield's sister village, Lydfield-in-the-Moor . . . she discovers that the murderer may be closer than she thought.